THE BOOK OF

Ralph

CHRISTOPHER
STEINSVOLD

Medallion Press, Inc.
Printed in USA

Published 2016 by Medallion Press, Inc.,
4222 Meridian Pkwy., Suite 110, Aurora, IL 60504

The MEDALLION PRESS LOGO
is a registered trademark of Medallion Press, Inc.

Cover design by Michal Wlos
Interior design by James Tampa

Names, characters, places, and incidents are the products of the author's imagination or are used fictionally. Any resemblance to actual events, locales, or persons, living or dead, is entirely coincidental.

Cataloging-in-Publication Data is on file with the Library of Congress

Typeset in Adobe Garamond Pro
Printed in the United States of America

ISBN 9781942546344
10 9 8 7 6 5 4 3 2 1

First Edition

For Marie-Juliette

CONTACT

I was at home in Washington, DC, when the solar eclipse occurred on January 28, 2021. At the totality of the eclipse, a message appeared on the moon. I watched through a digital camera rigged with a solar filter to protect my eyes. When those three words appeared on the lunar surface, I closed my eyes and shook my head.

The message was in plain English, but I couldn't process it. I kept peeking through my camera at it and turning away. I did a quick virus scan on my camera, but it was fine. In the end, I looked directly at the eclipse. As a scientist, this is embarrassing. Everyone knows you don't look into a solar eclipse, but like everyone else, I couldn't resist.

I stupidly looked through the camera again. I stupidly looked at the moon again. I collapsed on my ass and stared.

'DRINK DIET COKE' was writ bright across the moon.

The crimson letters across the blackness of the eclipse looked simply satanic. After the eclipse passed, the bright, grey glow of the moon made it seem more natural and professional, though there was no trademark symbol.

It would remain visible for a little over a year.

'DRINK DIET COKE'

It was the perfect message, and it did what it was intended to do.

Six hours after the advertisement appeared, Coca-Cola sent out press releases to every major news outlet on the planet. They denied all responsibility. All of it.

Like any normal person, I thought they were completely full of shit—lying to shield themselves from the worst implosion in the history of advertising. And like any normal person, I wanted to break something.

Within 24 hours, arsonists destroyed the Coca-Cola bottling plant in Liaoning, China, the largest bottling plant on the planet. The local police stood by and watched. Within 48 hours, rioters demolished bottling plants in Bangladesh, Libya, Indonesia, Pakistan, and Texas. #OccupyCoke was the dominant trend on Twitter, and humans around the planet used all social media available to protest the beverage-industrial complex.

Three days later, just as I'd been doing every day since, I was watching cable news. My phone rang right when CNN had a breaking news report: North Korea threatened to attack the moon with a nuclear missile. When I stopped chuckling, I picked up the phone.

"Markus?" It was my old friend in Congress, Bill Paterson, a former trial attorney.

"Bill, haven't heard your voice in a while. What's going on?"

"A lot, actually. As you've probably heard, Coca-Cola is still denying responsibility for their own advertisement," he said, sighing with disbelief, "and so we're putting together a rather large investigation team. We need someone to lead the forensic side of it. I've been making a case for you, and when we took a preliminary vote, you won."

"I'm not a forensic scientist."

"Markus, are you tired? We're not investigating a murder on the street. We're investigating something that happened on the moon."

"But you're not sending a forensic team to the moon."

"No one's going to the moon," he said. "I'm sure there's plenty of evidence here on Earth, somewhere."

"Why me?" I asked, looking out the window at the lunar ad.

"Well, you're certainly qualified."

"Thanks, but there are others more qualified."

"Markus, you're a fucking rocket scientist."

"I prefer 'fucking aerospace engineer.'"

I *was* a rocket scientist, but after joining NASA, I realized they weren't interested in building new rockets, because of funding, and I spent my time rechecking someone else's calculations. I considered leaving, so NASA appealed to another interest I had studied passionately: climate studies. They offered me the head of NASA's climate studies division, and I took it gladly. My colleagues saw it as a backward career move, but, for me, saving the Earth from environmental destruction was a dignified intellectual thrill.

"We both know I've been focusing on climate studies, so why me?"

He paused. "It's because of your falling out with NASA."

"I don't understand."

With a hushed tone he said, "Markus, no one here is saying it publicly, but everyone thinks NASA must have played a role. They had to be complicit in this. How could anyone put a huge advertisement on the moon without NASA knowing?"

"And since I got fired from NASA, that makes me trustworthy?"

"Precisely."

Four years prior, I saw the funding for my climate studies research sliced in half so that NASA could create a new research division, dedicated to SETI, the Search for Extraterrestrial Intelligence. Sea levels and carbon dioxide levels were rising, and NASA wanted to appease the public by searching for little green men. Dipshit SETI sympathizers acted as if finding a microbe on Mars was more important than saving the Earth's environment.

In a rather heated disagreement about this with the head of NASA, I took a globe of the Earth and smashed it through his office window. He fired me. Newspapers labeled me 'the mad scientist,' and I was lucky to get a part-time position as a professor after the negative attention.

"How do you think they did it?" Bill asked.

"You mean, how did they engineer the lunar ad?"

"Yes."

"I . . . I have no idea."

There were many solid reasons against funding SETI projects, and I was happy to present them to my colleagues at NASA, but my real motivation was not rational. The truth is I had a fear of aliens—I hated them.

I feared the aliens of popular imagination, the cold, grey ones: the humorless aliens with tall, oval heads, dull, skinny bodies, and dead black eyes. There were years of nightmares—as a child, my parents subtracted from my allowance the extra cost of keeping my light on at night.

Most of all, I feared we would become them.

Within me was a strange horror of humans evolving into purely self-interested, unemotional, and science-obsessed monsters—with no true love of laughter, art, or one another. In my dreams, aliens were cynical demons who coldly raped the Earth. At times, my fears were so strong and nightmares so visceral—I prayed to God for humans to be alone in the universe.

"I'll do it," I told him.

"I want you to be sure about this."

I smiled. "You're discouraging me?"

"No, but you must know what we're up against."

"Stop being a politician—what are you getting at?"

"Right this second, I'm being your friend. You *do* know President Shepherd was a former executive for Coca-Cola . . ."

Cindy Shepherd, the newly inaugurated U.S. president, was doomed by the controversy. As the former head of public relations for Coca-Cola, she was a primary player in every conspiracy theory available. For the year to come, gun sales and death threats against the president would increase above tenfold.

"Powerful forces are in play," he said, "and if the executive branch is involved—"

"Okay. I get it. Thanks for the warning, but stop being a friend. I *want* to do this."

"Good, but let's be clear what you'll do. Mainly, we want you to double-check any evidence we find. There must be plans or engineering schematics for the lunar ad somewhere, and we want you as the final judge. People will trust you, and with that in mind, I have to say, you'll be the public face of this investigation—the poster boy. And don't worry about the legal part of the investigation; we're covering that."

To be completely clear, our investigation was a criminal investigation. Back in 1967, the U.S. signed on to the Outer Space Treaty of the United Nations. If a corporation did anything on the moon without authorization from the government, it would violate the treaty. And, by Article VI of the U.S. Constitution, treaties must be respected as law.

"I've got federal judges calling *me*, practically begging me to request search warrants for Coca-Cola's headquarters—our probable cause is written on the fucking moon. But we have to act fast. They may start destroying evidence."

"If they're responsible, we'll find evidence. Someone will talk."

"What do you mean 'if'?" Bill said, laughing.

The next day, I, Markus West, was named 'chief scientist' of the congressionally sponsored forensic investigation into the lunar advertisement.

A week after the appearance of the lunar ad, the top executives at Coca-Cola faced the members of our congressional committee. It was televised, and the room was overfull with spectators and journalists. To his credit, the CEO of Coca-Cola, Carlos Heisenberg, appeared without any legal representation. Though well dressed, he was not well groomed—he clearly needed sleep and a shave, and there were rumors he was intoxicated. On his turn to talk, he brazenly pulled out a can of Diet Coke from his satchel, opened it, and noisily sipped as the crowd gasped.

"Do you maintain that you have no clue how this happened?" Bill Paterson asked.

"Yes," Heisenberg stated flatly. The *New York Times* said this was less credible than the seven tobacco CEOs who swore, before Congress in 1994, that nicotine was not addictive.

"An advertisement for your product suddenly shows up on the moon, and you really expect people to believe that Coca-Cola is not responsible?"

Heisenberg let out his breath and dipped his head. "You tell me, how could my company, as wealthy as it is, have the resources to do something like this? I cannot tell you how offensive it is, the very idea that Coca-Cola is somehow responsible."

"*You're* offended?"

"Congressman Paterson, before this, Coca-Cola was the most popular soft drink in the world . . . hell . . . Even Osama Bin Laden drank Coca-Cola. But since this so-called 'advertisement' showed up, our sales and stock have suffered dramatically, several of our factories have been destroyed, and my colleagues and I receive death threats daily. From my perspective, it's more likely a competitor or perhaps a communist conspiracy is responsible," he said and paused to take another sip from his Diet Coke. "For all I know, aliens did it."

Everyone laughed.

By the next week, mid-February, our investigation invaded Coca-Cola headquarters in Atlanta, Georgia. Walking into the main building through a throng of journalists and cheering protesters, my forensic team followed an army of FBI agents wielding the most permissive search warrants ever granted. Bill Paterson wanted me to be the public face of the investigation, and, as it turned out, the media did too.

I don't know if it was southern hospitality, or subterfuge, but Coca-Cola headquarters was eager to supply our forensic team with free drinks. Soon after, a journalist photographed me through a window drinking a can of Diet Coke. By the next day, that photo graced the cover of the *New York Post* with the headline, 'COLLABORATOR?'

Consequently, I ordered everyone on the team to stop drinking any soda whatsoever. Within hours, my demand was leaked to the press. The next day, there was an ugly photo of me on the cover of the *New York Post* under the headline, 'SODA NAZI—NO SODA FOR YOU!'

After that, the FBI threatened jail time and fines for anyone caught leaking any info to the press. The leaks stopped. Ultimately, our investigation ended sooner than expected, and I would announce our results at a press conference in October.

While the world waited for us, it was changing.

In March, the Cuban government began mass production of crimson-tinted eyeglasses. The glasses were an attempt to prevent citizens from seeing the crimson letters of the lunar ad and were required for going outdoors. They didn't work very well, but Cuban glasses became globally popular when Hollywood celebrities started wearing them. I owned a pair myself.

On May 1, the state of Washington banned all billboards, and many other states soon followed. An impressive development, but not new, as bans on billboards had already existed for decades in Vermont, Hawaii, Alaska, and Maine.

Untrue theories flourished. People imagined the advertisement was either being projected by lasers or somehow burnt into the moon by lasers. If you asked where these lasers came from, they would say 'satellites.' No satellites. No lasers.

While naïve explanations were easy to debunk, it was unclear what the correct theory was. By all accounts, the advertisement went from nonexistent, to appearing *all at once.*

In July, courtesy of NASA, we had forensic access to satellites orbiting the moon. We learned nothing. Our experts in computer forensics found trace evidence suggesting the lunar satellites were hacked, but they couldn't explain how it was relevant.

In August, an anthropologist exploring the Amazon found an isolated indigenous group profoundly affected by the lunar ad. They believed the advertisement was a cryptic message from a god. They tattooed 'DRINK DIET COKE' on their bodies, faces, and animals. The group was friendly enough to be studied, but only after the anthropologist was forcibly tattooed. Later, he would sue Coca-Cola for the tattoo on his forehead. This lawsuit was one among thousands claiming Coca-Cola's liability for damages.

The most common lawsuit involved whiplash—from a car crash or from double taking too quickly when seeing the ad for the first time. Several thousand people sued Coca-Cola for retinal damage from staring directly into the eclipse. Homeowners with beachfront property formed a class action lawsuit, arguing that the lunar advertisement ruined their view and devalued their home. Moon worshipping Wiccans filed suit as well.

All of these lawsuits were waiting on our investigation.

On October 12, eight and a half months after the lunar ad appeared, the commission held a press conference in Washington, DC. I stood at a small podium in front of the television cameras and reporters, while members of the congressional committee sat behind me, stiff in their suits. After a long introductory statement detailing the efforts of our investigation, I said the sentence that branded me forever.

"In conclusion, our investigation has found no evidence that Coca-Cola is responsible for the lunar advertisement," I said as gasps and nervous laughter sputtered across curious faces.

"Your investigation is over?" a reporter asked loudly from the back of the room.

"The investigation is over. Yes."

"Why end your investigation? Isn't it possible that with more time and effort, you might uncover something?" another asked.

"Our search warrants only covered Coca-Cola headquarters in Atlanta, and they've expired. We've searched through millions of e-mails, phone records, and internal memos. We've interviewed thousands of employees, from executives to janitors, and no one—"

"Just to be extremely clear," a reporter said, "you're saying

Coca-Cola is *not* responsible for the Diet Coke advertisement on the moon, right?"

"As far as the evidence is concerned, that's correct."

"So, then, who's responsible?"

"Our job was only to determine whether Coca-Cola was responsible."

"But *who* is responsible?"

I didn't answer.

"Dr. West, do you really expect people to believe that Coca-Cola is not responsible?"

Everyone laughed.

Two weeks after the press conference, our summary report appeared in print for the public. The Lunar Advertisement Commission's report was a 924-page testament to our own ignorance, and it appeared nine months after the lunar advertisement, coinciding with the greatest spike ever in newborn deliveries—maternity wards were overflowing globally.

I doubt any of these children were given my first name. Random pedestrians called me 'sellout' and 'traitor.' Restaurants openly refused me service. Friends and colleagues didn't return my calls, and I had no family to talk to. I couldn't read the news without seeing my name, so I stopped reading it.

Once, someone threw a baseball, but mostly people threw rocks, through my windows in the middle of the night. It was difficult to fall asleep, and it was difficult to stay asleep. I refused to see a therapist out of pride and drank a bottle of red wine every night, rarely leaving home.

Then, one morning in January, I woke up laughing. Maybe there was a dream I didn't remember, but I thought I knew the greatest joke in the world.

"Shut the fuck up down there," my upstairs neighbor yelled as he stomped the floor.

The joke was an absurd epiphany, and I was laughing so hard I must have been laughing in my sleep. The thought, the joke, was that *somehow* aliens were responsible for the lunar advertisement.

I kept this thought to myself.

That morning I scoured the Internet. Many people speculated that aliens were responsible for the lunar ad. Typically, these people also wrote about Freemasons, the Illuminati, Jews, Nazis, lizard people, Satan, and the Denver National Airport.

My own speculation was simpler, and I found many lonely comments scattered across the Internet that agreed. In the novel *Contact* by Carl Sagan, aliens transmit back to us the first televised transmission they detect from Earth—which is Adolf Hitler's opening speech at the Olympics in 1936. Similarly, I suspected the lunar ad was a primitive attempt at communication, basic mimicry of symbols the aliens sensed we approved of, but which the aliens themselves did not understand.

I was wrong.

CYLINDER

Exactly a year after the lunar advertisement appeared, I received a 4:00 a.m. phone call.

"Markus West?" a crisp, male voice asked.

"Yes."

"Sorry to be calling this early. This is Francis Holliday. We—"

"Apology not accepted," I said, yawning.

"Okay, I'm not sorry. I'm the national security advisor, and you are coming to the White House."

"Now?"

"*Now.*"

I thought it was just another prank call.

"What is this?"

"This is an emergency and we need your help. We can't talk about it until you arrive. Get dressed and look out your window. The Secret Service is there."

Francis hung up. When you have a doorbell and only hear violent knocking on the front door, something is wrong. When I saw the men in suits with handguns on my front lawn, I forgot about brushing my teeth. I got dressed quickly and opened the front door to find two agents staring me down.

"Sir, come with us."

I rubbed my eyes and walked toward their vehicle, which had another agent holding the door open for me.

"Do you have a cell phone, sir?"

"I left it inside," I said, slowing down.

"Good. Let's go," he said, putting a strong hand on my back and pushing me along.

I hopped in a slick, black SUV, which was moving before the doors closed. In short time, we were speeding through the morning darkness into the heart of Washington, DC.

The Secret Service agents were quiet. Wedged between two burly and conspicuously awake agents, I had to ask, "What's going on?"

"There's a situation at the White House," one said without moving his head.

"At the White House?"

"Above the White House."

His tone suggested I shouldn't ask. I didn't.

For one second, at 1:28 a.m., the power went off at the air-traffic control center of Ronald Reagan National Airport, near DC. When the power returned, an alarm went off. The alarm indicated the presence of an unidentified aerial object deep inside the prohibited airspace over DC. There was no detection of the object beforehand. Radar telemetry indicated an altitude of five miles and a creeping descent with no horizontal movement. Attempts to establish communication were unsuccessful. After exactly six minutes and eight seconds, the power went off again, then on again, and the object disappeared from radar.

The air-traffic controller immediately called the two other DC area airports, Dulles International and Baltimore-Washington International, but they had detected nothing. Before September 11, 2001, an air-traffic controller might not have reported such an event and just assumed the Air Force would be tracking it. But, before that terrible day, there wasn't a fifteen-mile-wide prohibited airspace over the capital of the United States. The official phone calls were made, and the machine of federal emergency awakened quiet and quickly in the midst of a sleeping populace.

NAIC, the National Air Intelligence Center, is the military entity whose main purpose is to detect foreign aircraft entering American airspace, but they never noticed the alien object. Neither did Andrews Air Force Base, Langley Air Force Base, Anacostia-Bolling, Fort Meade, The Naval Air Warfare Center, nor the Patuxent River Naval Air Station.

The unidentified object was a large cylinder. It floated upright and steady in the dark with no lights, and its downward trajectory was the White House.

I arrived at the White House around 4:30 a.m., still in the dark. As they rushed me into the West Wing, I saw Secret Service agents on the South Lawn, together with military personnel on emergency reassignment from the Marine Barracks in DC. Most of them had large binoculars pointed directly overhead. The president and first family had been evacuated before I arrived. The vice president's family had been as well.

The White House was near vacant, but not completely vacant. Officially, it is called a 'silent partial evacuation.' Silent, because the White House didn't want the press to know. Partial, because a complete evacuation is impossible to keep silent. The White House Secret Service was there, and the live-in staff remained as well. All other nonessential personnel were told to stay home.

The Oval Office was unrecognizable. The president's desk had become a breakfast buffet with bagels, cream cheese, water, coffee, mugs, and paper towels instead of napkins. A dozen pairs of military-grade binoculars lay scattered about the room, and anything of historical value had been put into emergency storage. Wires meandered throughout the room empowering various laptops and small machines I didn't recognize. An automatic rifle rested in the corner unattended. The main door to the Oval Office was propped open by a bottle of red wine, and no one was guarding the door.

In retrospect, it wasn't strange the president would let Francis organize our meeting in the Oval Office. Like many presidents, she only used it for show and did her real work elsewhere. But the room was desperate and amiss. On the ride over, I convinced myself there was an impending environmental catastrophe. When I saw the Oval Office, I thought we were at war.

I took black coffee, sat down, and slowly realized the fake blonde next to me was the secretary of defense, the legendary Samantha Weingarten. Just glancing at her woke me up.

Samantha was one of the six Navy SEALs in the 2011 raid on Islamabad, which killed Osama Bin Laden, and the story is, she planned the mission. Of course, her involvement was unknown until long after the event, and strictly classified, but about as classified as Israel's nuclear weapons. Multiple books and newspaper articles were written about her. Soldiers joked about her the way they joked about Chuck Norris. She became a darling of the military establishment, which eased her path into the political community where she was coyly referred to as 'Aunt Sam.'

Samantha was widely considered the most dangerous woman on the planet, and she was sitting next to me. When she recognized me, her eyes widened, but her mouth stayed still.

"Hello, everyone, I'm Francis Holliday, national security advisor," he said, introducing himself unnecessarily—he clearly needed sleep.

Before working in government, Francis was a professor of computer science at Stanford University. After September 11, 2001, he left academia to work for the National Security Agency. There he allegedly created the Stuxnet computer worm, which crippled Iran's nuclear centrifuges in 2010. Later, he left the NSA to work in the White House.

As national security advisor, Francis answered directly to the president and had an office in the West Wing. Strictly speaking, Francis had no authority at the NSA. But, practically speaking, he functioned as an unofficial second director of the NSA. He routinely used his old, high-level contacts and the influence of the president to get things done and find out information.

The national security advisor and the secretary of defense were the insiders of the Washington insiders. I wouldn't normally be in the same room with them unless there was a shrimp cocktail in front of me. But there I was.

Naturally, I wondered why I was there. Given what I was

about to hear, I should have wondered why anyone was in the White House at all.

"Francis, why was I told not to contact anyone? What's going on?" Samantha asked as she took off her black-framed Cuban glasses, revealing the cute little scar under her right eye. She faintly smelled of cigarette smoke.

Francis sipped coffee to give himself a moment to think—an old academic trick for professors who had lost their train of thought. He put his coffee down and eyed all of us slowly before continuing.

"As we speak, an object of unknown origin is descending toward the White House," he said, pausing to gauge our reaction.

"I'm sorry . . . What's happening?" Samantha said.

"We need to figure out what's happening. The president has deemed this a matter of national security, so all major decisions are to go through me, understood?"

A marine rushed into the room, handed Francis a wireless USB transmitter, grabbed his rifle from the corner, glanced at Samantha, and left from the door to the Rose Garden. Francis thanked him and plugged the transmitter into his laptop. After some fiddling, he placed the laptop on the table in front of us.

"Francis, what are you talking about?" Samantha said.

"Something unexpected is happening—unexpected in the extreme," he said, guiding our eyes to the laptop monitor with his open hand. "You are watching live footage from a high-altitude helicopter hovering two miles above the White House."

The monitor was on, but the unfocused footage revealed only the blurry black of night.

Using his smartphone, Francis communicated with the pilot of the helicopter. "Captain Hathaway, do you see it?"

"I see it."

"Captain, you're on speakerphone. Can you describe for my team what you are looking at?"

"Yes, sir. I am looking at a cylinder approximately 400 feet tall and 250 feet in diameter. The lower half of the cylinder is white, and the upper half is red. It is currently two miles above the South Lawn. The rate of descent is not constant."

"Thank you, Captain. Please position your camera for us. We need to see it down here."

"Affirmative."

When it came up on the screen, it was easily identifiable. The other two members of our team looked at Francis, nodded, and walked out of the room. I didn't know who they were and never saw them again. Judging from their casual dress and creepy, pale faces, they probably worked for the NSA. Only Samantha, Francis, and I remained. Francis couldn't look at us or the monitor.

"This is a joke," Samantha said.

"Is it?" Francis said without inflection.

Looking at the screen, I wondered if my eyesight was damaged from the eclipse a year earlier. I wasn't sure what I was looking at, but my eyesight was not the problem.

On the screen was a gigantic can of Campbell's soup.

"A giant can of soup," Samantha said.

"What's going on?"

"Chicken noodle."

Samantha turned sharply to Francis. "I'm not in the mood to play the fool. Can you please . . . Does this have something to do with the advertisement on the moon?"

"We are all playing the fool here. The eclipse was *exactly* one year ago today," Francis said, looking at me. "Captain Hathaway, please circle out to your left."

"Affirmative."

Circling to the left revealed the cylinder's promise of low sodium.

Francis grabbed the house phone and contacted the understaffed White House kitchen. The White House was only partially evacuated, and everyone remaining had to eat. My understanding is that only the executive chef was in the kitchen, and someone from Secret Service was responsible for delivering meals throughout the White House.

"Hello . . . Chef? Jules? This is Francis Holliday. I'd like to order up a can of Campbell's Chicken Noodle soup to the Oval Office . . . Just the can, though, uncooked . . . Yes. That's right. Don't cook it, just the can . . . and with low sodium if you have it . . . OK. Send it anyway. Thank you."

In less than a minute, there was a single loud knock on the open door of the Oval Office. We looked and saw the can of soup on the floor in the doorway and the back of the Secret Service agent already walking away.

Francis rushed over, picked it up, and looked at us as if he had discovered the Rosetta Stone. I didn't understand why, but Francis approached the cylinder as a puzzle to be solved.

"Captain, circle around the cylinder as slowly as you can. I need a full 360-degree view."

"Affirmative."

As the helicopter revolved around, Francis compared the big can of soup in the sky with the little can of soup in his hand. Samantha and I joined him. There was no propulsion device of any sort detectable. No way to view inside. No lights.

The ingredients, the logo, the inspection seal from the U.S. Department of Agriculture, the seal from the International Exposition of 1900, the fleur-de-lis, the recycling symbol, and the address of the Campbell's Soup Company were all identical. Even the dimensions of the cylinder were proportional.

Despite the similarities, there *was* an important difference. But at that moment, I didn't recognize the difference as important, so I stayed silent.

Naturally, I assumed the cylinder was a promotional stunt from Campbell's. But there were two glaring facts that didn't make sense. The first fact being my presence in the Oval Office—I still didn't know why I was there. I only had the vague suspicion that my experience with the lunar advertisement brought me there. The second fact was the level of detail on the cylinder—I couldn't imagine why someone at Campbell's would make a near-exact giant replica of a regular can. No one on the ground could've read even half of the detailed information on the cylinder. It was hard enough reading it off the computer screen.

"You're saying you have no clue where this thing is from?" Samantha said.

"No one does," Francis said.

"Not even NAIC?"

"Not even NAIC."

". . . How is that even possible?"

Samantha waited for a response, but didn't get one—Francis had no idea how it was possible. He hated saying, 'I don't know,' and wanted his silence to say it for him. It didn't work.

"Answer me," Samantha said.

With strange reluctance, Francis divulged the cylinder's lone discovery by Ronald Reagan National Airport. Samantha and I were stunned to silence—how could only *one* airport pick it up on radar? My first thought was that every airport and military installation with radar covering DC was simultaneously hacked—a possibility so unreasonable it was embarrassing just to think it, let alone say it.

"Have you tried dragging it off course, somehow?"

"It was the first thing we tried. We dangled grappling hooks from the helicopter, hoping to hook the cylinder and drag it away, but it wouldn't catch hold."

"What else have you tried?"

"We've only been here a few hours."

"Look," Samantha started, "I'm tired, and I'm tired of *this*. If this is some sort of joke, you better say so right now."

"If this is a joke, I'm not in on it. There are no major winds outside, so it should keep its trajectory, which is currently aimed near the South Lawn. If there is something dangerous in there, like a bomb, I'd rather it be high above us right now."

"You idiot. Nuclear bombs are not detonated at ground level; they are detonated a few thousand feet *above* the target for maximum damage," Samantha said.

Francis looked at me for confirmation. I nodded and he paled slightly. The atom bomb that destroyed Hiroshima detonated 1,900 feet above it. Nagasaki, 1,650 feet.

Samantha grabbed Francis's smartphone. "Captain, can you hear me?"

"Yes, ma'am. It is an honor to be taking orders from you, Miss Weingarten."

"Get serious, Captain. Do you see any person on or in the cylinder?"

"No, ma'am."

"Captain, take your flare gun and fire a warning shot across the bow."

"Across the bow . . . of a can? Ma'am?"

"You heard me, Captain."

Captain Hathaway increased his altitude above the cylinder. After a pause, a burning red flare shot out across the top of it. The shot landed near the edge, bounced, and fell over the other side. Nothing changed. I had to say something.

"Do you really think this is dangerous?"

"I don't know if it is dangerous, *which is why it is dangerous.*"

"Come on, obviously, this is some public relations stunt gone to hell. Francis, have you tried contacting someone at Campbell's?"

"I talked to the head of advertising, and she claimed total ignorance. Of course, if this is a PR stunt gone wrong, it would be natural for them to lie. I've got some people looking into it, but nothing's turned up. Personally, I don't think Campbell's is responsible."

"This feels like Coca-Cola all over again," I said.

"I'm not sure this is just another advertisement," Samantha said. "Francis, is Iran capable of something like this?"

"Like what? Intercontinental Ballistic Noodle Soup?"

With a quick hand, Samantha shoved Francis by the shoulder and he fell backward onto the carpet, landing on his ass.

"We don't know what the hell is in that thing, and it is hovering over the White House. Did it occur to you that maybe, just maybe, whoever is responsible made it laughable so that we *wouldn't* take it seriously?"

It didn't work for Francis, but humor, by nature, is disarming, and that is exactly what Samantha was worried about. She didn't want to be the secretary of defense who let a can of soup annihilate the White House.

Francis got back on his feet and played it calm.

"I apologize for the flip remark," he said. "But what are you proposing? Fire a missile at it?"

"We could easily knock it off course by a hundred yards, using an unarmed missile, and the White House would be fine . . . but you must have considered doing that . . . What are you not telling me?"

His body slumped in response. I was a spectator watching a game I did not understand, but I knew Francis had lost.

"It's classified," he said, turning away from her.

"You can't pull rank with me."

"You can walk out the door if you like. But I assure you, the president is familiar with this information and she agrees with the decision as well."

Knowing the president had agreed to not to attack the cylinder, she calmed—Francis couldn't lie about this, not with me as a witness. At that moment, I assumed Francis would've told Samantha if I wasn't there, and that, out of politeness to me, he did not pull her aside and tell her privately.

But he wouldn't have told her—he didn't know how.

"What am I doing here?" she asked, looking at me.

No doubt, Samantha wanted to call the president, but Cindy Shepherd was incommunicado at that moment, en route to a secure location. I got into scientist mode and called Captain Hathaway to ask him anything that came to mind.

"Captain, is there anything interesting you can tell us about the cylinder . . . something you can see that we don't see down here?"

The captain did not respond.

"Captain?"

"Sorry, sir. The answer is 'yes,' but . . . It might sound strange."

"Please. It may be important."

"The cylinder . . . doesn't seem to be affected by the wind . . . at all."

"How is the wind up there?"

"The wind is mild, but noticeable. Gusts have blown by, and the cylinder doesn't even wobble, not even a little. Very strange, sir."

"What do you think the cylinder is made out of?"

"I don't know, sir."

"Is it translucent?"

"What, sir?"

"Does light shine through it?"

"No, sir."

"Do you sense any heat off of it?"

"None, sir."

"Captain, how do you think it is staying aloft?"

". . . I have no good idea about that, sir."

"None at all? Even a bad guess would be pretty good right now."

"Perhaps a . . . highly contrived dirigible, sir."

"Thank you. Captain, fly back around and give us a clear shot of the bar code."

"Yes, sir."

We had ignored the specific numbers written on the bar code. When recycling cans, I often noticed that the numbers under the Universal Product Code, the bar code, were typically twelve digits. The cylinder had eleven.

The numbers on the cylinder were: 18663287687. I showed the numbers to Samantha and Francis. With a smile, Francis rewrote the numbers with revealing hyphenation:

1-866-328-7687

Taking the initiative, Samantha started dialing the toll-free number on her phone and Francis snatched her phone away.

"We should know who we are calling beforehand," he said. "Knowledge is power."

Samantha nodded quickly, and he tossed the phone back to her.

Francis called a liaison at NSA headquarters and requested a search for the number in every available database. While we waited for an answer, Samantha typed the number into Google.

Her search returned a few websites, but only one was

relevant, and it was at the top of the list. The strange website contained only one page: an oversized photo with superb resolution, far too large to fit completely on a computer screen.

Later, Francis had the website disabled—ensuring no one else could view it.

As the web page slowly loaded, the upper portion of the photo revealed an unusual view of Earth from space. I realized the photo wasn't from a man-made satellite, because the Earth was too far away. As Samantha scrolled down to view the lower parts of the photo, the round horizon *of the moon* came into view.

I gasped.

As she scrolled down further, the surface of the moon cut the field of vision in half. The sharp crimson letters of the lunar advertisement, unreadable from this close angle, were unmistakable. Feeling unsteady, I grabbed Samantha by the shoulder.

She stopped to look at me, squinting in confusion.

"Keep scrolling down."

As she scrolled, the granular surface of the moon came into the foreground close-up, revealing the long, dark shadow cast upon the surface of the moon from the being who took the photo.

My hand covered my mouth so quickly it slapped my face. My gut instinct told me the photo was real, but I was afraid to trust myself. When I looked at Francis, he turned away to hide a smile.

"This *must* be photoshopped," Samantha said.

"Keep scrolling," I urged. Near the bottom of the photo was a typed message:

For a good time, call 1-866-328-7687.

By then, the cylinder was a mile above the South Lawn of the White House. Tourists and residents were waking up, and the whole world would soon be talking. It was a good time to make a free call and find out who was inside the cylinder.

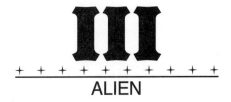

ALIEN

I got an outside line, dialed, and put on speakerphone. Francis didn't stop me. We waited about a minute, listening to a mixture of jittery clacks and clicks before the phone started ringing. Location traces for White House calls are automatic.

"Hello," a jovial voice answered.

"Yes, hello. With whom am I speaking?"

"Please call me 'Ralph.' Ralph!"

For a moment, I thought Ralph was eating something or the connection was faulty, but then I processed the strange bubbling sound as laughter. Ralph laughed for a full minute as we wondered what to think.

"Do you think 'Ralph' is a good name?" Ralph asked.

". . . It is a wonderful name."

Ralph laughed some more. His effervescent voice was an inviting swirl of international accents. There was a depth in his laugh that swallowed you inside.

"Ralph, are you inside . . . the cylinder?"

"I am. What is your name?"

"My name is 'Markus.'"

"That's a wonderful name. I will enjoy saying it often."

"Thank you . . . Ralph, are you in control of the cylinder?"

Again, Ralph laughed for an inappropriate amount of time. He seemed genuinely overjoyed to be talking, to anyone.

"That is a funny question. Markus, I want to ask you a question too. May I?"

"Okay . . ."

"Can I land my cylinder on your White House lawn?"

Samantha yanked me by the arm outside the range of speakerphone and spoke directly in my ear with an angry whisper. "*He is in restricted airspace. Tell him to take his cylinder and get the hell out. We can't have him landing on the lawn. And don't forget to mention he's going straight to federal prison.*"

As I mentally juggled ways of restating Samantha's meaning, Ralph interrupted. "Markus, is someone there with you? It sounds like a female, a woman. Are you flirting? . . . Is that a bad question?"

Trying to stay quiet, Samantha expressed her sudden irritation by taking a square pillow from the couch and throwing it at me.

"Ralph, don't land on the lawn. It is best if you take your cylinder and—"

"That's quite all right, Markus. I'll pleasantly land it on the street. I know how you people feel about your lawns. *I can't wait to touch them.*"

He hung up.

Francis immediately put the Secret Service operator tracing the call on speakerphone.

"We have a trace, sir, but it—"

"Please," Francis hissed.

"I'm figuring this out as we speak, sir. The toll-free number was established twelve months ago, and it looks like . . . It is an alternate access number for a Chinese communications satellite, ChinaSat 11. Looks like the Comsat got hacked."

"All right."

"We can't trace it any further. The signal's source could be coming from anywhere."

More than any of us, Samantha hated not knowing what was going on. She was used to asking questions and getting answers. "So the call relayed through a Chinese satellite, but the Chinese are not involved?"

"Correct. Hacking a satellite is not as impressive as it sounds. And something as innocuous as this would easily go undetected. It limits the possibilities, but not by much," Francis said. No one in the room thought the Chinese were responsible. The Chinese government was far too friendly with America, and far too humorless.

Francis's smartphone started beeping, and he activated the speakerphone.

It was Captain Hathaway. "Sir, we have a development."

"Yes, go on."

"The cylinder has an increased rate of descent, and it has shifted to the southeast. I suggest you look out your window."

"Thank you, Captain."

Looking up out of the bulletproof windows, we saw it, barely lit in the morning dark by dawn. It descended quicker than expected, floating and maneuvering without sound, and decelerated as it approached the intersection of Hamilton Place and East Executive Avenue, just south of the visitor's center.

It's embarrassing to admit, but I sensed a sublime beauty gazing upon the cylinder. A bubbling joy filled me just below the threshold of laughter as a dark silence flooded the room. Each of us picked up a pair of binoculars to view the delicate landing of the absurd at the southeast gate of the White House.

When I saw it, I knew—we were not the ones in control.

The unexpected guest had become the host, and somehow we were the ones that didn't belong. We were the homeless orphans peeking through the banquet window. We were the frills of the universe gazing upon something unspeakably more central than ourselves.

The cylinder landed, not with a thud or a bang, but with an impossible silence.

I turned to Samantha. "You still think this is dangerous?"

"No other option makes any sense."

OTHER

Francis answered his phone, and his face told us the president was on the other end. His palm motioned for us to stay as he moved out the door. Samantha and I were alone. I confronted her. "For all we know, this is performance art from a fine arts student gone off course."

"You're forgetting it wasn't picked up on radar. I doubt any art students have stealth capability."

"But can *anyone* avoid all of the radar covering DC? That's practically impossible, right? Which means it's probably some malfunction, a glitch."

"That's quite a glitch."

"In any case, why would it be a danger? You think it's a bomb?"

"Why not?" Samantha said as she took out a cigarette and casually lit it with a Zippo.

"If it's a bomb, why hasn't it detonated?"

"Maybe the bomber is waiting for the president to come back."

"But then we'll disarm the bomb before she returns."

"Okay. Maybe it will go off in a few minutes," she said, looking for an ashtray.

"With Ralph inside? Does Ralph sound like a suicide bomber?"

"Ralph is a loon on a phone. We don't know he's in there."

It was a fair point I hadn't considered. For all we knew, the cylinder was being controlled remotely, and no one was inside.

"The president and vice president are far away in secure locations," I said. "The White House is not a target-rich environment for terrorists at the moment."

"You're being narrow-minded. You have no idea what's in that thing or how powerful it is. There's the Pentagon, the Treasury, the Capitol Building, FBI headquarters, not to mention the White House . . . all of these things and more which your average terrorist would love to destroy."

"So then . . . Why hasn't it exploded?"

"It should go off any second now," she said, touching her hair.

"Then why are you here talking to me?"

Intending to soothe her fears, I only refined them. Francis came back into the room, and Samantha charged at him. "We must find out what's in the cylinder *immediately*."

". . . You can't smoke in here," he said. With a harsh smile, she grabbed Francis by the arm and tenderly dropped her cigarette in his fresh mug of coffee.

"We need to know what's in that cylinder, Francis. We need to know *now*," Samantha said. "Stop ignoring the danger."

"Look outside. Our people are on it," he said, placing his soiled coffee down.

Samantha picked up a pair of binoculars. "All I see are a bunch of scientists with hazmat suits taking air samples and marines with guns not using them. Look at all of them. They've got the thing cordoned off and most of them are more than twenty yards away."

"They are checking radiation levels carefully before they bring everyone else close. So far, there's no abnormal radiation. The FBI bomb squad is down there on standby, CDC is here too, and there are all sorts of dogs sniffing for anything dangerous. It is all being coordinated off-site by Homeland. This is under control," Francis said.

I picked up binoculars and like Samantha said, most of them were far away from the cylinder, but they were all working, and I sensed no hesitation. I spied the faces of the various breeds of dogs. None of them were barking.

"We need to get over there, break it open, and get inside. I'll get a giant can opener if I have to," Samantha said and rushed outside.

I started to follow as Francis grabbed my arm.

"Samantha can handle herself. We need to talk . . ." he closed the doors, ". . . about the congressional report on the lunar advertisement."

"Is that why I'm here?"

"Of course," he said.

"So there's a connection. I mean, besides both occurring on the same day of the year?"

"The NSA did a follow-up study to your investigation— classified—only I, the president, and the few who worked on it know. Samantha doesn't know. The director of the project was actually sitting on this study for a few weeks, afraid to tell me the results. But when I told him about the cylinder early this morning, he finally told me, and it is a damn good thing he did."

"Is this the classified material you didn't tell Samantha?"

"Yes."

"Why not tell her?" I was too naïve to expect the routine secrecy between such high-ranking government officials.

"Why not tell her?" Francis said. "You are missing the bigger questions here."

"Like what?"

He laughed hard and shook his red head. "You should be asking why anyone is in the White House at all—they've evacuated it, evacuated it completely, for a lot less."

He was right. In 2002, a single-engine Cessna flew too close and the entire White House was evacuated. A similar situation occurred in 2005.

He continued, "You should be asking why it is just the three of us. You should be asking why my assistant isn't here, and the same for Samantha. You should be asking: where's the CIA? If this is a possible terrorist attack, why is Homeland Security not in charge?"

I am no strategist, and Francis was making this glaringly clear.

"Okay . . . Why *isn't* Homeland Security in charge?"

"The short answer is: the president trusts them, but not enough. Samantha and I have very close, personal relationships with the president. And she trusts you because of your work in the congressional investigation, but in any case, I wanted you here for that reason."

"But you're still avoiding my question. Why not tell Samantha about this other report, the NSA report? For that matter, why not tell me?"

"Hear me out. I'm telling you now. The conclusion of your

investigation was that Coca-Cola did not create the advertisement."

"Of course."

"Our study concluded . . . No one could have created it."

I aimed my eyes at his and he didn't blink. My open mouth salivated and a wisp of nausea knocked me gently.

"You're serious?"

"Completely," he said, smirking.

"So, God made the advertisement," I said with no sincerity.

"I don't think so."

I promised myself that if Francis was joking, I would punch him in the gut. I mustered an angry face and stared at him. He opened his eyes wider and stared back.

The problem wasn't that I didn't believe him. The problem was that I already did. There was no humanly possible way to explain the lunar advertisement.

But, believing it and saying it are two different things. My composure dissipated as old nightmares heated my thoughts. Ralph would later say it was an important test for the individual to sincerely discuss the actuality of alien visitors. This was mine.

"Fuck off."

"Look," Francis said, losing his smile, "no nation on Earth could have done this and you know it—you, more than anyone, should know."

"How exactly do you come to a conclusion like that?"

"Easy. You ask the best minds available how they would create the advertisement. If they tell you it's impossible, you have to agree. Not a single engineer at DARPA or NASA could explain how it was possible. Without actually going to the moon, there is simply no feasible way to create the lunar advertisement undetected."

"So you're saying aliens did it."

"I didn't say that."

"You're implying it."

"Yes, but I'm glad you're the one who actually said it."

I shut my eyes and felt vindication but was afraid to let it show. Still, I feared Francis was playing an insane joke on me. The lunar ad had caused me enough humiliation.

"So you don't buy into any of the conspiracy theories about Coca-Cola? You don't think the president is covering anything up?"

"Markus, even if *you* told me Coca-Cola was involved, I still wouldn't believe it. Only morons believe in conspiracy theories. We live in a world where two nosy reporters caused President Nixon to resign. This is the same world where President Clinton couldn't get a blowjob without the whole world finding out. This is the real world, and in the real world, no one, not President Shepherd nor Coca-Cola, could possibly keep a conspiracy of that magnitude quiet."

As I considered his words, I picked up some binoculars and looked at the cylinder. I saw Samantha gesticulating furiously while talking to, or yelling at, someone from the CDC.

"This . . . doesn't make sense. Why would you authorize the research in the first place?"

"The report never mentions aliens. Officially, it was just a technical report about engineering, and those we asked didn't know we'd asked anyone else."

"You're not answering my question," I said.

"Markus, in all seriousness, I'm not obligated to tell you

anything, so don't be naïve. Suffice it to say, I had good reason to investigate this possibility."

Francis the scientist turned back into the national security advisor. His coldness put me in my place. I had been hoping to see this other report, but right then it was pointless to ask.

"Just to be absolutely clear, you are telling me there's an alien in the cylinder out there. This is our first contact with an alien species, and the alien decides to come down to Earth in a can of soup?"

"No other option makes any sense."

Francis picked up his phone that had been ringing. After listening a few seconds, he jerked his head up, picked up binoculars, and looked out the window.

"Something's happening."

He grabbed my arm, and we were running to the cylinder through the Rose Garden.

V

+ + + + + + + + + +

FRIEND

Putting a Geiger counter up to the cylinder revealed no hazardous radioactivity. In fact, there was *less* radioactivity near the cylinder than in nearby areas. The temperature around the cylinder was lower as well. Various detection dogs, trained to sniff out explosives, firearms, drugs, human remains, and electronic equipment, had been walked around the circumference of the cylinder—they detected nothing.

The FBI bomb squad was camped back on the South Lawn, on standby, in case evidence of explosives came into play. Using handheld devices I had never seen before, the CDC was checking the environment for pathogens and evidence of bioterrorism: anthrax, ricin toxin, plague, hantavirus, etc. The CDC had found nothing. The few marine officers stood outside the cordoned area, which was fifty feet away from the cylinder, while scientists and dogs did their work.

At this point, no one had actually touched the cylinder.

Everyone, except Samantha, was wearing a gas mask with a respirator. She was standing less than fifty feet away from the cylinder, just inside the cordoned-off area, when I approached her shouting at a young marine. Francis trailed several yards behind me.

"As the secretary of defense, Lieutenant, I am ordering you to shoot a hole in this cylinder. If you can't do it, surrender your weapon, and I'll do it for both of us."

The marine looked at his commanding officer, a major, who nodded. The lieutenant slowly pulled his sidearm from the holster while everyone else backed away. I could sense his reluctance behind the gas mask as he stared at his weapon. I wanted to say something, but there was no reason for anyone to listen to me.

Francis ran up. "Hold your fire, Soldier. Holster your weapon. Samantha, calm down."

"Don't tell me to calm down, Francis, and don't contradict me. You have no military authority here." She turned back to the marine. "I command you to stand your ground and fire one round into that fucking can."

Soldiers don't like to turn down challenges from beautiful women, and this was Samantha Weingarten. Francis put his head down and shook it. The marine released the safety on his sidearm and aimed an eye-level shot, square into the base of the 400-foot tall cylinder. I started to shake. Something inside me said this was completely wrong.

"No," I shouted and lunged at the marine as he shot, but it was too late. The single gunshot banged in my ears as the marine caught me by the neck with his free hand and forced me backward with a rough push.

When I landed on the ground, my eyes spun to the cylinder, but it was too far away. I used my binoculars to see the tiny black dot of a waist-high bullet hole on the white surface. All I had done was skew the marine's aim by a few vertical feet. When my eyes returned to the lieutenant, he had his gun aimed at my face.

"Thank you, Lieutenant. You may holster your weapon," Samantha said calmly while glaring at me. The lieutenant let his sidearm hover over my face a few extra seconds before holstering it.

I climbed off the ground and slowly moved in to inspect the bullet hole in the cylinder. While everyone else backed away, Samantha and Francis followed behind me. The three of us were less than ten feet away when I sensed something different about the air around the cylinder.

I kept moving. None of us said a word.

From less than five feet away, I realized the cylinder caught the bullet clean in its wall.

As the three of us stared at it, the lodged bullet was slowly ejected from the wall, seemingly forced out by something or someone inside. The bullet landed on the pavement, and I focused on the fresh, dark hole in the cylinder

I put one knee on the ground in front of the hole and placed my right hand on the cylinder for balance. Before I could react, the left side of my body smashed onto the pavement. With the wind knocked out of me, I couldn't even yell out the pain.

I didn't even remember the sensation of touching the wall.

I looked at Francis and Samantha. All I saw was their surprise.

A dog let out a bark from far behind. I looked back outside the cordoned-off area to see the crowd of gas masks staring at me. I waved my hand to indicate I was all right and stood up.

I placed my right palm on the wall of the cylinder again, not to lean on it, but only to feel it. The temperature of the wall was normal, and the surface was pristine, but the texture was somewhere between lubricated ice and pure nothingness. When I had tried to lean on it for balance, I had slipped so fast I barely felt anything before hitting the ground.

Startled by the unexpected sensation, I yanked my right hand away from the wall and rubbed it with my left, expecting to feel an oily substance. But there was no oil or anything. My hand was as clean as it was before touching the wall. I put my hand back on the wall to check again, waving and gliding my palm over the inexplicably slippery surface.

The wall was so unreasonably smooth it made me dizzy. I kept thinking there must be a thin film of lubricant covering the wall, but there was nothing. There was so little resistance on the surface it was difficult to feel the wall at all. When I attempted to put any pressure on the wall, my hand would instantly slip away. As far as I could tell, the wall was close to frictionless.

And there was another conundrum—if the wall was near frictionless, why didn't the marine's bullet ricochet? How did the wall *catch* the bullet so perfectly? If the bullet had ricocheted, it could easily have killed someone, which would not have boded well for the passenger of the cylinder—so, I thought, there was a conscious decision to catch that bullet in the wall.

Only Francis, Samantha, and I were near the cylinder, and I was the only one close enough to touch it. For whatever reason, none of us had said a single word.

I used my binoculars to look back at the dogs. Each was sitting and staring wide-eyed at the cylinder, almost hypnotized with open mouths and gently wagging tails. In the confusion, one of the detection dogs, an old German shepherd, became un-attended and had wandered near us.

The dog ran up, circled around us, sniffed the hole in the cylinder, let out a single high-pitched yelp, then sprinted away to a patch of grass. From afar, I could see the dog rubbing his head and face hard into the grass, as if to wipe off an invisible enemy that had attached itself to his face.

Samantha moved closer. She picked up the bullet off the ground and showed it to me. It was as undamaged as could be. As if the bullet had been shot into water.

"How?" she said and then instantly smiled quizzically. The sound of her own voice gave her pause. I smiled as I bent over again to look inside the bullet hole.

I could see nothing inside the hole but darkness and noticed the bullet hole was slowly shrinking. The wall, somehow, was repairing itself, and the hole was about to vanish.

I had an idea.

I knelt down quickly on both knees with my face up close to the hole in the cylinder. I looked back at Samantha, gave her a wink, put my lips flat over the tiny disappearing hole and *inhaled*.

I tried hard not to laugh when I heard Samantha gasp. When my lungs were full, I stood up, turned around, and in my best Donald Duck impersonation ever, I yelled back to the crew and asked, "Does anyone have a portable mass spectrometer?"

Despite the gas masks of the crew, I could hear healthy laughs—even the marine who shot the cylinder was grabbing his gut. A hazmat worker answered me by going to his van and pulling a spectrometer out. After activation, my suspicion was revealed to be correct.

The cylinder was bleeding helium.

In comparison to normal air, sound travels three times as fast in helium, which is why it raises the pitch of your vocal cords. It is why my voice, Samantha's voice, and the dog's bark were distorted.

More importantly, it became obvious the cylinder was a helium-powered blimp.

Samantha stared at me, her quivering lips resisting a smile. Francis patted me on the back and laughed, giddy with diffused tension. When I looked back at the hole, it was gone. I rubbed my finger where the hole had been moments earlier, and there was no trace of a scar, not even a bump.

The cylinder was *perfect*. No part of the surface was uneven, and the walls were inscrutably round. It seemed like the geometric ideal of a cylinder. I circled around but couldn't find a door.

I stared upward and around to get a feel for the humungous size of the cylinder and an old memory forcefully returned. There is a giant statue of a clothespin outside city hall in Philadelphia, and the giant can of soup gave a similar psychological effect to be near. It made me feel small. I remembered feeling the same visiting St. John the Divine in New York City, a large cathedral that dwarfs its visitors.

A flock of pigeons had gathered near the cylinder, impressively unimpressed. Francis swatted at a pigeon in the air that came too close. That pigeon flew over to the group and pecked at the face of another pigeon. This second pigeon, in turn, pecked another. I was irresponsibly mesmerized by this behavior when

Francis said something. His voice went from slightly effeminate to downright girly under the influence of the helium, which is probably why he said little as he handed me the phone.

"Hello?"

"Markus, could you stop making so much noise outside?"

"Are you really in there?"

"Your voice sounds funny."

"When are you coming out?"

"Whoa. Slow down, Speedy Gonzales. You want to see me naked?"

"How did you get Francis's number?"

Ralph laughed for half a minute and said, "I want to come out soon, but I gotta get serious with you. I must do something so your people know I don't want any trouble."

"So you're an alien," I said.

"Markus, you're embarrassing me."

"For all I know, you're some friend of Francis piggybacking on this whole event, trying to make me look like a fool. Why would an alien come down to Earth in a helium blimp disguised as a can of soup?"

". . . I've put a lot of thought into this. You got a better idea?"

"Why not show off your power? Impress us with some spectacular display of your superior knowledge and technology?" I said, expecting some banter in response.

Ralph paused.

"What a primitive response," he said slowly with a downward shift in tone.

The shade of his voice had turned black. His disappointment

was palpable, and it engulfed me, giving me nausea. His voice had the power to make you feel what he felt. Ralph was not human. He was angry.

"Is that *really* what you would do, Markus? *Really?* That's what you do when you meet people you're superior to? You show how superior you are to intimidate them? Is that a good way to make friends, Markus? *When was the last time you made a friend, Markus?*"

I got angry and hung up.

VI

TELEVISION

After further inspection and tests, the area outside the cylinder was deemed safe. A command post was set up near the southeast gate, where the FBI and CDC waited to inspect its interior. All military personnel were ordered to stand by inside the White House, and Captain Hathaway's helicopter was recalled to Andrews Air Force base in Maryland.

It was 9:00 a.m.

Pennsylvania and Constitution Avenues had been shut down from Fifteenth Street to Seventeenth Street, but the blockade should have been wider. Media, tourists, and local onlookers were prevented from coming close, yet, at a height of 400 feet, roughly six times the height of the White House, it was easily seen from afar.

Distant photos and video footage of the cylinder went viral immediately: Facebook, YouTube, Twitter, Reddit, HuffPo, Drudge, etc. At that point, it was only embarrassing for the government, and embarrassment was the least concern.

Samantha was going back to the Oval Office alone. I joined her. We ignored the curving driveway and walked straight across the lawn.

"Do your instincts tell you this is dangerous?" I asked.

"My instincts tell me this is hilarious. Did you hear Francis's voice with the helium? Ha. What a sissy bitch." It felt good to hear her laugh. "And you, you bastard, I almost burst out laughing when you asked for a spectrometer. But . . ."

"But what?"

"My head tells me this is dangerous. My head says we are being seduced."

We walked into the empty and quiet Oval Office. Samantha bent over to look in her bag when the TV flashed on.

"Watching TV's a good idea," she said. "We should know what people are thinking."

"I didn't turn it on," I said, spying the TV remote on a desk across the room.

Her eyes spun at me.

On channel 210 was a light and breezy morning show: weather, traffic, news, and call-ins. The commercial ended and the host, Tricia Tanaka, made it clear why someone wanted us to watch.

"By now, you know about the supersized can of Campbell's Chicken Noodle that floated down beside the White House," she said cheerily with distant footage of the cylinder in the background. "As promised before the break, we have a caller, Waldo, who claims to be *inside* that can. Waldo, tell us a little about yourself."

Tricia Tanaka didn't care if Waldo was inside the cylinder, but it made for good TV. I thought it was a prank, but when I heard his voice over the airwaves my gut melted.

Waldo was Ralph.

"Well, Tricia," Ralph said, "I'm from out of town, never been here before, and I'm looking to make some new friends in DC. I'm starting to wonder if this was the best option."

"Well, with an accent like that, I'm sure lots of ladies will want to meet you. Where are you from, Waldo?"

"I'm still from out of town, Tricia Tanaka, and I hope to meet lots of ladies and gentlemen. I'd much like to meet the president."

"Whoa. You are ambitious. Not sure what the first husband would say about that."

"I'd like to meet him too. I'd like to know lots of people, including you, Tricia. I know we've just met, and it is insane in an informal sense, but here's my number: 1-866-328-7687. Call me potentially."

"Oh boy, I bet you're gonna get a lot of calls now."

"That'd be great."

"This is quite a stunt, Waldo. Why do you want to meet the president so badly?"

"A whole bunch of reasons, but I would like to mate with her."

"What?"

"I'd like to have sex with her."

"Excuse me?"

"I'm sorry. My English is not very natural. I mean, I want to *fuck* her."

The show immediately went to a commercial.

"Call him. Call Ralph and tell him to come out," Samantha said, handing me her phone.

VII

+ + + + + + + + + +

USED

"**H**ello! Who's calling?" Ralph said, with heavy noise in the background.

"Ralph, it's me, Markus, I—"

"I'm sorry. I can't hear you very well. Please speak up."

"Ralph, it's me, Markus. Can you hear me?"

"I can't hear you. Speak louder next time."

"Can You Hear Me Now?"

"Ha-ha. Just joking, I'm unavailable right now. Please leave a message after the beep."

Beep.

I told him to call me.

Samantha rolled her eyes, lit a cigarette, and called the president. No one answered. She finished her smoke with me on the couch as we watched various news channels.

We learned nothing from TV, which was good. By then, every network, local, and cable news program was reporting on the event.

Reporters smirked as they made questionable puns. Fox News labeled the story 'SoupGate,' while CNN went with 'Chicken Soup for the Pol.' NBC was the first to report on the official 'no comment' response from Campbell's, and everyone else immediately followed. Most guessed it was a publicity stunt. But the best guess came from MSNBC, who suggested it was some form of street performance art by the infamous Banksy.

Again, I called Ralph, but he didn't answer.

The adrenalin was flowing, though neither Samantha nor I had slept. I yawned and tried to hide it. Samantha, looking at me, yawned and smiled. My heart beat stronger when her eyes lingered on mine. She brushed her hand against my leg. I had to tell her.

"There's something you need to know," I said, sitting back a little. "Something Francis and I know. I don't really know how to tell you—"

Without warning, she slapped my face.

I stood up and stepped back, glaring. Calmly, she stood up and put her face in mine.

"Say it."

I walked away from her, looked outside, and shut my eyes. "Ralph is not from this planet . . . He's an extraterrestrial, an alien."

I felt like the greatest idiot on Earth, but saying it relieved more tension than I knew. In response, she paced back and forth, occasionally breaking her pace to glare at me.

"Francis told me. The president knows," I said.

She picked up a bunch of pencils and casually snapped them as she paced some more. I was glad she didn't ask me how I knew. I sat back down and hid my face in my hand.

"I feel . . . used," she said.

She walked back over to me. "Stand up and look at me."

I did, and she instantly slapped me hard across the face, harder than before. I paused, closed my eyes, and let the pain run over my flesh.

On instinct, I slapped her face in return, knowing I had zero chances in a physical contest with her, but it was the only way for her to take me seriously. Calmly, she picked up a cup of water off the table, stood in front of me, and dumped the water on my head.

I did not retaliate.

She marched outside to the Rose Garden with her hand palmed over her skull. I picked up paper towels to feebly dry myself off and then overheard Samantha speaking viciously to the president. Under most circumstances, it would be unreasonable for the secretary of defense to call the leader of the free world a 'shitty bitch' and a 'devious cunt,' but in this case, tolerance is required.

When she was done, she walked back into the Oval Office, red-faced and lost.

"Sorry," she said.

There was a bottle of red wine by the door. She bent over and grabbed it. In short order, she took out a Swiss Army Knife from her purse, released the corkscrew, engaged it, uncorked the wine, and took one gulp. She silently offered the bottle to me, placing the mouth of the bottle near mine. I took a swig while my brain told me not to, then put back the cork.

"Why are humans such secretive assholes?" she asked.

Before I could answer, a phone on the desk rang.

The president has dedicated phone lines in the Oval Office. One is direct to the Kremlin, created after the Cuban missile crisis. Another is direct to Beijing, and it was ringing. Samantha picked up the phone immediately.

"Samantha Weingarten speaking."

It was Ralph. I moved closer to Samantha and put my ear next to hers. I took a tiny pleasure in the tickle of her blond hair against my cheek and took extra pleasure when she did not pull away.

"Hello, Samantha. It is pleasant to hear you. Is Markus there?"

"Yes, Ralph. Your *friend*, Markus, is here, listening with me."

"Hello, Ralph."

"*Markus* . . . Markus, I've been talking *to people*. They called to talk. I was talking to Tricia Tanaka on TV. My *voice* was on the television. I gave out my phone number, and people called *me*."

"We heard."

"I talked to a man from Maryland. He called me. I'm sure he was an African American. He used slang and called me his 'nigger.' It was wonderful. I was thinking about what I said, about the president, to Tricia Tanaka. *He* wanted to have sex with the president too. And a *woman* called me. She was a lesbian American, and she wanted to have sex with the president. I'm glad because I thought I said something bad."

"Ralph," Samantha started, "I'd like to get to know you better. Can I ask you some questions?"

"So . . . inevitable," Ralph said.

"What's inevitable?" she asked.

"Me, talking to the military. I was trained for this, but I'm nervous."

"Trained by who?" she said, but Ralph's response was laughter. "Ralph, don't be nervous. I just need to know that . . . We have nothing to fear."

"Samantha, I like you. This is where I ask how to convince you I'm not dangerous. Then, we discuss it. Then, you realize there's nothing I could do to convince you. All that matters here is what I *don't* do. Do you agree?"

"Agreed. So stop hiding in the cylinder."

"I'll be out shortly, but you need to understand, if something bad happens to me, your planet will be blacklisted."

"Blacklisted?"

"Meaning you won't be visited by anyone benevolent, and if someone nonbenevolent comes, Earth will be alone . . . bloody hell," Ralph said as he, apparently, tripped over something. "Listen, I'm gonna come out in about five minutes. I gotta get the music ready. This is gonna be awesome."

He hung up.

Samantha and I got up and rushed outside.

VIII

+ + + + + + + + + +
ENTRANCE

As Samantha and I ran to the cylinder, Secret Service agents were backing away from it. Samantha pointed ahead to Francis and we darted to him. When Francis saw us, he rushed to meet us. Worry covered his face.

"Strange noises . . . coming from inside the cylinder," he said, slightly winded. We stood halfway between the cylinder and the Oval Office.

A murder of crows had gathered atop the cylinder. Hundreds of faint caws and cackles fluttered high above as the crows left their slippery perch and flew south. Eyes were drawn in to watch the lid of the cylinder propping up, as if opened with an invisible can opener.

"Stand by," Francis said, speaking on a black walkie-talkie to the head of Secret Service, who, in turn, relayed commands to agents throughout the White House grounds.

A tinny ping reverberated through the air, and everyone froze in place with their palms stuck over their ears. Harsh, electronic breaks of speaker distortion and microphone feedback sliced through the air and pierced our nerves.

"Microphone check: one, two, what is this?" Ralph's voice

boomed into the air with an excessive degree of bass. His voice reached the distant pedestrian onlookers easily, and they cheered passionately with blank expectation, thrilled to have their schedule interrupted by the bizarre.

"HELLO. WASHINGTON! D! C!" Ralph screamed slow and loud to his new crowd. The cheering response from the distant throngs of spectators was overtaken as music radiated from the cylinder in a blaring auditory assault.

I only had to hear the first few toots of triumphant horns to recognize the theme song from the movie *Rocky*. I urge the reader to listen to Bill Conti's original score 'Gonna Fly Now,' at top volume, to best conceive this uncanny and unbearably loud event.

As the drama of the music increased, so did the height of the lid. Through my binoculars, I saw two tiny, dull, and silvery objects creep out over the edge of the lid from inside. These were Ralph's Earth mittens.

"TRYING HARD NOW. IT'S SO HARD NOW. TRYING HARD NOW."

As the trumpet-accompanied guitar solo launched, Ralph pulled himself up, slowly, floating, until his feet stood on the edge of the lid. Using binoculars, he was completely visible, in his Earth suit.

The suit was a dull silver color, like his mittens. If kindergarten students made a space suit for an alien, it would look like this. There were small words, in different styles, colors, and fonts, all over his suit—but I couldn't read them from afar. Pumping his fists in the air, he turned around to reveal the numeral '23' covering a large portion of his back—right under the name 'JORDAN.' And there were long, lustrous rainbow tassels on his arms and legs, glittering in the morning sun as he strutted like a rock star to the rhythm of the encouraging music.

He danced dangerously near the edge of the cylinder—but he had to be seen—not by the public bystanders, who could barely see him at all—but by us. A Secret Service agent close by couldn't resist smirking beneath his binoculars when Ralph pulled out from the cylinder an oversized American flag on a glowing white pole.

The flag was ten feet high and twenty feet long, dwarfing Ralph as he fought to wave it back and forth over the edge of the cylinder. As the tempo of the music increased, I heard Francis shout into his walkie-talkie the order to release safeties on weapons. I glared at him. He repeated the order three times, each time yelling into his walkie-talkie to compete with the deafening music. He pulled me close and yelled directly in my ear, "He's doing this on purpose. The music is so loud we can't communicate."

"GETTING STRONG NOW. WON'T BE LONG NOW. GETTING STRONG NOW."

The ludicrous behavior of this alien hid well his more truly alien features. The pink glow emanating from beneath the black-tinted visor of his helmet was inexplicable, and it weakly permeated his entire suit. Ralph, in his suit, stood about five feet tall, and though he wore his human-shaped suit well, he was not humanoid.

He bumbled about like a skilled clown, his movements abnormally exaggerated. It was like watching an astronaut on the moon. He did not walk so much as float and bounce, and he struggled to wave the gigantic flag, which yanked him wherever he waved it.

There was desperation in his movement as he tried to please his audience with questionable flag-waving. Watching him, one could infer that Ralph, even in his Earth suit, weighed little. I realized this just as Ralph started to crouch. When he did, he did not bend at the knee; rather, the entire leg of his Earth suit crumpled straight down.

"GONNA FLY NOW. FLYING HIGH NOW. GONNA FLY. FLY. FLY."

Ralph sprang up like a rabbit, shooting himself into the air, flag in hand. At the apex of his jump he was directly above us, halfway to the White House. He used his large American flag as a perfect parachute to glide downward toward the Oval Office. Midflight, the music ended.

Francis was about to say something into his walkie-talkie. I took the large, black walkie-talkie from his hand, threw it to the ground, and stomped on it with both feet, crushing it. Francis rolled his eyes and huffed, but he understood my fear. He grabbed my arm and got us running. Samantha trailed behind.

"Stand down! All units, stand down," Francis shouted in all directions as we ran to the White House, and Ralph wafted gently above us. He glided so slowly I reached his destination well before him, and well before Francis and Samantha.

I slowed my pace as I neared the Rose Garden. Francis's order was obeyed by everyone, except for the young Secret Service agent in front of me with his service pistol drawn, aiming skyward, directly at Ralph.

I approached him slowly, waving my hand in a soft up-and-down pattern to indicate he should lower his weapon. His hands only clenched his handgun tighter as I approached. The agent, red-faced, stressed, and sweaty, took his aiming eye off Ralph to size me up.

Within the speed of a glance, he knew I had no business telling him anything. He took his left hand off his pistol and stuck his arm out at me with his palm up. This Secret Service agent was the soon-to-be infamous Brian Summers.

"You are a civilian and have no authority. Back away," he said.

I ignored the gravity of his tone, stepped a foot closer, and asked, "Did you hear the order to stand down?"

"I am a Secret Service agent. I do not take orders from you or him."

"But—"

"Back off."

I could hear Francis yelling behind me, but Agent Summers did not listen. I looked around to see everyone on the lawn staring at us and moving in our direction. Luckily, the public was too far off to view what was about to happen.

We would only find out later what motivated his anxiety, and mine was growing as Ralph was twenty feet in the air and descending on us. With a firm aim on Ralph, Agent Summers glanced at me again.

"What the hell is that thing?" he shouted. "Someone tell me what the hell is going on here, or I am going to blow this thing out of the sky. I want a goddamn explanation, and I want one *right now*." He put his hand to his earpiece, listened, and shouted, "No." He then took out his earpiece and let it tumble to the ground, not once sacrificing his aim on Ralph.

I looked around for help, but no one was near enough. I was compelled to say something but couldn't think. Francis and Samantha were getting closer, but I couldn't wait.

Samantha had circled around and was sneaking up behind Agent Summers in his blind spot. I wanted to distract him with some deception, but the creative part of my brain had shut down.

All I could think about was the truth.

"He is an extraterrestrial, an alien. His name is 'Ralph,'" I said.

Agent Summers's head and aiming arm drooped abruptly when I said it. I broke his concentration, and he could not resist glaring at me with furious curiosity.

"Are you mentally retarded?" he asked.

Before I could respond, Samantha grabbed his arm, took his gun, and shoved his face into the ground. The subdued Agent Summers was instantly embarrassed and did not resist. In fact, he was delirious. The cold grass barely muffled his pained laughter.

Agent Summers would be sent home for the day, but the White House should have permanently released him for his behavior. However, his confusion was understandable, and dismissing a Secret Service agent in the wake of the cylinder's arrival would only increase scrutiny. The whole event would still need to be explained to the outside world, and at this point, I had no idea what story the White House would concoct.

While Samantha guarded Agent Summers, Francis and I got below Ralph's trajectory and caught him softly in a nest of arms. Ralph greeted our successful catch with the first hug of many I would receive. On the upper chest of his suit, right where a human heart would be, 'RALPH' was imprinted with a blockish angular font over a small American flag.

"Markus . . . Francis," Ralph said, "I need rest."

I realized something, and it stunned me. I looked at Francis.

"We didn't say anything to him," I said. "How did he recognize us?"

"Did you tell Samantha?" Francis dodged.

"Yes."

"Did she believe you?"

I looked at him, looked at Ralph, looked over at Samantha gawking at Ralph, and looked back at Francis. He smiled.

When I looked at Ralph's head to find a face, all I saw was an impenetrable pink glow beneath his visor. Around the edges of the pink liquid glow were thousands of thin tentacles of light, as thin as angel hair pasta. They seemed to reach out to me.

I hesitated to let go.

HUNGER

Ralph bounced slowly into the Oval Office and said, "Francis, I have needs."

"Tell me what you need," Francis said, strangely subservient.

"Canisters of helium and a class O visa."

Ralph's race primarily breathes helium. He can survive with oxygen, but he preferred helium respiration. Though a mixture of helium and other gases is often used in deep-sea diving, breathing pure helium will asphyxiate a human in minutes.

"I am very happy with how things happened," Ralph said, quietly exhausted. "I enjoy not being shot and must rest. Francis, it is good to finally see you. Enjoy your lunch."

Ralph then went silent and supine on a couch.

When Francis and I caught Ralph in our arms near the Rose Garden, I discovered the words all over his suit were commercial brand names of various companies. Ralph looked like a short, bulbous, race car driver with his sponsors all over his suit. Wonder Bread, Old Spice, Coca-Cola, Goodyear, and others, all prima facie sponsored Ralph.

He communicated and heard others through a device on

the front of his helmet. On closer inspection, the device had the brand name 'Fender' written on it. Of course, I didn't believe the device was made by Fender any more than I believed OshKosh B'gosh designed his Earth suit.

I continued to wonder how Ralph recognized Francis and me before we spoke. Francis was making multiple phone calls: to get helium, to make sure everyone was off the South Lawn, and to update the president. Samantha and I drew the rarely drawn, heavy drapes over the windows to help hide our new guest but left some window exposed for the sake of natural light.

"How did Ralph recognize Francis?" I asked Samantha. She looked at me and answered by pursing her lips, tilting her chin down, and staring at Francis while he talked on the phone with the president.

Besides Ralph, the other unexpected thing in the room was the fresh pizza on the table. Initially, the pizza was not mysterious. Thinking little of it, Samantha and I began to eat.

Samantha had been subdued by the situation. At this point, I think, she was just leaving everything to Francis and trying to keep her head straight. Francis, on the other hand, was comfortable with the situation beyond explanation.

"Who ordered the pizza?" Francis asked after getting off the phone.

I shrugged, took another bite, and paused when something on the table caught my eye. A small note card, the type that comes with a bouquet of flowers, stood next to the pizza. The outside of the card had one word written in script: 'Francis.'

I looked at Francis, noticed that he saw it, and he looked

at me. With my free hand, I picked up the card and read the interior aloud.

"I hope you like pizza," I read. "Love, Ralph."

Heads swiveling, our sights spun to Ralph, still sleeping. There was no way Ralph could have written the note since he came in the room.

Samantha and I looked at each other and put our slices down.

I thought I had missed something and needed sleep, but that was no explanation. The more disturbing possibility, too insane to suggest aloud, was that Ralph had made the pizza materialize out of thin air. Right then, none of us knew what Ralph was capable of.

With a weak smile, Francis picked up the house phone, called the kitchen, and put it on speakerphone. The executive chef, Jules, had a slight French accent.

"This should be interesting," Francis said as the other end picked up.

"Jules Marrant, speaking."

"Hello, Chef. This is Francis Holliday. Can you tell me who sent up the pizza to the Oval Office?"

"Is there a problem with the pizza? I made it myself."

"No, Jules. Thank you. There is no problem with the pizza. I just—"

"I can make another if you like," Jules interrupted. "I am not Italian, but I can make pizza, you know. I learned from the best. Dominic DeMarco himself taught me how to make the pizza."

"The pizza is fine, Jules, really," Francis said, "but who sent up the pizza to the Oval Office?"

"Eh, the usual people are not here. I had Secret Service bring it to you. The pizza is okay, no?"

"I don't care about the fucking food," Francis said. "I just want to know—"

Jules hung up on him. Francis rolled his eyes and called him back.

"Jules, listen—"

"*Non*," Jules said. "You listen to me. Someone who does not care about food does not call the executive White House chef. I do not call your office and tell you I don't care about your insecurity, monsieur, you understand? You talk to no one that way. I don't care if you are the president. You hear?"

"OK . . . yes . . . Chef, I'm sorry. The pizza is great. We are all enjoying it. I promise," Francis said. "But, Jules, I need to know: who *ordered* the pizza?"

"Your friend Ralph ordered the pizza."

The picture got clearer. We already knew Ralph had hacked the internal phone system of the White House—he was talking to Samantha and me on the Beijing line before he came out of the cylinder—so for him to order a pizza for us seemed plausible. But, as friendly as the gesture was, it was intimidating.

"So you spoke with him?" Francis asked.

"Yes," the chef said. "He called me this morning to remind me to have the pizza ready. I put the little note on it, just like he asked. He wanted a surprise for you."

"He *reminded* you?"

"Yes. He speaks very good French."

"Jules," Francis said, "*when* did Ralph order the pizza?"

"Wait, only a moment, please. I got the advance order here somewhere . . . *oui, deux semaines* . . . Two weeks ago he place the advanced order for today, the twenty-eighth. Ralph said it was super, super important to have the pizza today. He called sometimes to remind me, no matter what happens today, I had to make the pizza and write the note. I don't forget it, no way."

"Jules," Francis asked with a hollow voice, "have you met Ralph?" It was borderline insanity for Francis to ask this question. My mind would have exploded if Jules had somehow said 'yes.'

"We only talk on the phone," Jules said.

Francis, speechless, quietly hung up and stared at Ralph.

Obviously, to Jules Marrant, Ralph was just someone who worked in the White House. He might have assumed Ralph was Secret Service, or a secretary, or a politician—after all, he's a chef; it didn't matter who he was talking to. As long as the call came from an internal White House phone, Jules had no reason to be suspicious of Ralph, who, I had just learned, spoke French.

I looked over at Francis, his visage pale and limp. Ralph and Francis had been playing a game of cat and mouse, and the arrival of the pizza made it absolutely clear: Francis was the mouse. If there was a home court advantage, we lost it two weeks ago when Ralph ordered the pizza.

"Francis," I started, somewhat shaken, "we already know Ralph can hack into the White House phone system, but how could he know, *two weeks in advance*, that you would be in the White House, here and now? How does he even know who you are?"

Francis took a deep breath, dropped his slice on the table, and said, "He knows who all of us are. He knows because he's had access to the Internet for . . . I don't know how long. We are public figures, after all."

"And how do you know he's been on the Internet?" Samantha asked. Francis picked up the rest of his slice and threw it in the garbage. Finally, he began to explain.

"About three months ago, the NSA started getting chilling e-mails from an unaffiliated and unknown hacker. He called himself 'Ralph.' He kept sending his work, his hacking exploits, and we were blown away. Normally, I wouldn't be involved, but his work was too good to ignore. No one at the NSA could explain how he did it."

Francis stopped to gulp down a mug of warm water. Grimacing, he continued. "He hacked into big governments and big companies. He had hacked into *my* personal e-mail account, as well as the president's. I'd have to reveal classified material just to explain how near impossible that is. Suffice it to say, it was an unprecedented nightmare. But, as far as we could tell, none of the information was being used maliciously. In fact, he sent us a shocking amount of valuable information on people and nations America is unfriendly with."

"For example?" Samantha asked.

Francis glanced at me, then looked back at Samantha and said, "Ask me later . . . We could only think of him as a huge potential asset. We wanted to recruit him. After a series of e-mails, he eventually wrote that he would be coming to the White House . . . today."

"And you didn't tell us this why?" Samantha asked.

"He didn't mention anything about a soup blimp," he

said, glaring at Samantha. "In the e-mails, he promised more information in exchange for a visa, and I agreed. Obviously, I expected a more covert meeting, but White House security had been minimally briefed, which is why Secret Service wasn't completely caught off guard. I couldn't give them the full details, obviously, but they knew today was not going to be an ordinary day."

"You should've told me, Francis," Samantha said.

"I did not confirm it was the same Ralph until an hour ago when I spoke to him privately, when the two of you weren't around."

"You were careful enough not to assume it was the same Ralph, but not careful enough to tell the secretary of defense who Ralph might be," Samantha said, her volume escalating. "That's just genius, Francis, totally fucking clever, and when were you planning on telling me he was a fucking alien from *outer space*? No, I gotta hear it from Markus, and I'd bet you manipulated him into telling me."

Ralph awoke, and it saved Francis from the verbal assault Samantha was mentally preparing. I understood Samantha's rage but was too dumbfounded to share it.

ANSWERS

"**D**id you get the helium?" Ralph asked.

"It's coming," Francis said.

"I shouldn't need it, but I feel safer knowing it is near. And my visa?"

"You're serious?"

"Well, I would like to establish residency. Nobody wants me to stay in this oval room forever, and I would like to meet your president."

"You said you wanted to *mate* with her," Samantha reminded.

"We don't have to mate. We could just talk."

Ralph was a highly sexual being. None of us spoke of it at the time, but it was typically arousing being near him.

"Meeting the president will have to wait," Francis said. "And the visa can wait too. We have questions."

Ralph responded by reaching into his oversized chest pocket and pulling out two iridescent black sheets with white writing. His overly articulated handwriting oozed childishness. He would put a dot in the middle of every 'O' and put a circle, instead of a dot, atop the letter 'i.' Creepy smiley faces and other terrestrial doodles filled the margins.

"These sheets contain the typical questions asked during . . . this type of visit," Ralph began, trying to be serious despite his obvious excitement. "On this first sheet are questions I will answer. On the second sheet are questions I will not answer, but you may ask me why I won't answer."

"What do you mean by 'this type of visit'? What type of visit is this?"

"126-84."

"What does that mean?"

"Sorry, that's one of the questions I won't answer. Please look over the questions carefully. The list is here to make this part of our experience efficiently pleasant."

"But we can ask why you won't answer?" Samantha said.

"Correct."

"So, why can't we know what a 126-84 is?"

"We could spend all day discussing the nature of the 126-84, but it would be a waste, and there are more urgent matters. The short answer is: your people are carbon-based, more technologically mature than sexually mature, humorous, hairy, and violent."

"We are more mature technologically than sexually?"

"I've seen your Internet," Ralph responded.

I seized on the questions he wouldn't answer. Most were of a scientific nature. Dark energy, gravitons, P=NP, and many other subjects were off-limits.

"These are questions you must answer for yourselves, just as we did."

"Then what *are* you, and what are you doing here?" Samantha blurted.

"I am a *visitor*. It is my vocation. It is what I was trained to do."

"You're a tourist?" Samantha asked.

"Being a visitor . . . It's the funniest translation I can think of, though I should probably say 'xenoanthropologist.' It is one of the more dangerous professions. I must say I am overjoyed to have made it this far. In fact, I need a hug. You don't know how lonely it's been."

We all sat still.

"I'm serious. I would truly enjoy a hug right now, from all three of you. Be gentle, this suit is my only one, and it is a delicate form of protection."

I was already sitting close. I gave my fellow humans my best 'why not?' look, and embraced him gently, wondering if this was a joke. Samantha and Francis kept their distance.

"Can you survive without your suit?" Francis asked.

"I can, and I can breathe oxygen, but I prefer not to. It is mainly to protect me from your harsh and prickly environment, but this suit also protects you, of course."

Hug time ended as I stood up and backed off.

"Protect us? Should we quarantine you?" I asked.

The CDC had been outside testing the air around the cylinder for basic pathogens, but when Ralph emerged, I forgot all about them. Old fears and facts rushed to mind. Smallpox, brought by Spanish explorers, devastated the Incas and Aztecs. By one estimate, 90 percent of the entire native population of North and South America died from diseases brought by foreigners.

Ralph laughed at the suggestion of quarantine. He laughed for a full minute, and his whole being bounced while he did—as if his entire body was laughing.

"The likelihood of any difficulty is extremely low. I have been studying your genetic material, this DNA, for some time, and have taken all precautions to ensure I am bacteria free."

"I don't like this," I said, staring at Francis.

"Do you people really think I'd come all this way to poison you, to infect you?"

Ralph laughed but we didn't join him.

"We can't quarantine him," Francis said.

"What do you mean we can't?"

"It would get too many people involved, and this *must* be kept secret."

I was in no position to argue, despite how irresponsible it was. I told myself: if Ralph is benevolent, he would ensure our safety from any alien pathogens. And if not, the battle was already over—the enemy king was in the castle.

There was a knock at the window behind the drapes. I went over, peered outside, and saw two canisters of helium on a dolly. The marine who brought them was already walking away.

"You can leave the helium outside. I won't need it any day soon," Ralph said.

"How does this suit work?" I asked.

"Sorry. That's a question I won't answer. It's not much different than a human space suit, except maybe a million times more efficient," Ralph said. "I can live in this suit for over a year."

"But is there an exhaust?"

"No. No exhaust. My Earth suit is airtight."

"How exactly do you breathe? I mean, how does helium respiration work?"

Ralph giggled and said, "This I won't tell you."

"How do you know about our DNA? Have you visited Earth before?" I asked.

"Everything I've learned about your people I've learned through your Internet. I've been accessing it for about a decade, using satellites to wirelessly connect. I learned your English language in two weeks, studied your pornography for four months, and took a full year to analyze your music."

"Why haven't we picked up any radio signals from your people?" Francis asked.

"Because we don't want you to," he said. "Our radio transmissions are encrypted and masked, making them indistinguishable from common microwave radiation."

I wondered what his people were hiding from, but right then, I didn't want to know. By the end of our discussion, we'd all know.

"Has Earth been visited by aliens before?" I asked.

"Not that I know of, but I can't be sure. I'd rather not talk about this. Only kooky people on your planet speculate about such things."

I stifled a laugh, and he turned to me.

"Are you worried about anal probes?" Ralph was doing his best to deflect the gravity of the situation. He seemed desperate, maybe too desperate, to not be taken seriously. But his humor was a mask, and everything about him was unexpected.

His energy permeated us. I could feel him emotionally, sexually, and physiologically. I was more energized than usual—it seemed time moved faster around him.

I think his presence even sped up my digestion. Consequently, I had to use the restroom. I excused myself and avoided Francis's eyes to ignore any disapproval of my exit.

Alone in the restroom, I looked in the large mirror and saw a younger man. I jumped in the air and felt lighter. I grinned at my reflection, but my pleasure was punctured by a dark concern. It was a fantastic thought, but I had my reasons.

I wondered if Ralph could read our minds. The possibility stunned me, and I was ashamed for not considering it earlier. I stared into the bathroom mirror and spoke.

"Ralph, are you reading my mind?"

I was alone, but still felt the thrill of embarrassment. I stayed still for a minute, wondering if I might get a response. I did not.

When I returned to the Oval Office, Francis looked at me and looked back at Ralph. Samantha seemed to be choking on disbelief, and Ralph was giggling frantically, floundering on the couch.

With a heavy tone, Francis said, "Don't ask."

I didn't.

With trepidation, I said, "Ralph . . . I have to ask . . . can you read our—"

"No," Ralph said, and returned to laughing.

Samantha and Francis looked even worse as Ralph's giddiness overwhelmed the room, his capacity for laughter seemingly endless. When Ralph finally realized we were disturbed, he calmed and explained.

"No. I can't read your mind. Don't worry."

"Ralph," I said as if speaking to a naughty child, "we want

to trust you, but if you lie to us about how powerful you are, it will be bad for our relationship. There are national secrets in the heads of Samantha and Francis . . ."

"Trust me, I am no telepath. But . . . Like your successful poker players, my people are gifted at knowing what others think and feel. It helps to be near them and see them, feeling helps especially." Ralph's glow brightened, and he moved closer to me. "For instance, Marcus, I can tell that, for some reason, you are especially worried about mind reading, more than Samantha and Francis. And they *should* be more worried about it. But, somehow, you raised this question first. This tells me . . . a lot."

"What?"

"I don't want to make you angry. I should stop talking about this."

"Say it."

"I'm afraid to embarrass you. I want to be friendly."

After a pause, Francis diplomatically stood up and said, "Samantha, let's take a short walk outside." Samantha understood and went out the door to the Rose Garden.

"We're not going far," Francis said.

When I looked at Samantha, her eyes glowed with fear. Somehow, I realized Ralph had revealed, while I wasn't there, something personal about her. The same was about to happen to me and I knew it.

When they left, I moved close to Ralph. He reached out to me.

"Tell what you know about me. Do it."

He put his hands on my shoulders and rubbed his helmet against my chest.

"I have studied human mental illness. There is a certain delusion where one believes others are reading their mind. Someone you knew, someone you loved, had this delusion. This is why you thought to ask me. This is what caused your question. I am not wrong, am I?"

It wasn't a question. His uncertainty was pretend, a type of etiquette. He *knew*, somehow. I exhaled my tension with a long breath. I was no longer angry. I was shattered and serene—the tear dribbling down my cheek was my response.

When we were sixteen, my twin brother, Tom, woke me in the middle of the night. He told me aliens were reading his mind. "Shut the hell up," I said and hid under the covers. Tom knew my fears. I thought he was trying to scare me. I woke up the next morning, went to the bathroom, and found his corpse in the still water of the bathtub.

Ralph tightened his embrace.

The media's focus was brutal when we ended the investigation into the lunar advertisement. Of course, there were news articles on the Internet, about me, which Ralph could've read. One of them could've mentioned my brother's suicide, and maybe his schizophrenia. But for Ralph to know that Tom suffered this specific delusion, clinically known as 'the mind-reading delusion,' was either an amazing inference, or something I didn't understand.

"I do not feel pleasant," Ralph said. "I am unpleasant to have reminded you of these things. Please know, it's not that I am reading your mind . . . but . . . rather . . . the distinction between our minds is . . . very . . . slowly . . . disappearing."

When he said it, I believed it, and it explained why I wasn't disturbed. I wasn't disturbed because I could sense Ralph's intentions. I felt them—the way one feels an apple in one's hand. I sensed that he wanted to help us, and himself, but I couldn't tell exactly what his intentions were. In fact, I knew he was hiding something.

"The rhythm of your mind is so familiar to me. It is clear and strong and beautiful," one of us said, but I'm still unsure if these were his words or mine.

I wanted to remain in Ralph's arms . . . until I discovered his fear. When I located the horror in his mind, it surrounded my thoughts like a tornado. Ralph knew Earth was in imminent danger. As if I felt the future inside him, somehow I knew millions of humans were going to die.

I jolted violently and pulled away, tossing Ralph off the couch as I pushed him and lunged myself backward. My breathing was heavy, and my pulse raced as I heard Ralph sigh and watched him stand back up, slowly.

I glared at him, expecting an explanation, but he said nothing. Then I realized, the fear we had shared I no longer felt, because it was never mine to begin with. I was left with a weak sense that Earth was in danger, but it was purely speculative in my own mind alone, like the faded memory of a nightmare.

"I like you, Markus, a lot, and it is causing me to make mistakes. Our meeting is not an accident. There's a reason why I'm here, and the reason is . . . unpleasant."

"But you will tell us."

"Yes. But there is time. I am not joking when I say I need to get to know you better. The messenger of bad news is more likely to be shot the sooner he says it, you see? Please, for my safety and purpose, wait."

I heard Francis and Samantha talking. Francis knocked, and Ralph nonchalantly told them to come in. Respecting Ralph's position, I said nothing, and they didn't ask. The only option was to change the subject.

"What are your people like?" Samantha asked.

He responded like a child reciting a book report for his fifth-grade class. "My people are peaceful and scientific. Humor and art are a great source of recreation for us. We are silicon-based, just as you are carbon-based. This makes us very fragile."

To have the possibility of silicon-based life verified so casually was thrilling. Carbon is a great building block for life because it can form long, stable molecules. Silicon can do the same, but the result is much weaker.

"You evolved your physical capabilities long before developing your minds, and for us, it was the opposite. We were talking about geometry long before we could draw a circle on something more permanent than a sandy beach. Our species had been passive participants in the world for so long, we developed hardcore religious prejudices against manipulating common objects. Our early experimental scientists were ostracized by the ancient church . . ."

"That part we can relate to," I said.

"Oh, and violence, we didn't even consider violence until much later in our development, whereas you started violent and are slowly moving away from it. Your early humans would tend to get violent as a first response to frustration, whereas in my people, frustration causes us to slow down and think. Violence is typically the last thing we consider."

"How old are you?"

"I thought humans considered that a rude question."

Francis balked, "It is on the list of questions we can ask . . ."

"*I'm just fucking with you.* Francis, really, you are much too serious. I'd really love to relax here, and it would help if you could do the same. You've all said funny things, but none of you have *tried* to make a single joke since I got here."

"Please stop joking around and take this more seriously," Francis said.

"Francis, what do you want from me?"

"What do I want from you? *You're* the one who came *here*."

"Clearly, and now that I'm here, what do you want?"

"I want you to . . . Take this meeting more seriously."

"First and foremost, I want to be friendly, and friendly beings joke around with one another. I hope that isn't mysterious. You do have friends, right, Francis?" Ralph asked, and waited a quarter-minute until Francis nodded sternly. "Good. That is good to know. I want to know I can trust you. I want friends, and friends joke around. Blah, blah, blah. I'm an alien, but I don't want to *feel* like an alien right now. Don't you understand?"

I tried to steer away from the social awkwardness. I was browsing the list of questions we couldn't ask.

"Why can't we ask you what your people are called?"

"Well, that would actually be rather rude, now, wouldn't it?"

"I don't follow."

"Really? Well, look. If I told you I was a . . . Klingon, I'd risk being referred to as 'the Klingon.' I am a person, and I'm trying to make friends here. When there is a black person in the room, you don't refer to him as 'the black,' do you?"

"Well, no, we wouldn't, but this is different," Samantha said, looking at me.

"No. It is not different. I'm trying to fit in and feel very self-conscious being the only alien on Earth. I've spent a decade on your moon, alone. I need to feel a part of your group here. Is this hard to understand? It doesn't help to have to explain this. It's like I'm surrounded by children with no social sense."

It was strange to hear any being talk this way.

"So then, how old are you?"

"In human developmental terms, I'm a teenager, but I'll be 19,000 years old soon."

Evidently, one human year was equal to 1,000 years, developmentally.

"Really? How long can your people live?"

"We don't really know. It seems there is no limit."

"How is that even possible?" Samantha asked.

I answered, "It isn't as alien as you're thinking. There's a creosote bush in the Mojave Desert, and it is over 11,000 years old. And there's a certain jellyfish, I forget the name, but theoretically, it could live forever. Biologists call this 'biological immortality.'"

"Thank you, Markus. The small jellyfish you speak of is a hydrozoa called 'Turritopsis nutricula,'" Ralph said, astonishing us with his zoological knowledge. "At one point in time, we were just like you. We had males and females, and we'd have lots of sex all the time. But we've evolved far past primitive intercourse."

With a smile, Samantha said, "But you said you wanted to mate with the president."

"Oh, I do. I definitely do. But mating for me . . . isn't really intercourse. I mean, it isn't penis and vagina. Pardon my bestiality, but I could take any of the president's cells and use them to mate with her. I would subsume her DNA, and it would combine with my own, and the net result would be a genetic improvement. I'm sure of it."

"Wow," Samantha said. "So have you mated with anyone since you've been here?"

"What? How could I?"

"Well, if all you need are some cells, for all we know, you've already mated with everyone in the room. Our hair cells and skin cells are all over these couches, right? And the president, her cells must be scattered all over the Oval Office. You could be mating with her right now."

"Well, I could have done that, but I really want to ask first."

"Why bother to ask?"

"Because . . . That would be rape."

Samantha was drinking water and spilled some on her shirt.

"OK, Romeo," she said, "if your people don't have sex like humans, how do you reproduce?"

"Once I have mated enough, I will spontaneously produce another being with its own genetic makeup. I could even produce carbon-based beings," he said, turning to me. "In fact, I can mate with any living creature, and I do mean 'any.' In rare cases, my offspring can even inherit my knowledge. Exactly how and why this happens is something even my people don't fully understand."

"How many beings have you . . . produced?"

"Two thousand, three hundred, and ten."

To hear him talk about sex affected our libidos to the point of discomfort. More than once during these moments, Samantha and I stared in each other's brown eyes, and . . . I'm glad I was sitting down. Even Francis snuck sultry glances at me.

"Your smile is very pretty," Ralph said, facing Samantha.

I nodded as if I was fact-checking Ralph's compliment.

"Well, thank you, Ralph. That's very kind," she said.

"But do you know why?" Ralph asked. "Do you know why you smile? There's a special theory which explains it."

"Special?" I asked.

"As opposed to the more general theory, but we can't talk about that."

"Really?" I said with disbelief, expecting another joke.

"Allow me to demonstrate," he said as he stood up and approached the draped windows of the Oval Office. "Please, Markus, come here, near me."

I joined him near the closed drapes.

"Now, put your face up close to the drapes."

I moved in until my nose touched the fabric.

"Good. Now, tilt your head up a little . . . a little more . . . stop. Good. Stay still. Don't turn away."

Ralph grabbed for the drapes, pulled them back, and slowly fell over. The sun burst its rays in the room through the tall windows and covered my face, which reacted naturally to the bright heat.

"Now, what are you doing?" Ralph asked triumphantly, lying on the ground.

"Wincing," I said, my face clenched in the sunlight.

"Silly Markus," Ralph said. "Your cheek muscles are flexed, your dimples are showing, and your mouth is in the shape of a semicircle. You're smiling."

"But," Francis said, "what does that prove?"

"Well, it proves nothing to you, but it confirms the theory once more for me."

"What's the theory?" Francis asked. "And close the drapes."

Ralph picked himself up and tried unsuccessfully to close the drapes. I helped.

"Thank you, Markus," Ralph said. "Simply put, the theory is that smiling is a psychological metaphor for sun gazing."

"What?" Samantha said, smiling.

"What you call 'smiling' is basically the same way your face reacts when it looks directly at the sun. When you smile at someone, it is your mind's way of saying that this person reminds you of the sun. They make you feel warm."

"Oh," I said, as Samantha and Francis looked at me for explanation. "What you've found is that the way a face reacts to the sun is similar to how the face reacts when they are looking at someone they like, or something amusing. I mean, smiling."

"Exactly, Markus. That's what smiling is. And this isn't just on Earth, you see, because most beings have faces, and most live on a planet orbiting a star. Of course, there are some interesting exceptions, and not everyone agrees on what counts as a face, but you get the idea."

This theory of smiling was a small taste of Ralph's knowledge about psychology throughout the universe. Though intrigued, I focused the conversation on the subject that mattered to me the most.

I had agonized over the question for a year.

"How does the lunar advertisement work?"

"How did you get it to suddenly appear all at once?" Francis added.

"The lunar advertisement, as you call it, is composed of the most efficient solar panels known. They were all in place for a month, soaking up the sun's energy, before I turned them on. Before activation, they are almost completely transparent, which is why you didn't see them beforehand."

He added that he avoided detection from the satellites orbiting the moon by hacking them. We begged him to elaborate, but he would not.

"I imagine you are here to help us, to tell us ways to improve our world," Francis said. "Am I correct?" To Francis's ire, Ralph laughed. Ralph laughed long and loud, so loud I felt embarrassed for Francis and annoyed with Ralph.

He had tried hard to connect with us, to bridge the gap between his advanced civilization and ours, but here he faltered, and we could all feel the width between us.

"You want advice to improve your world? Really? Is it that mysterious? Okay, listen closely: take zero chances with your own environment because it's your only one for a long fucking time. Do you have any idea how many alien species we've found who made their home planet uninhabitable? Do you?"

His piercing voice seemed to bypass my ears and imprint itself directly on my mind. He was glowing red. I had to say something.

"Thousands," I guessed.

"That's right, Markus, thousands. Thousands of cultures gone, thousands of histories obliterated, and only a single-digit percentage escaped to find new planets. The others killed themselves . . . And all we could do was come along and write books about how pathetic they were."

I wished everyone could hear him.

"We have a special word for this," Ralph said in normal volume. "The best translation I can think of is 'suigenocide.' It's the saddest word in our language. Entire species destroyed because they could not think past their own little time period. They didn't care about future generations, they only cared about themselves, and somehow, no one else mattered. Our poets will write a song about them, but no one knows all the songs."

The word 'suigenocide' rang in my ears.

It was natural for Francis to ask how to improve our society, and I certainly would've if he hadn't. In any case, Ralph's lecture was stifling. We needed a different subject, and Samantha came to the rescue.

"Why the soup can?" she asked, pointing outside. "It seems so ridiculous."

"My dear, I did it precisely because it was ridiculous," he said as he slapped her knee. "I couldn't risk being perceived as a god. Many of your people are still tribal. It was the best way to introduce myself without causing global panic."

"You're saying you haven't caused a global panic?" Francis said. "What about the lunar advertisement?"

"I know well the trouble I've caused," Ralph said, trembling a little. "You must understand, there is a whole *science* behind visiting an alien species for the first time, and I'd be embarrassed if you knew how much thought I'd put into this. Considering all your xenophobic sci-fi movies, you know I couldn't just show up. A trigger-happy soldier might shoot an alien exiting a shiny flying saucer, but no soldier will shoot someone who pops out of a giant can of soup, especially if they are waving an American flag. It is simply too ridiculous."

"I thought you were making some Warhol reference," Samantha said after a pause.

"Andy Warhol! Oh my God. All this stress. I almost forgot," Ralph said as his arms fumbled for his chest pocket. "Markus, help me. I have something amazing in here."

I went over, opened his pocket, and peered inside.

"I don't see anything."

"Just put your hand in deep and search the bottom. It's in there."

"What am I looking for?"

"The moon museum," he said.

"What?"

"It's the moon museum. I found it on the moon."

"What?"

When I found the tiny object and took it out, I had no clue what I was looking at.

The so-called 'moon museum' is a tiny, ceramic wafer left on the moon during the Apollo 12 mission in 1969. It has six miniaturized drawings from six artists, including Andy Warhol and Claes Oldenburg. Why NASA agreed to take it and leave it on the moon is another story altogether.

After I pulled it out and gave it to Samantha, Ralph explained all of this.

"I was wandering on the moon, wondering how to contrive a way to come down and meet you, when I found the moon museum tucked inside the leftover equipment from your astronauts. I had no idea what it was, of course, but discovered it was the moon museum with a little Internet searching. It was the inspiration for . . . well, everything."

"So it *is* a Warhol reference," Samantha said to double-check.

"Yes. Warhol is someone my people would relate to. But, as Warholian as it is, the giant soup can is just as much Claes Oldenburg."

Andy Warhol, of course, was famous for creating art involving Campbell's soup cans and Coca-Cola products. And Claes Oldenburg is known for making gigantic sculptures of everyday objects. The giant can of Campbell's was, indeed, a tribute to both artists, but that's not all it was.

"Then what was the point of the lunar advertisement?"

"The lunar advertisement deflected any threat the cylinder may have otherwise created," Ralph said. "Your soldiers outside, what are they thinking? What do you think your Secret Service is thinking? And the people who saw all this on TV?"

"It's a fiasco. They think it's a public relations stunt from Campbell's gone to hell, just like they think the moon ad is a Coke ad which backfired," Samantha said slowly, as if she was figuring it out as she spoke.

"Exactly, and I needed them to think that, to ensure my own safety, so I could be right here, right now. Are you ready to know why I'm here?"

We quickly nodded.

EVIL

He did not laugh. Ralph's entire body went motionless. The usual pink glow emanating from beneath his silvery Earth suit faded to a shade of purple.

"At the visitor school, we have a saying: the most frightening thing in the universe is an alien who shows up at your door and says, 'I'm here to help.'" He paused for a laugh but didn't get one. He hissed and dropped his arms at his sides. His purple glow grew darker.

"I am here to warn you. I am warning you that you will be visited by a race of aliens that are . . . evil. In fact, the word my people use for 'evil' derives from our name for them."

He was bad at delivering bad news, and he shivered. Behind the drapes, a large cloud hid the sun and darkened the room. Insanely, I wondered if Ralph was somehow controlling the weather.

"Maybe this will be easier if you all have some wine," Ralph said as he reached out for the bottle, fumbled it, and gasped as it fell to the floor, staining the presidential seal on the carpet. Francis quickly got some paper towels to sop it up.

Ralph made new sounds, which I couldn't interpret at first, but it made me sad and frightened. The sounds were a type of crackling, a type of internal breaking, as if there were thousands of egg shells cracking open inside his suit.

"They will come, and they will not compromise . . . Things were not supposed to happen this way, none of this. We were never supposed to meet."

"Ralph," I said, "we need you to be clear right now. If there is some danger to . . . our people, you have to tell us."

"I have been calling myself a 'visitor,' but I was only here to study, analyze, and report back—the anthropological dangers of this encounter are severe. But, some time ago, I received a signal indicating they were near your solar system. I had to warn you. I had to concoct some scheme to come down here and tell you. I put the message on the moon to make you think your advertisers were out of control, so that when the cylinder arrived, you'd think it was just another crazy advertisement."

"Ralph, focus. These aliens, what do they want?"

"They will seduce many of your people. They have done it hundreds of times before, and have only improved their . . . charm. They too have evolved. You are lucky. They are not as violent as they once were."

As Ralph's crackling noises persisted, a tear leaked from my eye.

But Francis was unimpressed. "Sorry, but you're rambling. What exactly do they want?"

"They want to be seen as gods."

". . . And that's it?"

Ralph's sad purple glow turned angry red, and he slapped his mittens on the sides of his helmet. Without warning, a blaring scream emanated from Ralph's entire body and filled the room.

I cupped my ears and yelled out the pain. His scream lasted only a second, but it felt as if a concussion grenade had gone off in the Oval Office.

There was a hard, repetitive knock on the door and a voice spoke. I could not hear what was said, but I guessed.

"It's okay," I responded loudly, my own voice sounding foreign and dull through temporarily deaf ears. "Everything is all right."

We were not paying attention.

Ralph's scream was that of a mother who had lost control of her children. When my hearing returned, I spoke up. "Ralph, sorry, we understand *why* that is dangerous. But we want to know what else they want. Do they want our natural resources?"

"Once they are perceived as gods, whatever else they want won't matter. They will get it, and your people will give it to them. Expect chaos amongst yourselves. They will convert as many of your people as possible to their insane religion. That is what they want, and that is all they want. Beings that can travel light-years do not want for resources. I'm sorry, but it is rather primitive of you to think otherwise."

"Do they actually think they are gods?" I asked. "Or are they just con artists?"

Ralph paused, brightened, and said, "That's hard to say . . . You tell me, do the people of North Korea really think their leader is a god? Does the leader really think he is a god?"

Ralph implied he didn't know. But, in fact, he *did* know. These aliens did *not* believe they were gods, though they excelled at playing the role. Exactly how I know this cannot be explained at this point. I did not find out until two days later. In any case, Ralph's remark about North Korea was thoughtful enough, so no one pressed him on it.

"Who are they?"

"They are from a planet called 'Kardash.'"

"Wait a second," Samantha said. "They are from the planet *Kardash*?"

"Yes."

"So that makes them . . . Kardashians?"

"Yes. That is correct."

"Oh, come on."

Francis and I grinned.

"Ralph, is this another joke?"

"The Kardashians are pure evil. This is not something I could joke about. I don't understand . . . I'm embarrassed to not be laughing right now."

For future generations who may be unfamiliar, I'll explain. In 2007, a reality TV show debuted titled, *Keeping up with the Kardashians*. It followed the embarrassing adventures of *actual* humans with the last name 'Kardashian.' There was a whole family of them, and they made millions just for being human on TV.

Of course, I'm using the conventional spelling of the alien name, established by most media outlets after they announced themselves to the world. Only the *New York Times* bucked the trend by spelling the name 'Cardassian,' but stopped after learning this was the name of a fictional race of aliens from the *Star Trek* television series.

Despite everything, I'm convinced it was just a terrible co(s)mic accident that these aliens actually came from a planet they called 'Kardash.' The most comparable coincidence I can think of, a similar clash of names, comes from a terrorist group in the Philippines known as the Moro Islamic Liberation Front, whose acronym had a very different meaning during this era.

"I'm sorry if you think this is funny, but it is one of the few things I cannot laugh about. They are carbon-based life-forms, like you, but far more dangerous. They don't even come from a solar system. Kardash is a dark planet with a wide orbit around a small black hole."

Samantha broke out in disbelief and looked at me. "How is that even possible? Can something orbit a black hole? How come the black hole doesn't just . . . swallow it?"

I said, "It's definitely possible. As long as you are not too close, you can orbit it safely. In fact, most, if not all, galaxies are believed to have massive black holes at their center. So our solar system is, in effect, orbiting a black hole as we speak. The real surprise is how any form of life could exist . . . or be born there . . ."

"Yes," Ralph said. "It is surprising—we know of no other species like them. The ancient Kardashians had no eyes and were very much like your bats. They would fly and screech, using echolocation to determine the world around them and—"

"What? How can they learn interstellar travel? How could they understand something as basic as the electromagnetic spectrum without eyes?" Francis blurted. The short answer, of course, is that the Kardashians evolved just like any other species. But there is much more to their development than sheer evolution.

"Eons ago, when my people first visited other planets, we stumbled upon them. Much like the animals on your Galapagos Islands, we were ecologically naïve."

"Ecologically naïve?" Samantha said.

I answered, "He means they weren't used to predators. Many animals in the Galapagos Islands will just walk right up to you, unafraid. In practical terms, it means they stop being afraid and become more curious. Dolphins and humans are good examples."

"Yes. That's how my people were when they visited Kardash. I must stress just how naïve we were. On our home planet, no other beings attacked us, and we attacked no other beings. Our planet is essentially a planet of pacifists, not for philosophical reasons, but because of evolution and our environment. The beings on my planet never outpaced the resources required to live, so fighting over food or land never occurred to us. Every animal on our planet is a vegetarian, so to speak, though our plants are much different than yours. The very concept of a *predator* was a mere theoretical possibility, something philosophers talked about. For most, the idea of a conscious being purposefully attacking another conscious being with the intent to kill was a joke. My people believed, as an article of religious faith, that there could be no predators in the universe, that God would never let such an entity exist. They believed that everybody should like everybody. As a species, we were pathetically naïve. The small group of our people who visited Kardash . . . we never heard from again."

"But, how do you know about Kardash?"

Ralph's purple hue grew darker. The crackling noises within him increased.

"Millennia later, that same ship returned to our home planet. It did not respond to radio contact, so we assumed their communication system was inoperative. The ship had been gone for so long, this was easy to believe. We organized parades all over the planet and a homecoming party. Millions of my people were there to greet the returning ship. But when the Kardashians came out of our old ship, it was an immediate slaughter. There was no attempt to communicate. There was only an attack. This was the first time we had ever been attacked, by anything—ever—and it was my planet's first contact with an alien species. They slaughtered a quarter of our population, 1.5 billion of us, before they realized they could not gain nourishment from our corpses. All we could do was scream. The only thing they left us with was our concept of evil."

None of us could respond. This was Ralph's holocaust, his people's introduction to extreme malevolence. Though we should have, none of us wanted to inquire further. All of it had occurred millennia before Ralph was born.

"The shame of my people, our greatest error, was letting our ship fall into the hands of such a primitive group," Ralph said, facing Francis.

"Where is your ship?" Francis said.

I looked on the list of questions we couldn't ask, and spaceflight was one of them. It was obvious to everyone in the room that Francis was interested in obtaining whatever advanced technology Ralph might have.

"Imagine a caveman with a crossbow," Ralph said. "Imagine what would have happened if the ancient Romans had a single Gatling gun. Imagine if the Nazis had nuclear weapons before the United States."

"That's not an answer."

"I've disintegrated my ship and almost every trace of it on the moon. I can't risk the Kardashians, or anyone else, getting ahold of it."

Francis slammed his fist on the president's desk.

"Francis, believe me, you are not ready for our technology. It would only corrupt you. You wouldn't give a gun or an iPhone to a three-year-old, and there are good reasons for this. Of course, the shell of the blimp outside was part of my spacecraft. You may cannibalize it as you please. It shouldn't spoil you too badly."

"What is it made out of?" I asked.

"Hmmm," Ralph started, thinking aloud, "I'm not sure how to translate it. It is like your graphene, except stronger and smarter, I mean, programmable. But I won't tell you how to program it. You're not ready for that."

"Program it?"

"It can be programmed to take on almost any shape you can think of. The technology is ancient, but still elegant and useful."

"Will you at least tell us how you flew your blimp into the upper atmosphere without being detected by radar? Does it have some type of cloaking device?" Francis asked.

"No blimp that small has a cloaking device," Ralph said.

I smiled. Ralph's usual pink glow turned golden for a split second, then back to pink, as if to wink at me in his own way.

Ralph's reference to the movie *Star Wars* was lost on Samantha, and she glared at me when I snorted a tiny laugh.

"How will you return home?"

"I can't. This is why I asked for a visa. You won't deny me this, will you?"

Francis was exasperated. "Ralph, we don't know what to do with you. Don't you get it? Did you really think you'd start living a normal life here? What did they teach you at this visitor school of yours? Have you ever actually visited an alien species before?"

"Well, this is my first time, but I did go to one of the better schools."

"Ralph," Francis said, "we can't have you walking around in broad daylight. You must know this."

Of course, Ralph knew this. Ralph had no intention to roam in public. He wanted a visa as a sign of trust. He wanted something, some official piece of paper, which told him he was welcome on Earth.

"What am I supposed to do?" Ralph asked.

"I've got an idea," Francis said as he stood up and went to the door. "I'll be right back."

When Francis left, Ralph turned to me. It wasn't clear where his face was, but when he turned to you, it was as if his whole body was his face.

"Ralph, don't worry, nothing bad will happen to you," I said, but I didn't sound sincere because I wasn't. I had no power in the situation. Ralph turned to Samantha.

"Will you protect me?"

"The United States of America has no interest in harming a

friendly . . . person from another planet. I take it you will help us deal with these . . . Kardashians."

"Absolutely. That's why I'm here."

Samantha gulped down a glass of water as Francis rushed back into the room and shut the door. "This is what is going to happen. Ralph, you are going to spend the night in the bowling alley, and we are going to keep you there until we figure out what to do with you." President Nixon had a small underground bowling alley installed in 1969. "The bowling alley is out of the way, rarely used, and the president can come down and talk to you if she needs to."

Francis turned to me.

"Markus, I suggested it to the president, and she wants you to be Ralph's guardian." Ralph jumped on me and hugged me like a hairless, floating St. Bernard. I smiled and returned the warm hug. Something made it impossible to resist.

"There are only a few people who know about Ralph, and we are going to keep it that way. Are we clear on this?" There was no need to ask . . . Who would believe us? We nodded easily. "Ralph, were you joking about these other aliens? These Kardashians?"

"No."

"All right, when will they be here? How long do we have?"

"Three days."

Time seemed to stop for a few seconds.

Francis gripped his own head. "You are giving us *three* days to prepare for an alien invasion when you could have showed up sooner without all this comedic bullshit? What the fuck are we supposed to do, Ralph? *Did you really come to warn us or just mock us and watch us die?"*

Ralph's underlying pink glow returned, pinker than ever. Needing to be understood, he spoke slower. He tried all day to speak to us as equals, but now he treated us like the cosmic children we were.

"Whether I had come now or years ago, my advice would be the same. You can survive, but you must believe me, and you must follow my advice. The difference is between millions . . . and billions . . . dying. There is no other way."

"Do we have a fighting chance against them?" Samantha asked.

"A chance? Yes. But if you fight them, you will lose."

"Then what do we do?"

"Nothing."

NOTHING

"**N**othing," Samantha repeated after moments passed.

"Yes. They have weapons . . . If they wanted, they could destroy your entire planet. Please believe: you cannot win a fight against them. Anyone who engages them . . . You will see the consequences."

"They are coming here to attack, and you are telling us to surrender."

"I never said they would attack you, not a preemptive attack anyway."

The room was silent with confusion. Whatever trust Ralph had forged was melting.

"I've got a story for you too, Ralph, so now you listen," Francis began. "A dangerous horde of aliens is coming to enslave all the poor, pathetic Earthlings, and to make the job easier, they send in a scout, a cute and funny alien, to convince the stupid earthlings not to fight them. What do you think of that?"

"I don't like that story, Francis."

"Of course, you don't. Should we believe it's just a coincidence that you and these Kardashians just happened to show up around the same time?"

"It is not a coincidence. I knew the Kardashians would be in the vicinity, and I use 'vicinity' very loosely, of your solar system long before I came here to study you. My mission was twofold: to study your people, and take action in case, and only in case, they approached. It isn't my fault you let your radio transmissions blare all over the galaxy, like some dying animal crying out for a predator to extinguish your misery. I could have left a decade ago, saved myself, and let you fend for yourselves. I came here to help you, but I cannot force you to do anything. This is dangerous for me too, you know. It is one more reason why I needed this ridiculous charade with the soup can. They too have been monitoring your Internet, television programs, and whatever else you've let bleed out into space. The Kardashians will at least give you a choice, but if they find me here . . ."

I presented a tiny olive branch. "Francis, any beings capable of interstellar travel must be powerful enough to destroy us in any battle we can imagine. Even if you don't believe Ralph, you must believe we can't possibly defeat such aliens."

"Thank you, Markus," Ralph said.

"So what do you propose we do?"

"We have two options," I said. "If we attack first, we might fight the good fight, but we will lose. Hell, we couldn't attack the Russians without them retaliating and nuking half the planet. In my mind, it's obvious suicide. Therefore, we wait. We prepare, but we wait."

Francis started to take the idea seriously. Samantha stared at Ralph with her hand on her chin, silent. Her lack of objections held their own weight.

"Ralph, you told us these Kardashians murdered a quarter of the population of your planet, and you expect us to do nothing? This doesn't feel right at all," Francis said.

"That was so long ago, it isn't worth calculating in your years how long. They were savages, but they've evolved and matured, just as you have. They are less violent, thank God, but they are still tribal."

Samantha spoke up. "Ralph, why didn't you leave? Why did you come down here to warn us? Even if you convince America not to attack, other nations will."

"America is the most influential nation on Earth, and I want you to persuade other countries not to attack . . . but me . . . Why did I come and not leave? I did tell you, my species feels responsible for the Kardashians' technological development. Almost all their technology is based on our lost ship. Since then, all they have done is travel around the galaxy trying to convert people to their crazy religion."

"So that is really all they want, to convert us? What happens if we refuse?"

"If that is all you do, they won't harm you."

"They won't force us to convert?"

"No."

"If that's the case . . . What's the problem?" Francis asked. "They are just a bunch of interstellar Jehovah's Witnesses, and if we don't answer the door, they won't bother us?"

"They won't bother you, Francis, because you're too happy and clever to be seduced by them. But for all I know, two-thirds of the American population will convert. The Kardashians can be extremely seductive. We are not talking about slick-talking televangelists here. We are talking about arrogant aliens who claim to be prophets, and they have the power to convince humans they can do miracles."

I put in my two cents. "I have to say, we do have freedom of religion in America. If someone wants to join some whacky religion, there isn't much we can do, right?"

Francis and Samantha gave the nod to my constitutional reminder.

"Then what happens to the converts?"

"They'll become loyalists of the Kardashians, willing loyalists, and they are the ones you need to worry about. There is no telling what the converts will do to convert other humans."

"Wait . . . These aliens have some sort of policy where they won't force humans to convert, but the human converts will force others to convert? That . . . doesn't make sense."

"It makes as much sense as the followers of Jesus creating the Spanish Inquisition and the Crusades," Ralph said with a poignant snicker. "The Kardashians are dangerous, but they will only prey on your minds. The real danger will be the converts who will do anything for their false gods. And eventually, when the Kardashians are done, they will take the converts with them and depart Earth."

"And then what?"

"And then that's it. You'll never hear from the Kardashians or the converts again."

"All the converts will just go with them? Leaving everything behind?"

"The Kardashians will promise to bring them to heaven."

When Ralph said it, it all became clear and real. Francis and Samantha stopped talking. Until that point, it was as if we were adults debating a political issue in an afternoon coffee klatch. There's a reason why so many people believe in an afterlife, and part of the reason is a rest from the weariness of life.

"Why should we trust you?" Francis, like the rest of us, was tired, and his questions were getting sloppy. "How do we even know these Kardashians are evil? Maybe *you're* the devil, and they really are prophets . . ."

I suspected Ralph would be offended, but he simply did not respond.

"Who sent you?" Francis asked with accusation.

"Francis, calm down," Samantha said. "The truth is as Ralph said earlier, there's nothing he can do to fully gain our trust. It is all about what he doesn't do. And he hasn't really done anything except talk."

As Samantha spoke, Ralph stood up, took the scrap crusts of the pizza, and approached the windows of the Oval Office. I followed close behind. Just as Samantha was done speaking, Ralph grabbed for the drapes. I helped him.

With the drapes pulled back, everyone inside saw what was outside. At least a hundred ordinary pigeons, completely quiet and motionless, lurked right outside the Oval Office. All of their eyes pointed at us, and none of them expressed a shiver of fear when I pulled back the drapes.

"Could you help me," Ralph said quietly, pointing to the door handle.

I opened the door. With some difficulty, he broke the soft bread into smaller pieces and tossed them to the pigeons. But the pigeons were more interested in staring at Ralph than eating his bread. Samantha looked at me, and Francis turned away. I heard Ralph whisper.

"What I am doing you do not know now, but afterward, you will understand."

XIII

+ + + + + + + + + +
NIGHT

All of us, including Ralph, were exhausted physically and mentally, and the quality of our thinking was dwindling. Though much had been said, the president would decide the course of action.

"We are all worn down. I'm calling it a night," I said.

This we agreed upon.

Francis found plain white sheets to cover Ralph as we slowly led him to the bowling alley, though the inadvertent ghost costume didn't muffle Ralph's underlying pink glow. Every area we encountered, Francis would go ahead to make sure no one was in front of us. Then, we'd escort Ralph through, carrying him to make the trip quicker. Being mostly vacant, our path through the White House was straightforward and unseen. When we arrived at the bowling alley, there were two cots set up.

"Ralph, go inside and get comfortable. I have to talk with my fellow humans," Francis said. Ralph gave me and Samantha a warm hug, then bounced into his temporary shelter. Francis stepped outside with us and shut the door.

"I'm keeping Ralph company tonight. I need you two to get some rest."

"Wait a second," I said. "What is Ralph going to eat? What *does* he eat?" In the swarm of earlier questions, we had missed these practical matters. "How much sleep does he need? And what are you going to do with the gigantic can of soup outside?"

"Your job as guardian doesn't start just yet. *Take these.*" Francis put out his hands revealing two small, pink, and seemingly identical cell phones.

He stuck out his arm to me, but as I reached to take the phone, he paused and pulled it back. "Sorry," he said, then gave me the other phone. Despite everything, there was still a political hierarchy, and I was not at the same level as Samantha.

"This is the dedicated Ralph phone, got it? Don't use it for anything else. The relevant phone numbers are programmed in. Samantha, you stay at the White House tonight. Use one of the guest rooms. Same for you, Markus. I'm going to get some rest and catch up on my more terrestrial work. Good night."

He closed the door. It all felt too quick. I felt an urge to stop him, but I didn't. I knew I'd be alone with Samantha.

Given our choice of guest rooms in the White House, I was aiming for the Lincoln Bedroom. It was Lincoln's original office in the White House. A holograph of the *Gettysburg Address*, signed by Lincoln, was on the desk. I had to see it.

"I'm sleeping in the Lincoln Bedroom," Samantha said as she brushed a few hairs out of her face and smiled. "What about you?"

"Oh, I was hoping to sleep there too."

"Well, that is quite forward of you, Dr. West. Should we get some wine?"

"I meant—" But I didn't say what I meant. Samantha put

her hand in the cup of mine. "What *did* you mean?" she said in my ear.

"I meant . . . Yes."

It was a silent walk to the empty White House kitchen, and I took every chance to glance at her. Any opportunity to brush my body against hers was taken. Finding the wine racks, I took an Australian Shiraz for our one-night bedroom.

I opened the door to the Lincoln Bedroom as she opened her jacket and took it off. With the door open, we walked inside, and she dropped her jacket on the floor.

I uncorked the wine and poured quickly as she snuck up behind me and touched my neck.

"Full glass?" I asked.

"Yes."

We took our glasses to the bed and sat close. A teenage delight of anticipation warmed me, and the red wine felt like pure liquid health in my veins—a blood transfusion from Dionysus. We drank greedily and stared at each other in silence.

"This is . . . wild," she said, licking the corner of her lips with the tip of her tongue.

I rubbed her lower back and moved closer. She rubbed my thigh.

"I mean . . . I am feeling . . . really . . . wild."

We slammed the rest of our wine and stared at each other. She burped and laughed as I placed our glasses on the floor. I kissed her, and she whispered in my ear.

"Do whatever you want to me . . . *use me.*"

MORNING

I awoke the next morning with a shake.

Out the window I saw a Chinook heavy transport helicopter towing the monstrous cylinder away. High-tension towing cables, linked to the base of the helicopter, sprouted out from within the open lid of the cylinder. Multicolored tarps had been lamely connected and draped over the cylinder, but it was futile. Throughout the day, residents of America took pictures of the towed cylinder as it flew overhead, and uploaded them to social media sites. Putting all the locations of the amateur photos together, it was clearly headed west. The last photo was taken in southern Nevada.

"Hey, handsome, where's the coffee?" Samantha said. "My God, where's the cylinder?"

"They just towed it away," I said, as if it were an illegally parked can.

"*Francis* . . . Listen, Markus . . . Things got pretty wild last night. I want you to know—"

"Don't worry your sexy little head."

"Wait, I want you to know that I'm not always like that . . . in bed, I mean."

I smiled, unsure what to say. But it confirmed that Ralph's presence, somehow, sexually excited her too. I hugged her and kissed her forehead. I wanted to stay in bed with her all day.

"What did Ralph tell you yesterday, in the Oval Office, when I was in the restroom?" Samantha smiled, and I pressed. "He told you something personal, about yourself, didn't he?"

"He told me that he knew . . ." she started to say, but her words blurred into laughter. She pulled the white covers over her head and continued. "He knew I wanted to . . . *mate* with you."

We laughed as a knock hit the door.

"Can I come in?" Francis asked.

"No," we barked. Basic decency overrode national urgency, and Francis left. We looked at each other like naughty teenagers.

"Take it easy. I'll fetch some coffee," I said.

Taking my shirt from the desk revealed what I had forgotten: the holograph of the *Gettysburg Address*. I tried to sound like President Lincoln and read the start aloud, "Four score and seven years ago our fathers brought forth upon this continent, a new nation, conceived in Liberty and dedicated to the proposition that all men are created equal."

Samantha applauded and smiled.

"Get the coffee, Abe, and a sewing kit for the buttons on my shirt, you animal."

I got dressed and headed to the kitchen. I was not surprised to be intercepted by Francis. There was intensity under his tired face.

"No sleep?" I asked.

"Not much."

"How was Ralph last night?"

"Not as much fun as Samantha."

"It'd be nice if you kept that quiet."

"If you can stay quiet about Ralph, I can stay quiet about you and Samantha."

"That's a deal . . . You learn anything interesting from Ralph?"

Francis smiled. He had learned many things and was enjoying trying to pick just one. The academic in him resurfaced, and he brightened.

"Ralph showed me his numeral system, the standard symbols his people use for numbers. It's geometric and far less arbitrary, very different from ours," he said, and I raised my eyebrows. "Our symbol for one, the single vertical dash, is their symbol for two."

"So what's their symbol for one?"

"Just a single dot, a period," he said, then his phone rang, and he answered. It was the president, and Francis immediately walked into an empty room nearby and shut the door. I now wish I had asked about Ralph's numerals more, but was distracted by the thought of my night with Samantha. Francis returned and snapped me out of my reverie.

"Looks as if I'm out of a job," Francis said, smiling.

"What?"

"The president has asked me to step down, and I've agreed."

"I don't get it. This is punishment for something?"

"No, no, no," he said. "There's no way I can deal with this and remain the national security advisor. The president wants to keep all of this in a tight circle, and she wants me to manage the circle, so I'm stepping down."

"But, won't that look . . . suspicious?"

"Suspicious? What will people suspect . . . aliens? I have people monitoring major and minor news sources. Journalists and bloggers are talking about soup and art."

"Right . . . but still . . . a big can of soup lands on the White House lawn, and suddenly the national security advisor resigns? Won't people think that is . . . strange?"

"If Ralph's time line is right, these aliens will be here in two more days. By then, no one will be thinking about me. So let's talk about you. The president wanted me to double-check with you: you still want the job, being Ralph's guardian?"

"Yes."

"OK. We're going to find Ralph a place to live. It will be in the middle of nowhere. Your job, for now, is enrichment."

"Enrichment? You mean, what zookeepers do to keep the animals from getting bored?"

"Precisely."

XV

RELEASE

Francis had fabricated a simple press release for the White House. It was an elegant piece of misinformation about the cylinder, released the day of Ralph's arrival, but I didn't see it until the following day, January 29. It distracted the public enough in the short term, but would cause problems as time went on.

The press release in full:

The White House
Office of the Press Secretary
January 28, 2022

For Immediate Release

Statement by the President on the Occasion of International Creativity Month

The White House teamed up with a well-known but secretive European street artist to give the American people a hearty January surprise while bringing awareness to International Creativity Month. Our friend prefers to remain anonymous (but feel free to guess), and we thank him for his outstanding participation.

The press release requires some remarks.

First, January really is International Creativity Month, and the public had no problem believing the cylinder was a piece of art. Also . . . I can't resist mentioning that January is National Soup Month—I learned this from Ralph.

Second, the release fit with the theory that Banksy, the famous international street artist, created the cylinder. With his typically surprising, and illegal, public displays of art, Banksy was an easy target of speculation. And, since Banksy's actual identity is still a mystery, it was impossible to deny he was responsible.

Third, January 28, the day the cylinder arrived, is the birthday of Claes Oldenburg, another international artist. For many years later, experts in the art world would enjoy correcting those who thought Warhol was the dominant inspiration by informing them it was *obviously* a tribute to Claes Oldenburg.

Claes Oldenburg is internationally known for making gargantuan statues of everyday objects: a ninety-six-foot-tall baseball bat, standing on edge, in Chicago; a forty-foot-tall ice-cream cone, seemingly dropped upside down on the roof of a building, in Cologne, Germany; a fifty-nine-foot-high needle with thread in Milan, Italy; the forty-five-foot-tall clothespin at City Hall in Philadelphia; a forty-one-foot-tall trowel in the Pepsico Sculpture Garden of Purchase, New York (and another one in the Netherlands); a fifty-foot-high handsaw sticking in the Earth in Tokyo; a giant blue pickax stuck in the Earth in Kassel, Germany; near eighteen-foot-high shuttlecocks in Kansas City; and a variety of other everyday objects, each scaled upward to hundreds of times the normal size, sprinkled around the Earth.

Fourth, the release never actually mentions the cylinder and is short on details. When one deceives, it is best to do so minimally. With less lies, there are less ways to be found out.

But not everyone was satisfied with the press release.

INQUIRY

I left without saying 'good-bye' to Ralph, expecting to see him again soon.

At home, something unusual happened and it scared me. My home phone rang.

"Hello."

"Hi. Is this Dr. Markus West?"

I did not recognize the voice. She sounded young and worn out.

"Yes."

"Hi, Dr. West, I'm Alice Higginbotham from the *New York Times*, and I was hoping I could ask you some questions. Is this a good time?"

I petrified. I took a moment to put on my game face . . . and remembered I never had one. As a grown man, I was fully capable of making an excuse and hanging up, but the questioning voice of a young woman awakened my professorial manner.

"What is this in reference to?"

"I'd like to ask you some questions about your experience at the White House yesterday."

I paused and said the worst thing possible.

"How did you know I was at the White House?"

There was a pause, and I heard the worst thing possible.

"I won't reveal my sources, Dr. West."

"Your sources . . ."

"It is a matter of journalistic integrity not to reveal one's sources, Dr. West, and I would bring shame upon myself and the historic integrity of the *New York Times* should I disobey this essential rule of journalism."

Alice Higginbotham was a pot-smoking college student and an intern for the Arts Section of the *New York Times*. Of course, I didn't know this, and right then, it felt as if she was Woodward *and* Bernstein. She wasn't even majoring in journalism. She studied art history at NYU. She didn't know I was at the White House, but when I asked her how she knew, she knew.

Her bosses at the *New York Times* had been trying to get a quote from anyone who was at the White House the previous day. When they failed, they kicked the job down to her. Spunky, persistent, and thorough, she compiled a list of everyone working for the White House, searched for any number she could find, and called them. When that led nowhere, she called me out of sheer desperation—she thought that *maybe,* because of my involvement with the lunar advertisement, I might be involved with the cylinder. She gave everyone the same leading line she gave me.

"What exactly do you want to know?" I said.

"Are you familiar with the press release from yesterday regarding International Creativity Month?"

"I read it."

"Why won't the White House reveal the identity of the

European street artist responsible for the . . . large can of soup . . . in front of the White House, I mean."

"Well, you know how these artists are; they don't want to look too connected to the establishment and government and whatnot."

"Do you know the identity of the artist?"

". . . I believe that's classified."

"Classified?" she asked, slowed by her own surprise. "Why would it be classified?"

"I'm not sure."

"Is this some kind of . . . What are you hiding?"

"I have to go."

"Wait—"

I hung up in panic. The phone rang again, and I ran outside for a walk.

I had no idea how much Alice Higginbotham knew, but I knew I made the situation worse. After a short walk to mellow my mind, I used the emergency phone Francis gave me and called him.

"Markus . . . *Ralph, stop. Please don't do that,*" Francis said. I could hear Ralph giggling in the background.

"I . . . I screwed up. I just got a call from a reporter at the *New York Times* . . . Somehow she knew I was at the White House yesterday. How the hell did she know?"

"What did you say to her?" Francis whispered, seething. I told him the details of my phone call with Alice. "Markus, listen . . . *Ralph, stop . . . Stop tickling me.* . . . Markus, Ralph says 'hello' . . . I'm going to make a quick phone call and get right back to you . . . *Okay.* Wait, Markus, Ralph wants to talk to you."

"Markus," Ralph shouted.

"Hi, Ralph."

"Markus, cheer up, old bean. Francis is going to get me a house, my own house."

"Sounds good, Ralph."

"You sound down in the dirty dumps. What's wrong? I thought you'd be happy."

"Why would I be happy?" I asked miserably.

"Well, I heard you and Samantha—"

"Fucking hell, Ralph. *How did you know?"*

"I didn't, but now I do. Ha. Oh, Francis wants to converse with you. See you."

I punched a wall just hard enough to hurt myself.

"Markus, I just talked to my contact at the *New York Times*, he doesn't know anything about it, and there's no Alice Higginbotham on the payroll. Are you sure you were talking to an actual reporter?"

I didn't answer. I told him to wait as I googled 'Alice Higginbotham' on my smartphone and immediately found her Facebook page. The large pot leaf used as a profile picture irked me, but when I noticed she was just an intern for the Arts Section, thoughts of murder and suicide juggled in my head. Wearily, I told Francis, and we came up with a plan as I slowly walked back to my place.

"You sure you're okay with this? Lying to the *New York Times* is nontrivial."

"I don't see much of a choice."

The phone was ringing when I opened my front door.

BASEBALL

"Hello."

"Hello, Dr. West. It's Alice Higginbotham again. I'd really love to ask you some questions. Is that okay?" she asked, desperately nice.

"Yes, that's fine. I should apologize. I was quite agitated before. I was cooking and burned myself . . . and my linguini."

My lies were getting off to a bad start.

"These things happen . . . Anyway, I should apologize too—cold calling you like that and barraging you with questions—I'm sorry if I came on too strong."

We exchanged a few uncomfortable but easy pleasantries, which leveled the playing field. Once I agreed to answer her questions, she was more forthcoming about herself, what she knew, and how.

"Earlier, you said the identity of the artist was classified. Why classified?"

"You have to understand, I was there for unrelated matters and was just as surprised as anybody else. I did hear it was classified. Apparently, this was a condition of the artist, who demanded anonymity."

"Who told you it was classified?"

"Oh dear, I don't even know who I was talking to. There were just a bunch of us standing around, a marine, some Secret Service, a gardener, and the secretary of . . . maybe agriculture? I'm not sure—we were all just gawking at the damn thing. It was all highly amusing."

"So, you can't confirm it was Banksy?"

"Who?"

"You've never heard of Banksy? He's a British . . . Forget it . . . There were reports of soldiers in gas masks at the scene. Can you confirm this?"

"Yes, there were a few marines and some workers from the CDC as well."

"The Centers for Disease Control? Why?"

"Oh, there's something you have to understand . . . This is funny. You see, the White House was taken by surprise by all this too. The artist had agreed to do some sort of street art, that's what you call it, right? 'Street art'?"

"Yes, please go on."

"The artist had agreed to do something for this International Creativity Month, but no one knew exactly what was going to happen. When the big helium blimp showed up, the White House was just as surprised as anybody. The Secret Service got a real bug up their ass and wanted to be extra sure the cylinder was safe. Frankly, I'm surprised no one got shot."

"Was the artist arrested?"

"No."

"Where is he now?"

"I don't know."

"Did you see the artist? There's some distant video footage of someone or something jumping off of the top of the can."

"Someone or something is right. I still don't know who or what that thing is," I lied.

It was just one of the many questions on her list, but I was relieved to hear it. Because of the height of the cylinder and the blockade around the White House, the distant pedestrians couldn't easily see Ralph with unaided eyes. It still seems like luck that no one got any decent footage of him that day.

"Can you confirm that the . . . theme song to the movie *Rocky* was playing?"

"Umm, yes. It was one of the songs from *Rocky*. It wasn't 'Eye of the Tiger,' it was the other, more instrumental, one."

"Other news outlets reported rumors there was some sort of partial evacuation of the White House, is that true?"

"I really don't know, but if it had been a partial evacuation, they probably would have told me to leave. I wasn't there for anything crucial."

"Thank you. Can you confirm that the artist is male?"

"No, but I have to suppose the cylinder was made and operated by a large team, not just one artist. I suppose there were some females in that team."

"Why would you suppose that?"

"Sheer probability."

"I see. Where is the artwork now?"

"The cylinder? I don't know. I heard some say they might install it outside the Smithsonian, but I'm not really the one to ask."

"Who else might be a good person to talk to about this?"

"The president; it was her pet project."

"Umm . . . How about someone more accessible."

"Maybe the Secret Service? Sorry, I can't think of anyone else."

Our conversation was dwindling, and I was feeling like Keyser Söze. I was nervous the whole time, but sure it barely showed. She was nowhere near the truth, and, of course, she wouldn't have believed it anyway. She just wanted some good quotes, and I gave them. Lying was easy because it was mostly true. She paused and I took a drink of water, expecting a satisfying good-bye.

"I hope I've helped," I said. "Is there anything else you'd like to ask me about?"

She was shuffling some papers, getting distracted, and taking her time. "Yes," she started, ". . . one second . . . I wanted to . . . ask you about . . . *RALPH.*"

If temporary insanity exists, I experienced it the moment she sternly blurted his name.

I dropped the phone and envisioned myself in a nightmare. I expected the walls to dissolve. I expected assassins to walk in the door and kill me. I needed to destroy something to regain the sense of reality I normally held tight. I grabbed a stack of pens by the phone and threw them at the wall, but felt nothing. I took the baseball I kept and threw it straight through my kitchen window. Echoes of shattering glass urged me to yell as I grabbed the phone off the floor.

"How Could You Know About Ralph? How Could You Possibly Know Anything About Ralph? Who The Hell Told *You*

About *Ralph,* You Goddamn Impossible Bitch?"

I felt release as the silence drifted and my pulsing anger calmed. I had been imagining her talking to me in a cubicle in some office space in Manhattan. She was in her dormitory.

I heard a curious cat meow.

"Ralph is my cat . . . He jumped on my lap and surprised me . . . Mr. West, who did you think I was talking about? Who's Ralph? Is Ralph the artist? Ralph Steadman? Wait, isn't Ralph Steadman dead?"

I gently hung up the phone and wished I were dead.

XVIII

✦ ✦ ✦ ✦ ✦ ✦ ✦ ✦ ✦

FIGHT

I sat down in my armchair and hated myself for several minutes. I ruminated on my stupid explosion and tightly gripped the arms of my chair.

I screamed, "Ralph. Ralph. RALPH."

I felt slightly better.

For a few seconds, I imagined murdering Alice Higginbotham. Quickly ashamed, I hated myself for thinking about killing her. I wondered what to tell Francis and then wondered if *he* would kill Alice Higginbotham. All she knew was a name, and suddenly I feared for her life.

All Alice knew was that 'Ralph' was a name of importance. That's all she knew. She could not have considered the truth, not at this point. There was no persuasive reason to think the name 'Ralph' would show up in a *New York Times* article about the cylinder . . . but there was no guarantee it wouldn't.

In my effort to navigate the political intrigue, I let go the one secret I didn't want the world to know. I wanted to talk to Francis, Ralph, or Samantha, but couldn't talk to any of them. In my vexation, I decided to get exceptionally drunk. Normally, I would have stayed home, but every second at home reminded me of the phone call. Instead, I went to a bar.

Here is where I become unreliable. I remember going to an old dive bar with bare brick walls, the kind where the locals don't even know the name because the sign fell off the storefront a decade ago. All that remained was one of those small, rectangular neon signs that said 'BAR,' and that's all anyone needed to know.

I remember lots of empty chairs, a pool table, a broken Wurlitzer, and a bitter, grey bartender. I remember a chalky tasting glass of cheap, red wine. I remember politely complaining about the quality of the wine, and the bartender calling me 'an asshole.' I remember five quick glasses of Jack Daniel's on the rocks, followed by many more shots of straight Jägermeister that I don't remember so well.

I was talking to a fellow customer, a transient old biker, and I was arguing. I don't think he recognized me. He was convinced the lunar advertisement and the cylinder were signs the corporations were taking over. I argued that only aliens could be responsible. At first, the biker thought I was joking, but as my explanation became more elaborate, he thought I was mocking him.

I remember yelling Ralph's name and being called 'crazy.' The argument turned awkward, then loud, then physical. There were pushes and punches. I remember pain in my face, gut, and hands. I remember the taste of blood. I remember sirens and darkness.

I woke up the next morning on a hard floor, alone, in a dark room. I had a wrenching hangover, bad breath, and torn knuckles. My right shoulder ached because I didn't sleep properly. I saw a black eye in the crappy metal mirror which barely reflected.

My shoes, socks, wallet, keys, phone, and belt were missing. A lanky cop with a fat mustache walked to my cell and turned on a painful light. As my eyes adjusted, I could see him looking at me with suspicion as he handed me a box with everything I was missing.

"What happened last night?" I asked with a dry throat.

He huffed as he opened the cell and said, "Don't ask a single question. Just go."

I looked at him inquisitively, which apparently was too much of a question. He pulled me up and pressed me against the wall. "Get the hell out of my precinct, you fucking lunatic."

I gathered my things and got the hell out.

I picked up the *New York Times* and a decaf Red Bull from a deli and sat on a dusty stoop nearby. The article, with Alice Higginbotham's name listed as a contributing author, was on the front page underneath a distant color photo of the cylinder on East Executive Avenue.

Alice must have been thrilled with her scoop. She went from a lowly intern to a contributing journalist for a front-page article in the most respected newspaper in America. I read the article, which cited my name as a source, and smiled when I was done. I read it again to double-check. No mention of the name 'Ralph,' no surprises. I felt like Dick Cheney, and she was my Judy Miller. I wanted to hug her.

I checked my new pink cell phone and saw too many missed calls from Francis. Then it hit me. The phone must've had a GPS device in it. This is why my phone was different from

Samantha's. Francis had no problem tagging me with a GPS device, but he wouldn't have done it to the secretary of defense. I visualized Samantha righteously punching Francis in the groin. The thought brought some cheer to my weary face.

Francis had been trying to reach me, so he tracked my location and figured out that I was in jail. After a few official and awkward phone calls, I was released on my own recognizance. I had to call him.

"Markus."

"Thanks for bailing me out."

"There was no bail. They never found whomever you fought at the bar, and they were going to let you go eventually. All I did was expedite, but you can thank me later. Have you seen the *Times*?"

"Yes, and I think I did a pretty good job with Alice."

"Well . . . yes and no . . . From the standpoint of national security, it's beautiful. But, politically speaking, you fucked up," he said as he gave me a moment to figure it out. I didn't.

He explained, "Characterizing the Secret Service as being surprised by the cylinder was something of a surprise to the president. It doesn't look good. I mean, it looks awful."

"Jesus Christ."

"You made her look irresponsible, Markus, as if she's willing to sacrifice national security for the sake of some artistic statement. Her political opponents are writing editorials about her this second, and they'll be online by noon. It is all very ironic, of course."

"Ironic?"

"Well, by protecting national security, and by that I mean

Ralph, you've made it look as if our national security is a joke," he said with a laugh. "Look, Markus. Personally, I don't care, and the president understands. Ralph says we will detect the Kardashians by tomorrow night at the latest, so by then it won't matter. But, for the moment, the president has a small battle on her hands because of you. On top of everything, she has her *live* interview scheduled tonight for *60 Minutes,* and they *will* ask her about it."

It was her first one-on-one live interview since she came into office. It became the most-watched live interview in the history of television.

"Oh, God, can she cancel the interview?"

"We considered it, but it would look terrible. Right now, people are asking too many questions, and the only way to stop them is to start answering."

"Can she ask them to not ask about the cylinder?"

"Of course not; do you have any idea how strange that would look?"

"Of course . . . Sorry, I'm pretty messed up. What do I do?"

"Forget about all of this, go home, clean up, and be ready to go to Ralph's tonight."

"Ralph's?"

Most people know exactly where they were on the night of January 30, 2022. I was in the abandoned military barracks of Fort Ritchie, Maryland.

HOME

To escape the Nazis, thousands of German Jews immigrated to America before World War II. Many joined the war effort after the Japanese bombed Pearl Harbor and were trained as intelligence officers at Fort Ritchie, Maryland. They were then sent *back* to Europe to interrogate prisoners of war. In 1989, Fort Ritchie officially closed, and at Samantha's request, there was zero red tape in commandeering a portion of it for Ralph's new home.

Ralph got his own renovated barracks, encircled by a cyclone fence over a mile in circumference. At any given time, there was only one guard—which surprised me, but secrecy was Ralph's best protection, and the area was uninhabited for miles. The guards didn't know what they were guarding and were warned to never go inside the perimeter unless to pursue an intruder.

The night shift guard was Lieutenant Frank Barber, an old friend of Samantha's. Frank was a quiet, burly, and aging Navy SEAL with more hair in his mustache than on his head.

The two-floored barracks were quickly refurbished so that Ralph's home was Ralph-proof. The old windows were replaced by unidirectional windows—that is, the new windows were one-way mirrors, which gave them a fucking tint, and allowed Ralph to look out without anyone looking in. Lieutenant Barber would periodically scan the grounds with the night-vision binoculars he wore around his thick neck, and Francis didn't want him peeking inside Ralph's home.

All sharp edges were sanded down to protect Ralph's only Earth suit, and a fluffy wall-to-wall shag carpet extended to the ceiling and up the stairs. The upper floor, really an attic, contained a makeshift helium room, loosely enclosed with thick plastic, where Ralph slept on a waterbed. Here, in his helium room, Ralph could comfortably stay and sleep without his Earth suit, though he kept his helmet on at all times, for reasons explained shortly.

A simple hose connected a canister of helium, from outside, to a valve in Ralph's little plastic bedroom, upstairs. Again, the helium was not actually necessary. Ralph could breathe oxygen. But the helium made him comfortable.

The cover story for the whole operation did not make sense. But, if all went well, only the guards would know the cover story. The cover story was that NASA was doing experiments to find a better treatment for Alymphocytosis, also known as Glanzmann-Riniker syndrome aka severe combined immunodeficiency.

The disease is better known as 'bubble boy disease,' named for the young victims who spend their lives in a sterilized plastic bubble insulating them from infection. As an immunodeficiency disease, it is like AIDS, except congenital and typically worse. Those who have it in the extreme form can die of almost anything, e.g., the common cold.

Now, the reason the cover story *seemed* to make sense was because NASA, in 1977, had actually designed a special suit for the original bubble boy, David Vetter. This was explained to the guards. NASA's bubble boy suit was similar to a space suit, and more importantly, it resembled Ralph's Earth suit. In the off chance a guard might see Ralph, they'd believe Ralph was someone testing out the suit.

All the same, the cover story did not make sense. There was no reason to have armed guards, and it was too mysterious why the secretary of defense and the national security advisor would be involved in a NASA project of a medical nature. If anyone asked, the unofficial response would be that a close friend of the president had a son suffering from the disease.

This cover story bothered me. However, both Samantha and Francis assured me that, in the intelligence community, in this type of situation, this is how it is done.

"The bullshittier, the better," Francis said.

When you want guards to take their watch seriously, you tell them a story that reeks of bullshit. Then the guards know it really is important, because they know they are being lied to. And they won't ask questions, because they won't want any more bullshit.

Francis used an interesting example to argue the point: Area 51. Area 51 is a detached part of Edwards Air Force Base in Nevada, the existence of which was not even acknowledged by the U.S. government until 1995. It is notoriously claimed by conspiracy theorists to contain the remnants of a crashed alien aircraft. The main reason for the conspiracy theory, Francis confided, is because the alien aircraft rumor was the cover story leaked to the guards. Even today, the area is patrolled by guards armed with M16s, and the senior guards are still being told the same bullshit. When I asked him what was really going on there, he simply said 'research and development.'

Francis couldn't resist telling me a rather ironic piece of classified information. "Area 51 does contain alien technology *now*," he said, because this is where Ralph's cylinder was ultimately taken.

Alone, I drove north up I-270 out of DC about an hour and a half. As I approached Fort Ritchie, pavement and sunlight became scarce. It was a dark blur of dull, abandoned barracks, blank, grassy fields, and nameless dirt roads. On the side of one old building I saw a faded 'Loose Lips Sink Ships' propaganda mural from World War II. I thought of Alice Higginbotham and gripped my steering wheel tighter.

If nowhere had a middle, this was it. I was sure Ralph would be safe.

Approaching the small guard post, I saw a dead, fat raccoon on the side of the road, its red blood shining in my headlights. In retrospect, I'm sure it had been shot. Lieutenant Frank Barber stepped out into the light, looked at my face, looked at his clipboard, looked at Ralph's new home in the distance and then back at me.

"Give me your phone."

He meant the pink phone Francis gave me. I handed it over, he used some type of scanning device on it, and handed it back. His gaze caught mine, and I could tell he wanted to talk. Frank Barber was a quiet man, quiet because he thought all men should be quiet. He was accustomed to being sure of himself, and something had tweaked his confidence.

"Proceed."

I started to drive up the thin driveway when something neon green flew down in a flash onto my windshield, covering the center of it. I floored my brakes and froze as my car skidded tight on the gravel. In my rearview mirror, I saw Lieutenant Barber rushing up.

"Is everything . . . What the hell is that?" he asked, reaching for his sidearm.

"Everything is all right, Lieutenant—it's just a luna moth."

If you'd never seen a luna moth, you'd react the same. They are so big and green and strange, people often assume they're not real on a first encounter. The one on my windshield was abnormally large, with a wingspan over a foot. The strangest part was the timing. Luna moths are not seen at that time of year.

"There has been some unusual . . . animal activity in the area . . . sir."

Lieutenant Barber reached to remove the moth when a shrill screech blared above the car. All I saw was a flying sheet of brown feathers with talons. A beautiful bald eagle hurled itself onto the car, wingspan spread over the windshield, and snatched the delicate green moth in its feet and launched back up into the night.

"*Bald eagles don't hunt at night,*" I said, as if to argue away what just happened in front of my face. When I looked up, Lieutenant Barber was crouching for cover beside the car with his sidearm drawn. A half minute of welcomed silence passed.

"You weren't about to shoot a bald eagle, were you?" I asked with a smile.

"Negative, sir," he said, rubbing his bald head with the palm of his hand.

"Thank you, Lieutenant. That will be all."

But the lieutenant stayed.

"Sir?"

"Yes?"

"Permission to speak freely, sir?"

I made a minor calculation in my head and sighed.

"No. Permission not granted . . . Good night, Lieutenant."

". . . Good night, sir."

I rolled up my window and proceeded up the driveway, slowly. It was rude as hell to dismiss the lieutenant's desire to talk, but I was too afraid of any questions he might ask. After what happened with Alice Higginbotham, I had to avoid situations where I'd risk revealing information about Ralph.

As I pulled closer to Ralph's place, I saw a dozen or so birds on the roof, mostly crows. Judging from the bouncing movements, silhouetted against the moon, the birds were having sex.

More captivating than the birds were the sounds emanating from Ralph's new home. When I turned off the ignition, I stopped to listen. Rhythmic muffled yells and moans burst through the walls to fill the air so loudly I feared Lieutenant Barber might hear.

I assumed Ralph was watching pornography at maximum volume—the woman's voice was obviously amplified. As I walked closer to the entrance, I heard another voice, a quieter one, syncopated with the female's pulsing moans of pleasure.

The other voice was Ralph's. The couple's outbursts were not all incoherent moans. Words were being spoken, but I couldn't understand them. I proceeded to the front door with a slow caution.

I was ten paces from the door when it cracked open. Illumination behind the door drew a skinny rectangle of light outside, and from a shadow I knew something was moving behind the door. Two wild raccoons were on their way out. They scampered by me casually onto the soft grass and into the darkness.

Inside, my eardrums were pounded by the sounds of sex amplified throughout the house, and I was surprised to see four white rabbits in the center of the room *not* mating. An empty bag of Doritos lay nearby.

"*C'est bon. C'est bon. Oui. Oui. C'est bon,*" she screamed repeatedly. "*Oh, oui. Oui. Vas-y, ne t'arrêtes pas, continue. . . Oh, oui, oh, c'est bon. . .*"

When the French woman finally exploded, she and Ralph spoke softly to one another for a few minutes while I waited downstairs. I scared the rabbits outside and then cleared my throat loudly to let Ralph know I had arrived. After another minute, Ralph bounced downstairs to meet me, chipper as ever.

"*Salut,* Markus," Ralph said, greeting me with the accent of a native Frenchman.

"What was all that about?"

"Oh, I'm sure I shouldn't tell."

"Ralph, I'm your guardian. You shouldn't keep secrets from me."

"Yes, of course, but one shouldn't kiss and tell, isn't that right?"

"I think we can make an exception, under the circumstances."

"Well, that was my new friend Stéphanie. I was teaching her how to have phone sex."

"Why was it so loud?" I asked, somehow managing to ignore every other question raised by Ralph's statement.

"I hooked the speakerphone up to the stereo system. I find it much more erotic this way, don't you?"

"I . . . How do you even know her?"

"We met online last night in a chat room for lonely people. I like her."

"I hate to ask," I said, hating myself, "but she does *not* know you're an alien, right?"

"No. I told her I was a secret agent. She didn't believe me, but I had to tell her something. She just laughed when I told her that. She has such a great laugh. You should hear it. You want to talk to her? Let's call her back."

"My French is *trés terrible*."

"It's okay, she speaks English too. She's really good."

"No. Ralph, really, I'm not talking to her. I'm just trying to understand—who is she?"

"Oh, she's a nice Parisian, unhappily married. Stéphanie really needed a friend. It was sad . . . a smart and sexy-sounding French woman who doesn't know much about sex. We chatted online, then on the phone, and the next thing I know, she's putting a courgette in her *trou du cul*. I think she's Catholic."

Amid the swarming ludicrousness of the situation, my conscience hung on the idea of Ralph having phone sex with a married woman. I dodged my masculine curiosity—which wanted to know how he could seduce a woman so quickly. As Ralph's terrestrial guardian, moral instruction seemed more appropriate.

"Ralph, you really shouldn't be . . . facilitating that sort of thing."

"Facilitating?" he asked.

"She's *married*, Ralph."

"Oh dear," Ralph said. "I hadn't really thought of it like that."

"Like what exactly?" I said, wanting to be sure Ralph understood.

"Like, she was cheating on her husband," he said, sounding guilty. "I don't want to break up her marriage."

"No, you don't," I said. "Even though it was only over the telephone, I know her husband would be angry. You must realize this."

My concern for Ralph exposing his alien identity had metamorphosed into a concern for saving an anonymous marriage across the Atlantic Ocean. For a moment, I thought I had made my point.

"But I was trying to help her. I think you're wrong, Markus. Her husband wouldn't be mad."

"Why not?"

"Because I'm an alien with no penis."

Ralph had an inhuman capacity to gain pleasure from other's pleasure and was constantly interested in giving pleasure. Lost in my own head, I wondered how pleasurable life was on Ralph's planet. Certainly, human life had become more pleasurable over the centuries, so a more advanced life-form would experience even more pleasure, on average.

I recalled how he described his home planet in the Oval Office—no violence and no competition for resources. Perhaps he was overidealizing his home planet; being homesick could do that. But his planet sounded suspiciously like heaven. For a quick second, I laughed nervously, wondering if Ralph was some outrageous angel. The thought flickered in my mind and distanced me from him.

"You don't think I'm a bad person, do you?" Ralph asked, holding my hand.

I didn't answer. Flustered, I decided to drop the conversation about Stéphanie.

I returned to another matter, more immediately practical.

"Why were there raccoons in here?" I asked.

"I fed them. I would have fed the possums too, but they got scared."

"We're doing all this to protect you . . . Raccoons can be dangerous."

"They live here. I don't mind. I like them. Can I get a golden retriever?"

"I'll ask Francis," I said insincerely.

"Markus," Ralph started, changing his tone, "you look banged up. Are you okay? Did Samantha hurt you?"

"I'm okay, thanks. I got into a fight last night at a bar."

"Violence?" he said, shaking a bit. "What happened?"

"I'm not sure. I was drunk. I don't really remember . . ." I started and then, surprising myself, decided to say something personal. It had been on my mind ever since I met Ralph. I knew I'd tell him, eventually.

"Ralph, there's something I want you to know—"

"About your fight? I don't want to hear it. Don't try to impress me with your barbaric ways of violence."

"No, not that. It's about me."

"Then don't worry. You can tell me. I like you," he said.

". . . I've always had a fear of aliens," I blurted. "Not just a fear, a phobia. Since I was a kid, I've had nightmares, painful nightmares, about aliens . . ."

Ralph went silent for a moment.

"Are you afraid of me?" he asked.

"No, not you."

"Do you like me?"

". . . Yes," I said and Ralph laughed at me.

"This fear of yours . . . It is important," Ralph said, sounding serious. "We are very lucky to have met. This is a good sign."

". . . Well, yes, it has importance. I mean, it has affected me since childhood. I'm still somewhat afraid of the dark because of it, and . . . It isn't easy to say that."

"Yes, of course. *Of course* it is important to you, but I mean, it is important for reasons that may go beyond you."

The downstairs half of the barracks was bare. The only thing that stood out was the empty bag of Doritos on the carpet Ralph had been feeding the raccoons with. Ralph did not eat Doritos. The carpenters must have left a bag behind.

"Come upstairs to the attic with me. The downstairs is uneventful."

With my guidance, Ralph floated and bounced himself up the refurbished stairs. He proudly introduced me to his entertainment center: an all-access satellite television, stereo system, and a PC with DSL Internet access running through the old phone lines. He put on some hip-hop music and began jumping and twisting.

"Just put your hands in the attic and wave them like you're apathetic," Ralph rapped.

"We're not dancing tonight, Ralph," I said as I turned off the stereo. "Tonight, we are going to watch television like normal people do, to enrich their lives. And we're going to discuss ways to keep you busy."

"I must say, I have seen thousands of hours of your television. I get the basic idea."

"I'm sure, but tonight, the president is doing a live interview on TV. We should watch."

"Cindy will be on the TV? She's so dreamy."

"You're on a first-name basis with the president? When did you speak with her?"

"She visited me in the bowling alley. We didn't bowl or anything . . . I suppose she needed to see me with her eyes. I like to look at her eyes."

"What did you talk about?"

"Oh, you would have been bored. It was mostly the sort of things we talked about in the Oval Office the other day."

"Okay, but what about the Kardashians?"

"There's too much uncertainty right now, but she agrees with the most important thing."

"Meaning?"

"She won't preemptively attack the Kardashians when they come, and Samantha agreed. Strangely, Francis kept suggesting a preemptive attack, but I was just being the Kardashians' lawyer."

"You were being *what*? The Kardashians' lawyer? What are you talking about?"

"Ha," Ralph shouted, delighted by his own verbal mix-up. "Oh dear, I mean Francis, *he* was just playing devil's advocate. Ha. What a boner. Please forgive and forget. Oh dear, in any case, your females are much more rational when it comes to applying violence. I believe we are all very lucky."

Relieved, I turned on the television, and we waited for the president's interview to begin. Ralph moved over to his computer and began to type. It was difficult for him to type with his Earth mittens.

"Darn human keyboard," he groaned. I could tell from his hand motions he wanted to take his mittens off.

"The interview will start any minute."

"One second. I'm just updating my Facebook status."

"You're on Facebook?"

"Of course," he said, "aren't you?"

I was still surprised with how familiar Ralph was with our Internet. I was naïve.

"I would very much enjoy a Cray supercomputer. Do you think that can happen?"

"They're very expensive."

"Money is no problem," Ralph said, strangely casual. I was inclined to ask him exactly what he meant, but the interview started.

The Oval Office looked nothing like it did two days prior when Ralph arrived. In fact, it looked its usual stately self. Even the wine stain on the carpet had vanished.

Gwen Ifill was interviewing. After a simple exchange of pleasantries, the two pant-suited women sat down across from each other on couches. On the table in front of them lay refreshments: A plain glass of water for Gwen Ifill, and for the president, a glass of Diet Coke with lemon.

"Madame President, I have many questions for you, but I am compelled to start with the most recent. In an article today in the *New York Times*, Markus West was quoted saying the Secret Service was *surprised* when the gigantic can of chicken noodle soup showed up on East Executive Avenue," she said, pointing. "Is that true?"

"I think it is safe to say that no matter how much you prepare for a 400-foot-tall can of soup to float down near the White House, it will always be surprising," the president said, causing Gwen Ifill to smile. "There was indeed some miscommunication and misunderstanding which Dr. West keenly picked up on, but overall, the situation was under control. There were no real surprises."

The president's response was perfect. With a few words, she defused any malevolent curiosity into the subject, and as a perfect coda to her great lie, she casually took a drink of Diet Coke.

"I'm impressed with how efficiently she yields a falsehood," Ralph said.

"I have a few more questions on the subject, and my friends in the art world would kill me if I didn't ask you," Ifill started with a small smile, "Madame President, who is the artist?"

The president smiled and took one last sip from her soda. Ifill smiled expectantly, but within seconds, her interest and tone shifted.

"Madame President, are you all right?"

The president had a sour look on her face as she sniffed her drink. Her eyes became crossed and unfocused. Her glass of soda slipped out of her hand. The interviewer reached out to hold the president.

"Do you smell almonds?" the president asked, breathless.

I stood up and shouted, "NO" at the television.

The president collapsed to the carpet as the Secret Service rushed into view from different angles, bumping and jostling the camera. Male and female shouts and screams exploded as Gwen Ifill's face expressed the shock her audience felt.

"Turn it off," a strong male voice yelled offscreen. "Turn it off."

Seconds before the camera cut off, the president spoke her last weak breath into the microphone still attached to her lapel. The name was unmistakable.

". . . *Ralph* . . ." she said.

Ralph's glow grew purple as the president's eyes closed for the last time.

CRASH

I turned off the television. I was afraid I would smash it if I left it on.

"I don't understand. Will the president be okay?"

"No. She won't be okay."

"Not at all?"

"Ralph . . . She's gone."

"Gone?"

"She's dead, Ralph. Dead."

"How can you be sure . . . Maybe she just got sick."

"She drank from her glass and said something about smelling almonds, then collapsed. *It was cyanide poisoning.* It smells like almonds and kills immediately."

"But maybe she'll be okay . . . You don't know."

"Whoever was clever enough to put cyanide in her drink would be clever enough to put in enough. It may take an hour for the White House to announce, but she's gone . . . *Damn it.*"

By the next day, the full story was clear. As with the assassination of JFK, a plethora of conspiracy theories developed, but the official story was correct. Initially, the assassin, Secret Service Agent Brian Summers, was thought to be another victim. His body was found not far from the Oval Office. He too died from cyanide poisoning, but he was his own Jack Ruby.

The suicide note in his home, also a note of confession, revealed it all. Sandra Summers, his wife, was critically injured in a car accident seconds after the appearance of the lunar advertisement and died later from internal bleeding. Like so many, he blamed Coca-Cola and became increasingly angry with the president for defending her former employer. Wanting his job, he kept silent.

When the cylinder arrived, Agent Summers unraveled. He didn't know about Ralph, but he knew the White House press release was a lie. He assumed the cylinder was a public relations stunt from Campbell's gone wrong and was certain the president was covering for them. In the twists of his mind, she had to pay.

"Why did she say my name?"

If I could have picked the worst word for the president to utter before death, 'Ralph' was it.

"Markus, she called out to me. Maybe we should go. Maybe we can help."

"Can you bring humans back from the dead?" I asked half-seriously.

"No," Ralph said.

Ralph's crackling noises punctuated his speech. He was acting like a child, and I didn't feel like comforting him. He was scared and I was angry.

"Markus, I don't feel so well."

"Really? You don't feel so good? None of this would've happened without you," I said, surprising myself with such cruel words.

"I have a terrible feeling. It is what you would call 'nausea.' I have not felt this in . . . decades. Markus, I'm scared. I don't know if I will survive this . . . failure."

I held his arm, and he turned toward me. Suddenly, black tidal waves folding and crashing invaded my thoughts. I pulled away, and Ralph fell over me. Something inside Ralph was *falling*.

"Keep holding me . . . Do it . . . *Please*," he moaned.

The crackling noises Ralph emitted were sharper and louder than ever. Holding him, I felt the crackling more than I heard it. Like a dream, my mind used symbols to interpret something I could not understand. I was awake, but my senses idled as Ralph's feelings overrode my imagination. I envisioned a planetwide earthquake with mountain ranges for teeth breaking out into space and chomping the moon in half.

A sudden deafening thud extinguished my senses. Whatever was falling inside Ralph had crash-landed, and was so loud I feared Lieutenant Barber would hear. I didn't know if the thud was imagined or real, but either way, my whole mind went numb. I maintained consciousness, but I couldn't hear, see, or feel.

Slowly, my senses returned, and I was uncertain how much time had passed. I looked at a motionless Ralph, his glow black and shiny. Fearing death, I called his name.

"Ralph."

No response.

"Ralph?" I said, gently shaking his frail body.

". . . Markus . . ." Ralph groaned with a bare whisper, his voice radically different.

"Ralph, can I do something?"

"I am survived . . . we stay . . . me rest . . . we talk."

At that moment, I did not know what Ralph had endured, but I knew it was over. He was convalescing and had lost his spritely demeanor.

My pink cell phone rang, and I immediately thought it was Samantha. It was Francis.

"She's dead," Francis said with a cold whimper. I could hear the shock in his voice.

"We saw it. Ralph and I were watching."

"I can't believe she's dead. Someone poisoned her."

"It was cyanide."

"How did you . . . oh, I'm talking to a scientist. Look, Markus, I don't know what's going to happen now."

"What do you mean?"

"What do *you* mean? The president is dead, and now the vice president will take over. He doesn't know about Ralph or any of this. How the hell am I going to tell him what's happening? I can't even begin to think how that conversation starts."

"Don't do it alone. You should take Samantha with you, and I'll go too if you think it will help. He's got to believe if all three of us tell him."

"I can't think about that right now."

"This is something you should sleep on. I should go—something happened with Ralph."

"What?"

"I don't know. All I can say is . . . He had a negative reaction to the president's death."

"*What* happened?" Francis pressed.

"I think he's blaming himself."

"Oh . . . Look after him tonight. Don't let him go suicidal on us. We need him more than ever now. Look after yourself too. I've gotta go."

"No problem."

"Good night."

I returned to Ralph, whose dull black glow had turned a shade purple.

"Can you talk?"

"I can," Ralph said, sounding a little better.

"What *was* that? It sounded like something inside you . . . collapsed."

"Something did collapse."

"What was it? What was that thud?"

"It was my ego."

"Your ego?"

"It crashed."

HUMILITY

I t seemed like just another joke Ralph might make, but his tone was morbid.

"You're telling me I just *literally* heard your ego crash?" I asked.

"Yes. It is different for us. It is easier for humans to hide embarrassment and shame, but my species can't hide it like you do. When reality takes a nice chunk out of your ego, humans often deal with the pain for years. For us, it is more immediate."

"I know you're in pain, but . . . I don't understand."

"It is like . . . Some of your animals have skeletons on the inside, like humans, but some have exoskeletons, like a lobster. Similarly, my ego is external; call it an 'exoego' if you like, and I can't hide it when I'm hurt, mentally. If I wasn't wearing this helmet, you would see my ego directly, and that would be mortally embarrassing. It may sound funny, but I'm not joking: masks are a fashion necessity on my planet."

"So, psychologically speaking, you're a crustacean," I said, attempting humor.

"Exactly," Ralph said, completely serious. "I don't want to dwell on our differences, but our mental pain is typically much more severe and sudden than yours, and I truly envy you for this. My people can literally die of embarrassment, disappointment, or shame."

I instantly recollected some of my greater failures: vomiting on the first day of kindergarten; rejected by the first girl I ever asked on a date; waking up in a jail cell.

"What would happen if I did see your ego directly?"

"It would kill us both," he said.

"Ralph . . . I'm sorry . . . but that sounds completely ridiculous."

Taking no offense, he tried to help my understanding. "Think about how difficult it was for my people, when we learned that most other beings have their psychology neatly hidden inside a head," he said, followed by some more lingering crackling.

"OK," I said, "all things considered, you're an alien, and I should expect radical differences between us . . . But why would it kill us *both* if I saw your ego directly?"

"I would literally die from embarrassment. And you . . . Your psyche would crumble from second-hand embarrassment."

I paused in thought. Being human, I knew what it's like to be so embarrassed I wanted to die. And I understood the concept of second-hand embarrassment—feeling embarrassed for someone else. But, I've never felt so much second-hand embarrassment that I wanted to die. I wondered if any human ever has, but Ralph's people really are that sensitive.

He continued, "If you saw my ego directly, and do not ask me to explain, you would instantly feel *everything* I've ever regretted or feared. That's thousands of years of information, and your mind would implode. If one of my own people saw it, they too would die from second-hand embarrassment. It would just be too much. This is why we all wear masks."

"But you're not born wearing masks," I said.

"No, but a child's mind is pure. There's no danger being exposed to it. In fact, a child's mind is one of the most beautiful objects in the universe. It's a rather somber rite of passage, in my culture, when a child gets their first mask."

"And all this, your whole reaction . . . This was brought on by the president's death?"

"Well, my belief she's dead. You convinced me. You talked to Francis?"

"I did. She's gone."

Ralph responded with some residual crackling.

"You don't hate me, do you?" he asked. If I had said 'yes' in an angry tone, he might have crumbled and died on the spot.

"No. We're in this together. And in any case, it is good to know even an advanced species fails sometimes," I said.

"You have no idea."

"How exactly does your ego collapse?"

"The same way egos collapse throughout the universe," Ralph said, mystified I would even ask. I looked at him and shrugged my shoulders.

"Markus, we need to talk. I haven't been entirely truthful with you."

"You've lied to us?" I was not in the mood.

". . . Yes," he said with pain. "But the Kardashians are real, and they are coming. You'll be detecting them, at the latest, by tomorrow. And I'm afraid, with the president gone, of what will happen. Oh, Markus, it was so beautiful. I was going to save Earth, or most of it. Everything was going so perfectly: the lunar ad, the cylinder, meeting the president, and convincing her not to attack the Kardashians. Now, I honestly think we're . . . This is not good. Your vice president will take power now and . . . He is a man of war . . . He doesn't even know I exist, and I don't see him going along with my advice."

Ralph's uncertainty raised many questions, but I could only ask one.

"What have you been hiding?"

He paused. "You remember, in the Oval Office, when you asked me if the Kardashians truly believe they were gods? Or were they just con artists? Do you remember?"

I nodded.

"I convinced you I didn't know."

"I remember."

"That was a lie. I do know. They do not believe they are gods. They are as evil as can be, and they know it."

I expected him to elaborate, but he didn't.

"All right, but does that really change anything? And why would you lie?" I asked.

"What you need to understand . . . the differences between my people and the Kardashians . . . the difference is . . . philosophical," he said, still struggling with speech.

Ralph paused to gather his thoughts. There must've been a lot because he paused for ten minutes. But I did not want to wait. I was disturbed and seething with bad energy. Knowing

Ralph had suffered, my anger with him had deflated. But I was in no mood for his jokes, flippancy, and alien innocence. I was tempted to go outside and talk to Lieutenant Barber. I wanted to commiserate with another American, another human, over the death of my president.

I thought of people all over America talking and crying. I was irritated to be excluded, and I was angered to imagine the president's harshest critics welcoming her death.

I bet most people would love to talk to an alien and find out what they believe is important. But at that moment, I was not in the mood for a philosophical discussion.

My president had just been assassinated, and a primitive part of me felt under attack as well. Yet Ralph was hinting at some insight, and while I waited for him to say something, I convinced myself the Kardashians were to blame for everything that had happened in the last year. I told myself, if talking about this will save lives, I should stop thinking about myself and listen.

"On my planet, there is a specific ritual we have before talking about this. I wish I could perform the ritual now, dearly, but I cannot. We don't have the proper masks and paraphernalia, so it will be difficult for us . . . There is no easy way to go about this, so I'll just ask you . . . Markus . . . in all seriousness . . . Why do you think we are here?"

"What?" I blurted with an angry laugh.

"What do you believe? Why do you think you are alive?"

"What do you mean?"

"I'm talking about what you call 'the meaning of life.'"

". . . I usually avoid these conversations."

"You don't think this is important? I think about this all the time," Ralph said.

"I do think about it . . . but I don't want to talk about it."

"That's a good sign, but you must indulge. This is important. Do you want to know what is really going on or not?"

"Of course, I do."

"Then answer my question. Do you think life is just some silly accident, some meaningless cosmic coincidence, or do you think there is a deeper purpose?"

Ralph was serious and I had to answer. I was acutely afraid of embarrassing myself. I didn't want to seem shallow, but I didn't want to sound like a kooky earthling either.

"I hope there is a deeper plan, but that's about it. Whenever I hear people talk about this, they are usually too sure of themselves. It seems useless to talk about, because no one can really know."

"No one knows, but I can tell you what we believe, what we *and* the Kardashians believe. Keep in mind, I'm not here to convert you. You just need to think about it if you want to understand why all this is happening."

"You're not saying you're in league with the Kardashians . . ."

"No. But there's a basic belief system we share. In fact, every civilization we've surveyed eventually comes to the same basic belief system. I hate to sound like an ass, but to me, and almost everyone throughout the galaxy, it all seems rather obvious. But I won't be offended if you don't accept it. Not all of it is easy to hear."

"Then start with the easy part."

"All right. Now I will ask you a truly ancient question," Ralph began with a tiny spark of glee. "If the universe does have a purpose, why is it so big? Why is there all this extra empty space which doesn't do anything? The sheer size of the universe makes life seem rather insignificant, because we are all so ridiculously small."

"So . . . You're telling me there is no purpose," I said.

"You don't get it."

"No. You're just making me skeptical."

"Darn, I hoped you would see it. My dear Markus, the purpose of the grand size of the universe . . . is to make us *feel* small," he said excitedly, though I didn't catch the significance.

"Well, if that's the purpose, then OK, but . . . So what? That just sounds—"

"It is only part of the purpose . . . You don't see it?" he said, grabbing my arm. He wanted me to understand without saying it. By touching me, he was hoping I could *feel* the answer from him. I closed my eyes and recalled the cylinder and how I felt standing next to it—dwarfed by something so much larger than myself. I knew what Ralph wanted me to say.

"You're saying that the universe is so immense . . . to humble us?"

"Yes," Ralph said with excitement. "Humility is the key—the key to *everything*."

I never heard Ralph say anything more seriously. But I was not persuaded. The thought seemed too easy. And it wasn't clear how this was relevant to Earth's safety.

"But isn't it a little too big? I mean . . . Does the universe really need to be as big as it is?" I said, pointing outside at the sky. "Half the size would still be equally humbling, right?"

"You don't understand how big egos can get," he said.

"You're serious?" I laughed. "You're saying that the universe must be as big as it is . . . in order to keep my ego in check?"

"Not just your ego, my dear Markus, but all the egos of all the minds scattered about the universe. You look at the universe and see mostly empty space. I look at the universe and see a spacious zoo of comically different beings, each with their own egos that need to be kept in check. So yes, that is what I'm saying. In essence, the universe is an exquisitely efficient and maximally elegant, ego-crunching machine. That is what it does."

FALLING

alph approached the window while I considered his words.

"Oh my God," Ralph said slowly, staring at the sky.

"Ralph?"

"Please," he whispered, "do not speak."

He stood at the window and pressed his helmet against the glass, his vision aimed up into the night sky. He slowly tilted his head downward, only to quickly tilt his head back up again, then gradually tilted his head back down once more. For two long minutes he repeated this motion while I stayed silent.

I stood up and walked to the slightly tinted window next to him, trying to see what he saw. I hoped he had only seen a wild animal, but he was not focusing on the ground, and I could see no birds in the sky. In fact, I saw nothing moving. It was too dark, but Ralph's sight and hearing were much better than a human's.

"I can see them. *I can see them,*" Ralph said with an intense whisper. "Markus, you have to help us. *Turn off all the lights in the barracks. Do it now.*"

I jumped down the stairs and raced to flick off the light

switch near the front door. Then, quickly and quietly, I hustled back upstairs and turned off the upstairs light. The only light remaining was the subdued neon glow from beneath Ralph's suit and the moonlight shining through the scattered white clouds.

I was too scared to ask what he was looking at. I considered calling Francis, but thought it was best to stay quiet and hide. Since the window glass was unidirectional, no being outside could see us. Nonetheless, it was wise to switch off the lights— with less light pollution inside, we, or at least Ralph, could better see what was outside.

I stayed crouched by the window next to him as he continued his strange head motions. Ever so slowly sloping down and then quickly angling back up again, repeating this movement continually with his helmet rubbing firm against the glass. He did this for so long without speaking a single word—I wondered if he had been hypnotized. I peeked out the window expecting to see the end of the world, but all I saw was the tiny blinking taillight of an airplane disappearing far away. Yet he was not watching that airplane.

"Ralph . . . I'm frightened."

The repetitive motion of Ralph's head stopped. Suddenly, Ralph swiveled his entire body toward me, and I fell backward, startled. In silence, he stood over me, looking down into my eyes. He knelt down in front of me with his helmet inching closer and closer to my face. In the dark, with the tinted visor of his helmet inches from my eyes, I could see what was inside his helmet more clearly than ever. I could see thousands, if not millions, of miniscule strands of light reaching out to me, all flowing together as a coordinated swarm of spindly tentacles.

"I'm so sorry, Markus," he said with a voice that tightened my muscles.

Transfixed by what I saw beneath his visor, I noticed a change in the pattern of all the shimmering hairs of light, and Ralph's usual pink glow switched to golden. As I stared, he manipulated his tiny tentacles to form a message.

"Don't be afraid," he wrote across his golden face.

"What are they doing?"

Ralph's head pulled away from mine and looked away. He stood up, looked out the window again, and looked back at me. As I peered into his visor, I saw the long golden filaments rearranging themselves. There was no written message this time. Behind his visor was a golden human face, gently formed with his thin silicon tendrils. I looked closer at his new face and saw a darkened patch under the right eye. It was like looking into a golden mirror—the face he had formed was my own.

"*What are they doing?*" he asked, staring at me with my own face, mocking me. As if the pain of my fear wasn't enough, Ralph unleashed a cruel laughter that shook my mind to its edge. The desire to escape possessed me.

Bewildered, I ran down the stairs in the dark. Misjudging the unfamiliar stairs precipitated a fall, and I dove to the ground floor on my knee and shouted out the pain.

I gazed back up the dark stairs at Ralph's golden head, laughing even harder at my misfortune. The pain in my knee immobilized me. I gave up running away.

"Are they coming for us?" I shouted, not caring who might hear.

To my surprise, Ralph's laughter calmed completely, and his golden glow turned back to pink. He turned the upstairs light back on.

"Markus, no one is outside."

"Then why the fuck have we been hiding this whole time?"

"I wasn't hiding."

"Then why did you want me to turn off the lights and stay silent?"

"Well, I couldn't do it, but I tried to hear them. Weren't you able to see them with the lights turned off? You couldn't see them this whole time?"

"See *them*? See *who*? What the fuck are you talking about? I couldn't see anything. What the hell have you been staring at this whole time?"

Ralph laughed.

"Your pronouns are truly confusing . . . Markus . . . I was staring at the tiny snowflakes falling . . . I've never seen natural snow before . . . What on Earth did you think I was looking at?"

XXIV

+ + + + + + + + + +
PROGRESS

Radically disabused, I limped outside on my aching knee while Ralph tried to stop laughing. I couldn't see it through the tinted windows, but when I walked out the door, I discovered the exceptionally light snowfall Ralph had been gazing at with his extraordinary sight.

With no wind, the sparse and tiny snowflakes traveled straight to the ground where they melted on contact. I was amazed Ralph thought he could hear them.

I laughed aloud at myself in the dark, mentally replaying what had just happened with a corrected perspective. When Ralph said, 'I'm so sorry, Markus,' he was apologizing because we were sitting in the dark the whole time, and he knew I had a fear of darkness.

While I stood outside feeling silly, I heard the door open behind me. I turned around and saw a golden bright light from behind it.

"Markus, are you out there?" Ralph asked in a strange voice, deeper than usual. He was breathing oxygen, instead of his preferred helium.

"I'm here."

"I've taken off my Earth suit and I want to come out. I don't want to scare you though. You promise you won't be scared?"

"I'll be fine."

"I don't want you to think I look weird."

Almost naked, Ralph was unexpectedly shy. To prevent me from seeing his ego directly, Ralph kept his helmet on as he stepped into the darkness which he illuminated.

"You sure I don't look like . . . some scary monster?"

Ralph looked like a five-foot tall, radioactive jellyfish wearing a helmet. This description, though reasonable, is incomplete. Ralph was beautiful, and I could have stared at him all night. His body was millions of glowing and prehensile silicon hairs, which coalesced together with inexplicable coordination. When he moved, he flowed as if under water.

"You look beautiful," I told him, and he glowed brighter, as if blushing. He was enchanted by the snowflakes and seemed to dance among them as he bounced up and down rhythmically.

"You've really never seen snow before?"

"Only in the lab. It doesn't occur naturally on my home planet; too much fire. I mean, it is too hot. It is one of the reasons I wanted to come to Earth. These tiny water crystals are so cute. They are tickling me all over."

Viewing his floating dance amid the snowflakes, I realized how light he was without his full suit. A strong gust could've blown him away like a dandelion. It was a risk for him to be naked outside. But he adored it.

"Earth is so beautiful," Ralph said.

His delight in the moment was a forgetful rest from the

reality of the night. Cindy Shepherd had been assassinated, the future was uncertain, and in my morbid mind, I wondered if we deserved what was coming.

Ralph was convinced the purpose of the universe centered around one thing: humility. When I reconsidered his conviction, it angered me. In fact, I feared he was mocking me—because it seemed obvious humans have only gotten more arrogant.

"I've been thinking about what you said about humility."

"Does it strike you as implausible?"

"Ralph, if humility is the purpose of the universe, then the universe is doing a shitty job."

"Oh, you don't sense the progression? You think humans are more arrogant than, say, a thousand years ago?"

"Of course, we are. Everyone's always complaining about how narcissistic everyone is. Do we really need to go through all the evidence?"

"Markus . . . There was a time when your culture thought Earth was the center of the universe. Every culture in the *universe* starts off believing their planet, *their Earth*, is the center of the universe. Slowly, painfully, they realize their home star, *their sun*, is better placed at the center. Then, just like your culture, they go further. They realize their sun is just another star. They discover there are trillions of planets, and their little solar system is just one among billions in their galaxy, and their galaxy is just one among billions of galaxies in the universe as a whole. There's a reason why the universe has no center, and every culture realizes why, eventually. We all go through the same progression, and it is painful, but it is progress."

"Bullshit," I barked, annoyed with the all-too-pretty historical picture he painted. "Most humans don't think about any of that. They don't think about stars and galaxies. They think about food, money, and sex." I'm not normally so cynical. In fact, I hated these words, but it felt good to say them. "Maybe it is humbling for scientists, *maybe*, but most humans are not scientists. They are too busy thinking about where their next paycheck is coming from. You are being way too intellectual."

"Markus . . . Your species, like all species, will become more and more scientific; it is inevitable. Three thousand years from now, the everyday human will be a scientific genius compared to now. And more importantly, more of your population than ever will be *compelled* to think about the stars and galaxies."

"*Maybe* . . . But in the meantime, we have religious fundamentalists who think the universe is only a few thousand years old, they deny evolution, they think their religion is the only real one, and everyone else is gonna burn in hell."

Ralph laughed a little. "Oh yes, it is funny, isn't it. Those same people will agree with me about how important humility is. How lucky they must feel to be born into the one true religion. It would be truly comical if only . . . Well, no, I'm sorry, it is quite amusing."

"You're laughing, but their arrogance convinces me you are wrong, and obviously religious fundamentalism isn't the only type of arrogance."

"You will move past it. Trust me. Everyone does. In the meantime, yes, you have to deal with all sorts of primitive arrogance. But there are many signs that are reassuring. For example, your people are deeply curious about the possibility of alien life. I see it in your movies and books, your NASA and your SETI. It is all very encouraging."

"So what?" I said. "What's that got to do with humility?"

"I'm surprised you don't see this. Obviously, it is arrogant to believe that one's people are the only people in the whole universe, as if the whole universe was created just for you."

I looked up. Seeing the stars made it difficult to disagree.

"Of course, the final step will be to embrace the multiverse," he said.

My head snapped to look at him. "The *multiverse*? Are you joking?"

"Markus," he said, sounding exasperated, "just as it is arrogant to believe that one's religion is the only real one, and just as it is arrogant to believe that one's planet is the only one with life, the final form of arrogance is to believe that one's universe is the only universe that is real." He paused and said, "Though perhaps I've said too much."

Right or wrong, the claim was too far-out. Instead of responding, I thought about it. Sensing my mind was full, Ralph went inside to put his Earth suit back on. When he returned, I realized how Ralph fit in his suit. He did not have humanoid limbs, but he could fashion his thinner-than-angel-hair-pasta tendrils to form arms and legs. In any case, I was more at ease to see him in it.

"Ralph, I'm not saying I'm a convert, but I'll stop arguing with you. But I still don't see what any of this has to do with the Kardashians . . . Do the Kardashians agree with all of this?"

"Yes, but they have different . . . tremendously different . . . ideas about how to increase humility. That's what we really need to discuss," he said, lowering his voice to a whisper.

"You sound too serious, as if you are telling me some big secret."

"Markus, so far, what I've told you is something we tell our children. But there is more, something we don't tell our children—something we are forbidden by law, our law, from telling them. I was only told 2,000 years ago. Morally speaking, I can't even tell you."

"Don't get mysterious with me."

Ralph leaned back and laughed slowly. There was a great distance in his laughter, and I wondered just how long he could maintain his laugh. He touched me gently, and an image of him examining me under a large microscope flashed in my mind. I stepped back and glared at him.

"You don't know how dangerous it is to have this many secrets," he said in a low tone. "Markus, keep in mind, I learned how to build rockets before humans learned how to write. There are things I could tell you, right here, right now, and you would either go insane, or kill me, if you believed it. There are facts I could demonstrate, mathematical truths I could prove to you, and if you told others, it would shatter your civilization within a month."

I was in no position to argue, but I was annoyed. "Are you going to tell me what you have in mind or not?"

"This may be unwise to discuss."

"Then why mention it?"

"Because, Markus . . . Do I have to say it?"

"What?"

He paused.

"This has been the most disastrous event of my life. All my training, all the planning, and it all just imploded in my stupid alien face. Don't you see that?" he said, gesticulating incomprehensibly. "If I can't rectify my mistakes, I may go down in history as the worst xenoanthropologist ever. I thought I could do this on my own, but the president is dead, and Earth . . . I need help, Markus, *your* help."

"Ralph, I'm sorry, but what can I do?"

He paused again.

"Go home, rest, and come back tomorrow night," he said slowly. "This night is too much. Your country is in mourning. You should be with your people." We both knew it was my job to stay, but we both knew I wanted to go home.

"Don't worry. I'll be fine, and I'll talk to Francis," he said.

When I drove out of the complex, I said 'good night' to Lieutenant Barber, who responded with no words and a glare.

DREAM

I drove home slowly, running through the night's conversation repeatedly in my mind. Strangely, I barely thought about the assassination. As I approached my place, my mind fixated on my bedroom. When I unlocked my door, I bypassed my nightly ritual and aimed for bed, fully clothed. I lost consciousness before my head touched the sheets.

Before I awoke, I experienced an intensely vivid dream.

I was under water, unafraid, looking up at the sky. I felt slow and amazed by the world around me. I couldn't close my eyes, but there was little to look at. I could open and close my mouth freely. I was breathing water, and I knew I was a fish.

I looked for the sun, but there was something blocking my view. Every time I moved, it moved with me, hiding the sun's warmth from my face. The object was dark and crescent-shaped. I twisted, turned, and swam my fish body about. But, no matter how I maneuvered, the crescent-shaped object eclipsed my sight of the sun.

All I could see was this frustrating crescent, teasing me with the sun behind it. I hated the crescent-shaped object and tried to attack it. I tried to bite it with my fish mouth. But it anticipated my moves and evaded, as if it knew my thoughts.

I gave up trying to destroy it, and I gave up trying to see the sun. I focused on the crescent-shaped object and saw it was attached to something—a fish. It was the tail of some fish.

Some rude fish used his tail to block out the sun. I swam back and forth, hunting this maddening fish, but wherever I swam, I was alone. And whenever I looked back up to see the sun, his tail blocked my view.

I was too slow to catch the mysterious fish, so I gave up trying to find him. Instead, I used the sun to focus on the tail of this infuriating fish. With my watery eyes, I slowly traced the body of the fish attached to the tail. As I woke up, I realized the crescent-shaped object, the tail, was my own.

The ceiling light above my bed was on all night.

"Oh, babe. Oh, baby. Oh, BABY," my upstairs neighbor yelled.

"Ay, Papi. Ay," his Hispanic wife screamed.

I remained in bed and stared at the ceiling light, wondering if their own kids had heard them. I contemplated yelling at them for being loud, but felt too good to do it.

I was abnormally awake. My eyes gawked at the ceiling light as I lay on my back. I slowly got up, drank two glasses of water, went to the bathroom, and took a shower.

I meditated on my strange dream as I went through my morning ritual, the ritual I had before the lunar advertisement. It ended with me checking the news and then my e-mail. Of course, today's news would be different. The cable news networks, typically sensationalizing the most trivial news story, were lost in the midst of an actually sensational news story. Though I felt sick to listen, I left the TV on in the background and read the news online.

Brian Summers's identity as the prime suspect was leaked to the press to calm the unnerved public. It would take until late afternoon for the full story to come out at a press conference hosted by the Secret Service. Despite straightforward evidence, conspiracy theorists went full ragetard on the blogosphere.

One theory was that the president poisoned Agent Summers, then herself—because of a love triangle with a mysterious lover named Ralph. Another theory involved the Coca-Cola Company—she was going to expose the truth about the lunar advertisement, but Coca-Cola's assassins killed her first . . .

I was reading a respectful memorial article when the web page went blank. It became pure white. Neither the web page nor the website had crashed, and I was still connected to the Internet. I started checking the web pages bookmarked in my browser. They all loaded instantly, and they were the same, each a blank sheet of whiteness. There was no error message because there was no error. I had never seen anything like it before and assumed there was simply something wrong with my computer.

After only twenty seconds, the whiteness stopped and the Internet functioned normally again. I did a virus scan. Nothing was detected. What I didn't know was that almost everyone on the Internet had the same experience. The duration of the event was so short, barely anyone on the planet bothered to mention it to anyone else. Considering what happened later that night, it was obviously a preliminary test—the Kardashians were checking their control over Earth's communications infrastructure.

Francis had left a number of messages on my pink cell phone, but I refused to listen to them until I had completed my ritual. I checked my inbox and found two e-mails. One from Francis, and an apparent piece of spam with the subject heading: 'PENIS TOO BIG? HERE'S THE CURE.'

I almost deleted it before I noticed the sender: Ralph18663287687@gmail.com. The body of the e-mail was awkward and direct:

Markus,

They're here. Image file attached.

Call Francis immediately. We must talk. There are secrets you must know.

Love,
Ralph

I started downloading the large file attached, labeled, ???24. jpg, and I wondered how Ralph, Francis, or anyone could know the Kardashians were in the solar system without the whole world knowing. I called Francis.

"They're here," he said without a greeting.

"Ralph just told me. Have you talked to the vice president about him?"

"McAllister was at an Asian business conference. His plane is landing as we speak, but let me worry about him. Have you seen the image?"

"Downloading . . . one second."

"There are other images, but this is the most convincing."

Their spaceship shined pure optic white and seemed entirely smooth. Not a single symbol, indentation, or shadow was visible on the outer shell. Two large spheres, propulsion mechanisms, I presumed, lay in the rear of the ship. Protruding out from the spheres was a long cylindrical fuselage. No wings, no windows, no ornamentation visible. I chuckled a little.

"This isn't funny," Francis said correctly.

"How large is it?"

"Each of those spheres . . . is the size of the Earth."

The diameter of Earth is nearly 8,000 miles. The logistics of building such a spacecraft instantly staggered my imagination. The vehicle, amusing seconds earlier, struck me humorless when I contemplated its size and what lay inside. The length of the fuselage was approximately 25,000 miles, making it as long as the circumference of Earth. What first looked like a spaceship . . . now appeared as a bomb whose target was Earth.

"What's the little dot next to it?"

"Pluto."

With such overwhelming size, people assumed the mass of the ship was proportionally as great. But the so-called Kardashian mothership actually weighed relatively little. It was like a distended blowfish, or a blimp. The functional part of the mothership was a minute fraction of the ship itself, and the rest was mostly empty space. The humungous outer shell was made of the same light, malleable, and programmable substance as Ralph's cylinder. It was smoke and mirrors, a contrivance, designed to impress us into submission.

"Where did this photo come from?"

"Keck Observatory. It's in the wild."

By 'in the wild,' Francis meant he had no control over it, which meant it could go viral. Astronomers at the Keck Observatory in Hawaii were doing research on Pluto's moons and accidentally captured the first images of the Kardashian ship. They knew it wasn't one of Pluto's moons or a comet. At that point, the image was circulating through academia, and, of course, their colleagues thought it was a joke. No one took it seriously. If I hadn't known Ralph, I wouldn't have either. Regardless of the image from Keck, even an amateur astronomer with a high-end telescope could see it if they looked in the right place.

"That's not all," Francis said. "There's no evidence yet, but Ralph says there will be many more ships, smaller ones. I've got someone looking, but it's difficult to search effectively and discreetly at the same time."

"Jesus Christ."

"I have to ask . . . What did you and Ralph talk about last night?"

"As if every word we spoke wasn't recorded," I said, feeling clever and then remembered we had talked outside of Ralph's residence as well.

"Yes, of course, there is a recording . . . moron . . . but that doesn't mean I'm listening to it every night. I have better things to do, and there's no way I'd authorize anyone else to listen. So are you going to tell me or waste my time?"

I paused.

"He told me the meaning of life."

Francis paused.

"Write me a full report on that," he said and hung up.

I didn't think he'd read my report, but I was on the payroll, so felt obligated to write something. With coffee and cream, I spent the afternoon summarizing my conversation with Ralph about humility.

Next, I wanted to do something normal, figuring this may be my last day on Earth to do so. I let my first draft sit to go grocery shopping—though I didn't need anything. I had hoped the mundane activity would be a soothing escape from the events circling my life.

I went out the door to my car on the street and noticed a black SUV, an apparently unoccupied Cadillac Escalade with New Jersey license plates, parked on my block. The area was residential, far from the tourist attractions, so Jersey plates were unusual. I drove five blocks and then saw the black SUV following far behind. I called Francis.

"Am I being followed?"

"Why would anyone follow you?" he said with a blank tone.

"Can you not be a cagey asshole and just answer directly?"

"No one is following you," he said and hung up.

I continued to the supermarket at a busy, brick strip mall a few miles from home. The black SUV followed but hung too far back for me to spot the driver. Arriving, I parked close to the stores, and in my rearview spied the SUV backing into a spot at a far corner of the oversized, suburban parking lot.

I turned off the engine and immediately launched out of the driver's seat. Running, I aimed for the parked SUV, hoping to glimpse the driver. But it was getting dark. Before I got close enough, the SUV sped out and fled the lot, narrowly missing a minivan as it exited.

I turned around with clenched fists and aimed to shop. Along the way, I saw an event, which I know Ralph would want me to include. A middle-aged woman who ran the tanning salon was outside feeding some stray cats, and a black girl bumped into her. The older woman snapped, "Watch where you're going, ya' dirty welfare nigger." The girl glanced at me and just laughed. If I had been in a better mood, I might have laughed too.

Hunger and aggravation made it difficult to shop properly. I wandered around the store, constantly checking if someone was watching me. If I did see someone eyeing me, I looked away. When the supermarket became too crowded, I left without buying anything.

My heart felt choked. I feared I had somehow been poisoned. I got some cheap Chinese take-out next door and headed to my car.

Before leaving, I scanned the parking lot. The black SUV was absent.

I did not see the SUV on my drive back. I opened my front door slowly and quietly checked every room and closet in my place. Then, feeling safe and alone, I sat down and ate my shrimp almond ding. A full stomach calmed my head.

On the news, I learned the vice president had officially become the new president of the Unites States. John McAllister, a former five-star general, was inaugurated in an undisclosed location. No media, though photos were available to the press— revealing far fewer witnesses than those present at Lyndon

Johnson's inauguration on Air Force One after the assassination of JFK.

I reread my report for Francis, edited it, and e-mailed it. I took another long stare at the image of the Kardashian ship. Before seeing that image, I had hoped the Kardashians weren't real; that they were just another joke. When I reviewed it, I knew my expectations were worthless. The only person on Earth who knew what to expect was not human. I had to talk to him.

I went out on the street filled with suspicion. I didn't see the black SUV on my block, but that wasn't good enough. I couldn't risk being followed to Ralph's. I walked around the block, and after two right turns, I saw it, from the back. The engine and lights were off.

I found what I was searching for and stood still. The supermarket parking lot had been filled with people. Here, there was almost no one, and it was night. There was no shortage of parking spots in front of my home; the SUV was deliberately parked around the block so I wouldn't see it.

Looking around 360 degrees, I saw a middle-aged couple holding hands, an old man walking his dog, and a teenage boy with a hooded sweatshirt—no one worthy of suspicion. I continued my approach to the SUV.

Seeing no one inside, I took a closer look. It was an older model, and the interior was dusty. Peeking inside revealed nothing. Most people have a few personal items lying around in their car . . . an air freshener, a hat, a lighter, music, a piece of clothing, something—there was nothing at all.

I tried Francis again.

"Francis, someone is definitely following me."

"No, they're not."

"I have the license plate. Just check the New Jersey Department of Motor Vehicles."

"No one from Jersey is following you."

"Just check the goddamn plates."

"Just check it? Markus, you're an idiot. You ever heard of the Driver's Privacy Protection Act? What you're asking is illegal."

He hung up.

I reminded myself I was not trained to deal with any of this and was probably lucky to not find the driver. If they wanted me dead, I'd be dead. It was Francis monitoring me, and he wouldn't admit it, I told myself.

I walked back around the block and got in my car. As I drove to Ralph's, I took every opportunity to check my rearview mirror. I pulled into random parking lots, twice, and waited ten minutes, intending to throw anyone off my tail.

I assumed the driver had switched vehicles and was behind me, somewhere. This assumption was correct. The person who had been following was *directly* behind me—in the back of my own vehicle.

BROTHER

A quarter of the adult population of Earth watched the president's live interview in the Oval Office, including Alice Higginbotham. When Alice heard the president whisper 'Ralph' just before death, she inferred this was the same Ralph I screamed about on the phone.

While there was speculation over the president's last word, few concluded it was meaningful. Doctors specialized in palliative care were interviewed on TV, all declaring, based on years of anecdotal evidence, that last words were often random and nonsensical. But, Alice knew better.

When she knew there was a connection between the president's assassination and the cylinder, her curiosity was impassioned. Her parents in New Jersey let her borrow their old SUV. She then drove to DC to spy on me.

My address and home phone were unlisted, so how did Alice know them?

The short answer: I was *doxed*.

'Dox' is Internet slang for information on personal documents. When you get doxed, this means your information is exposed and freely available on the Internet—typically posted on sites like Pastebin. It is a way for hackers to attack anyone they don't like. Because of my global unpopularity, everyone wanted to dox me.

In my case, my home phone number, address, Social Security Number, and the make and model of the car I drove became public knowledge. Even my credit card number was exposed briefly. Thankfully, I convinced the credit card company I did not order twenty Jennifer Lawrence hermaphrodite blow-up dolls from Japan.

I changed my home phone number several times, but it kept getting doxed, despite being unlisted, so I just stopped bothering to change it. Eventually, the prank calls and unwanted pizza deliveries stopped, but the information was still out there when Alice searched.

She discovered I drove a 2018 Lexus Hybrid RX. Then searched and found, on the Internet, instructions on how to break into that exact make and model of car. I'm sure she only planned to search it, but when she knew that I knew I was followed, plans changed. She broke into my car and hid snug in the rear of it.

Oblivious to my stowaway, I continued to Ralph's.

Reaching the barracks, I slowed at the gate. Lieutenant Barber nodded without looking at me, and I continued up the driveway. It was night, and I saw no lights on inside.

The pervasive animal activity from the previous night had vanished. The night before, Ralph was joyous from his successful journey to Earth, and the wildlife adopted his enthusiasm.

Now, the mood of the forest was quiet and cold.

I parked my car and turned off the ignition. The only available light source was the night sky. The moon, still beautiful despite the lunar ad, struck me calm.

I approached the entrance, but then heard Ralph outside.

"Over here, Markus," he called from the grass.

He was near the other side of the barracks, laid out in the strangely plush and healthy winter grass, staring at the sky. His usual pink glow was now a blackish purple. His voice was deeper, and I wondered if he had been breathing oxygen. I walked over to him silently and lay next to him.

"My mind has healed well," he said. "I am . . . better."

He sounded older.

"Better?"

"I am . . . humbled," he said. "I was arrogant to think I could do this on my own. It was arrogant to think everything would go as planned."

Moments passed and I said nothing. I wanted hope, but I could not convince myself. Ralph was the guide and he was lost.

"I'm afraid, Markus. I fear it will be my fault. I was sent here to study, and now I may be entangled in your . . . genocide."

'Genocide' echoed in my mind as a furry animal approached, a plump young raccoon. With moonlit eyes shining through a black mask, the curious animal looked more playful than hungry. Ralph looked at the raccoon and waved to shoo him. It scampered away without a second approach.

"You enjoy looking at the stars?" Ralph asked as he raised his hand and swept it across the sky. He knew the answer.

"Of course, I do."

"One of these shining points of light could be a Kardashian ship," he said. "Light can be so deceptive."

His hand fell slowly back down to the soft grass. "Markus, there is something I must say. I was afraid to say it last night."

I nodded.

"Last night . . . I almost died. This is not exaggeration. I was humbled severely last night, and you cushioned the blow just enough."

"I don't really understand."

"It is not mysterious. It was the threshold of mental annihilation, but you comforted me."

He was deflated to admit it, and I still didn't understand.

"Now," Ralph said, "symmetry demands I guard your life as if it were my own. You are a good being, Markus. I must look after you. There is a deeper connection now. We must protect it."

His tone was too serious to question or even respond to.

"We are brothers."

"Brothers?"

"On my planet, all friends become brothers."

I wondered if he meant it literally, as if by an extraordinary feat of alien genetics, one could actually make a friend a brother. My mind wondered, but my gut agreed.

We were not equals, but we were more equal than before. I could not explain it, but somehow we had humbled each other, and this made us brothers. Of course, I was still the younger brother by about 19,000 years.

"Together, maybe, there's a way."

"All right," I said, "what's the plan?"

"The plan is to find a plan. You still don't really know what's happening, I'm sad to say. The rules of the game are not what you think they are, and the stakes are greater than you imagine."

MISTAKES

"I need you to focus," he said. "Do you understand how humility works? Do you see how and why I was humbled last night? Is it obvious?"

"I think so," I said. "You made a mistake."

"Yes," Ralph shouted, as if I said something amazing. His purple glow pulsed and brightened. "That is exactly it, Markus. Exactly! I became something I did not want to, and it humbled me. It is so simple, frightful, and beautiful, is it not?"

"I understand what you're saying, but . . . I don't share your enthusiasm."

Ralph laughed the way I'd imagine a lion laughing—a deep, slow laugh that rolled over me in waves. He reacted like a dog owner teaching his pet a new trick. Like the dog, I was not impressed.

"You understand, but not completely," he said. "This is where you need to take the next logical step. To me, it is obvious, but for your people, it may be difficult."

"You made a terrible mistake, and it humbled you; it's a good thing. I get it."

"Now we are getting somewhere."

"I'm sorry, Ralph, really, but that's obvious. Of course, you can learn from mistakes; of course, mistakes can be humbling. What are you trying to say?"

"I wish you said it. If mistakes can be humbling, then what should we do?"

"Stop avoiding them?"

". . . You need to go further . . ."

He did not want to preach. He wanted to talk. I was less argumentative than the previous night, but I was just as lost. Instead of thinking aloud, I shut my mouth and thought.

A minute passed while I searched my mind and Ralph waited patiently. When someone lives thousands of years, waiting a few minutes for another to think is nothing. But it did me no good. I tried to think like Ralph and failed.

I stopped thinking and looked at Ralph lying calm in the grass. His whole being seemed to smile and pulsate, like a rolling silent wave headed toward me.

We were motionless, but I felt guided, and I noticed I was holding his hand. I closed my eyes and saw a black tsunami silently rushing toward me. When it hit, a hot flash of pleasure gripped me tight, then released and washed over me.

"Are you saying we should purposefully make mistakes?" I asked, laughing.

"Ah," Ralph said, pinker and sharper than before, "the primitive mind awakens."

The claim seemed odder than anything. And since it was Ralph, I had to wonder if he was joking. Of course, he wanted to be doubted. He wanted me to think.

"We should purposefully make mistakes?" I repeated,

resisting a smile and trying to comprehend. "That's not obvious."

"No, it isn't."

"So . . . Should I ram my head into a wall, over and over again? Or deliberately become a heroin addict?" I said.

"No," Ralph said with strength. "Making the same mistake over and over again, like an addiction, means you're avoiding a more important mistake that needs to be made."

"Okay, so you don't mean just any mistake."

"Of course not. What's difficult is to make the right mistakes."

"Wait," I said, "what do you even mean by a 'mistake'?"

"I mean it loose: when you become what you don't like."

"So then . . . Should I become what I hate?" I asked, wondering if I had gone too far. "Should we become what we hate? To try to become more humble?"

Ralph grasped my hand, and I waited, but he said nothing.

". . . That's just perverse," I said.

Ralph's pink glow brightened.

I took a pause without interruption from Ralph. We stayed silent, both focused upward at the sky. I found myself staring at a particular star in the sky, isolated from the others. I kept a soft focus on it and imagined Ralph looking at the same star. Then, something unexpected happened.

The star blinked and disappeared. With wider eyes, I stared at the spot where it had been, but it didn't return. There are many reasons why a star might disappear, but I imagined the star had collapsed and turned into a black hole. I envisaged the star becoming the complete opposite of what it once was, and by ridiculous chance, I saw its last light after traveling thousands of light-years to Earth.

I thought about the eclipse and the lunar ad, and then Ralph made a bunch of variously pitched hissing sounds. Apparently, it was whistling, or he thought it was.

"Can you stop making that noise?" I said.

He laughed. "On Earth, if someone's whistling annoys you, you ask them to stop or move away from them. On my planet, we are taught to join them."

"I couldn't make those sounds if I wanted to."

"That's not the point."

"Oh."

"On my planet, if a youngster has a problem with authority, we give them a position of authority. One's hatred of authority melts rather quickly when one sees how difficult it is."

"I'm not sure that would work on Earth."

"It works well enough," he said with a sigh. "As children, we all hate our parents, to some degree. The best way to get over it? Have kids and become a parent yourself, to see how difficult it is. You probably think the point of having and raising children is to prolong the survival of your species, but that is merely a beneficial side effect. The deeper reason is to humble yourselves, because there are few things more humbling than raising kids."

I laughed a little.

"My point is, becoming what you hate," he said, "can help you to forgive those you hate."

"How far are you taking this?" I asked.

"What do you have in mind?"

"Well, if I hate Nazis, should I become a Nazi? If I hate murder, should I become a murderer in order to *understand* them?

You're not saying that, are you? That's . . . insane."

He laughed as he rolled over and hugged me, straddling me, his glow pinker than ever. He tried to tickle me unsuccessfully as I pushed him, and he bounced horizontally across the dark grass.

"Ralph, tell me you think that is crazy."

"I love you so much, Markus."

"Answer the question."

With his strange joy, Ralph inched closer. Again, I pushed him away with force. His glow dimmed as he bounced.

"I'm feeling very weary of all things alien right now."

"Of course, that's crazy," he said.

"So why are you so excited?"

"Now you know the difference between my people and the Kardashians."

"You mean . . ."

"Yes."

"Oh God."

"Yes. My people do all sorts of things for humility. We risk becoming what we hate in all types of ways to embarrass ourselves and gain humility. But, my people are not violent by nature. We would never go that far."

"And the Kardashians . . ."

"Exactly. They believe that by *becoming* monsters, they can learn to be at peace with monsters. They think that by acting intolerant, they may truly understand those who are. They are coming to Earth to act as terrible as possible, just to fulfill this twisted purpose. Become evil, to overcome it, like a reductio ad absurdum of evil itself."

"But . . . how?"

"They will take the worst of Earth's culture and twist it back at you in force—expect the ultimate forms of mockery. They will seduce your people with great trickery and power, appealing to the worst of what you know."

"But . . . How will they do it?"

"I . . . could only guess. We've tried to stay away from them. It's too dangerous for us to track them closely, but we've found planets they've . . . visited. They always cater to the worst elements of the planets they visit and will similarly tailor their guile for earthlings."

"How often do they do this?"

"Each Kardashian is obligated to do it at least once. For them, it is like going to Mecca."

"I'm afraid to ask . . . but . . . Why don't they just destroy us?"

Ralph turned away and said, "They need to leave behind witnesses . . . What they have planned is far worse than annihilation."

Some statements deserve a silent response. Some claims need to breathe and linger in the air without question. My greatest childhood fear, which stalked me into adulthood, was creeping toward Earth. With his bizarre and unexpected ways, Ralph had extinguished my fear. He was the perfect counterexample to my phobia. But, at that moment, I needed the fear. If Ralph was afraid, I should be afraid, but I was too afraid to ask what was worse than annihilation.

Now I know.

XXVIII

+ + + + + + + + +

STARTING

Lost in thought, I barely felt my pink cell phone vibrating against my thigh.

"Francis is calling," Ralph said, pointing to my pocket. I answered reluctantly.

"Turn on the TV," Francis yelled.

"What channel?"

"Any channel."

I stood up and told Ralph to follow. He waved his arm, motioning me to go on.

"It's starting," Ralph said.

I left him on the grass and rushed upstairs. Turning on the TV revealed the same blankness I had seen on the Internet earlier—a steady image of unpolluted white. I clicked through channels and saw the same bright white nothingness without sound.

"How long has it been like this?" I asked Francis.

"Four minutes."

I turned on the radio. On each station I checked, FM and AM, there were no sounds, not even noise, only fresh silence. Satellite radio had the same silence on every channel.

"Did Ralph say this would happen?" I asked.

"I was going to ask you the same," Francis said and sighed. "He's been giving great intel on the Kardashians, but never mentioned this. Let me talk to him."

"He's still outside," I said, glancing out the window. "Pluto is around four billion miles away. Am I naïve . . . How can they do this from so far?"

"You're not entirely naïve . . . but I'm guessing Ralph didn't tell you," Francis said.

"Tell me what?"

He inhaled and exhaled. "I need you not to panic. I can't lose you right now, do you understand? You're one of the few people I can talk to about this."

"Whatever it is, just say it."

"Markus, I'm trying to be gentle here. Ralph told me you have some . . . phobia of aliens. Was he wrong?"

"Just fucking tell me."

"Markus, they're already here."

My mouth froze. My right hand started to shake and I steadied it with my left.

He continued, "Most of them, I mean the one's we've observed, are the smaller ships I had mentioned earlier today."

"What do you mean 'most' of them? How many are there?"

"My resources at NASA are limited. I don't have much authority over there, and it's been hard to coordinate and contain—"

"Answer the fucking question."

"They seem to be . . . everywhere, but we can't check everywhere all at once. I only have access to one satellite. It's designed to see into deep space, not locally. It works, but it's the opposite of being myopic. Extrapolating from what we've seen so far . . . There's at least a thousand ships."

For a moment, I couldn't talk. A tear came to my eye and I let it run down my cheek. My emotions seemed to give up, but my mind kept moving.

"How could no one notice until now?" I asked, but I knew the answer.

"No one was looking. Barely anyone studies the empty space right around Earth, because . . . Well, most of the time it's empty. It's a blind spot. Frankly, I'm surprised you're asking. Are you okay?"

"No."

"Markus, it doesn't matter. Even if someone had seen them, they wouldn't know what they were looking at. We can't see them directly, but I've been working with a few people at NASA, and they're there. The ships barely reflect visible light. But they show up on thermal infrared easily, just as Ralph said they would."

I sat down and stared at the blank television, dizzy with questions.

"Ralph tells you all this, but not about what they are doing to our TV?" I said.

"They want our attention. It's probably why our phones aren't knocked out, so people can call and tell others . . . And there's more. The top 1,000 most popular websites are all blank, total whiteout. All other sites are normal. It's good to know they have limits, but still . . . This is overwhelming."

"Is there any way to stop it?"

"Nothing short of shutting down the national grid or

pulling the plug on the goddamn Internet. We can't even get the Emergency Broadcast System to work. Can you please get our resident alien on the line?"

"Hold on," I said as I cracked the tiny attic window an inch. "Ralph, get up here. We need to talk to you."

Ralph did not respond.

"Markus," Francis shouted in my ear. I looked at the TV.

In black numerals, '1:00:00' appeared on the white screen.

00:59:59

00:59:58

00:59:57

Every channel was the same.

They wanted our attention—and they got it. For the next hour, anyone awake told somebody else. North Korea was on high alert, but most countries relaxed their defenses when they understood this was happening all over the planet. The accessible Internet raged with speculation about elite rogue hackers disabling the world's communications infrastructure, and, of course, aliens.

By this time, the image of the Kardashian mothership near Pluto from the Keck Observatory had gone viral. Keck had posted it on their own website, stating the image was genuine. Following up on Keck, five other observatories had recalibrated their telescopes, produced similar images, and were freely sharing and discussing them.

Francis was furious at Ralph's silence and even angrier Ralph hadn't warned him. He ordered me to "interrogate" Ralph and hung up. I went back outside and stood over him, supine and relaxed on the grass.

"Why the fuck would you tell Francis but not me that the Kardashians are already here?" I asked.

"I hoped Francis would tell you. I was afraid how you'd react."

He was terrible at delivering bad news.

"How much time is there on the countdown?" he asked.

". . . You knew this would happen."

"This is standard engagement protocol for the Kardashians."

"What happens when the countdown reaches zero?"

"They will broadcast their transmission, a message."

"Ralph, Francis is suspicious. Why not warn us they'd take over our communications?"

"Because then you would've tried to prevent it, and you'd fail. Waste of time."

"But you know how to prevent it?"

"Well, yes. But, then, they'd know I'm here, and that can't happen."

"You just have an answer for everything."

"Markus, be serious. How much time is left on the countdown?"

"Less than an hour."

"That's not enough time."

"For what?"

"For you."

"What does this have to do with me?" I asked.

He paused, looked at the moon, and said, "There is something special about you . . . between us . . . I can't explain it without sounding like some kook. Your language is so . . . impoverished. I need to think. Please, sit down. It will make me more at ease. My people are not good in stressful situations."

I sat and stayed silent in the cold grass waiting for Ralph's thoughts. I looked for that vanished star, but the light was still gone. I stared at the empty space where it was, wondering if the starlight had been blocked by one of the thousands of alien spacecraft surrounding Earth.

The pink cell phone Francis gave Ralph vibrated in his chest pocket. He took it out, looked at it, and shut it off.

"On second thought," he said, looking over at the barracks, "let's take a walk."

He ended our path at a lonely tree twenty meters away and turned to me, the visor of his helmet inches from my face.

"What would you sacrifice to save Earth?" he asked.

I stared at him.

"Would you sacrifice your life?" he pressed.

"Yes."

Ralph's glow brightened.

"There are things I want to tell you. But you cannot tell another human. So we need to make an agreement—right now."

"Tell me."

"If you survive what's coming, you must go to ****."

The last word was a melodic hiss.

My eyebrows rose.

"My home," he said.

XXIX

+ + + + + + + + + +

LAWS

The rational side of me needed more time, but there was none.

"I agree," I said. Then, questions I had ignored raced to consciousness. *What will happen when I get there? How would we get there?*

"I must ask again. You sure about this? You may never return."

"Am I sure? No. I'm agreeing anyway."

"Markus, even if I die, you must try to find a way there."

"How on Earth would I do that?"

"Just promise."

I reaffirmed my promise, and Ralph hugged me as tightly as possible.

"And don't worry about how we get there or where you'll stay. You'll be a celebrity and everyone will have sex with you. So don't worry about any of that; it's taken care of. Trust me."

I trusted him. It was the biggest, strangest promise I ever made, and I only considered it for a minute. The promise was a gateway. Ralph had secrets, and he wouldn't have told me otherwise. It was far from clear, at first, why Ralph told me these things, but I was about to get a crash course in what he called 'universal psychology.'

"You need to understand how the Kardashians think," he said. "For this, you must understand some basic psychology. There are psychological laws obeyed by all species in the universe. In fact, these laws hold in all possible universes—"

"Ralph, slow down. Let's stick to this universe, okay?"

"You're right. I'm getting ahead of myself. We'll start with the second law."

"Wait . . . What's the first?"

"You're not ready for the first law, and we don't have time. The second is more important right now," he started. "This second law relates to envy, a phenomena underdiscussed by your psychologists. So that we are clear, when I say 'envy,' what does that mean to you?"

"It's when you have a . . . negative emotion toward someone who has something you want or is something you want to be."

"Exactly. Envy is when you hate someone, and at the same time, want to become them."

"I wouldn't put it that way."

"Why not?"

"That sounds too strong. 'Hate' is a strong word for humans."

"Markus, don't make me a philosophical nit who qualifies everything he says—there's no time. When I say 'hate,' I mean the whole spectrum of dislike, irritation, fury, alienation, and all those negative feelings. Whether it is pure rage or minor annoyance, this is what I'm talking about. Envy is when you hate someone and you want to be like them, either because they have something or are something. Any other way of looking at it is primitive sugarcoating."

He rarely spoke with such strength. It made me cautious. He paused to face me, waiting for a question, but none came.

He went on. "There is something basic about hatred, in all its forms, which your people do not understand. There is barely any human awareness of what I will now say. This is the second law. In the strongest and simplest terms: All hatred is envy."

". . . *All* of it?"

"All of it."

"That's . . . hard to believe."

"It's not obvious, nor easy to believe, but you must understand—"

"But what does that mean?"

"It means . . . however angry or annoyed you are with someone, a deeper part of you wants to become them. In fact, the stronger the hate, the stronger the desire, the need, is."

I was about to ask a question, but Ralph anticipated.

"Of course, most of the time, you're not aware of this desire to become what you hate, but the desire is there, lurking unconsciously. It will satisfy itself one way or another."

This claim, the second law, has bothered me deeply. If there is one claim that has haunted me, it is this: All hatred is envy. When Ralph first said it, I laughed.

"Ralph . . . This is getting too abstract."

"Look, let's say someone attacks you, hits you—what is your natural response?"

"To hit back, to retaliate," I said.

"Exactly. You are attacked, you hate it, and so you attack back, thereby becoming what you hate. Revenge is mainly a desire for symmetry. Let me ask you: when a child is a bully and attacks his peers on the playground, what's the most likely explanation?"

"Probably being bullied at home."

"Right. The child is bullied at home, hates it, then repeats the behavior with his peers. He's becoming what he hates. It's the second law in action."

"All right . . . but that's a small amount of evidence for an extraordinary claim. Hate and envy are just too different."

"Why do you say that?"

"It just doesn't feel right," I said. "I mean, hate just feels different than envy."

"*It just doesn't feel right,*" Ralph said, whining in a squeaky little girl's voice. "*I mean, hate just feels different than envy.*"

"Why are you being an ass?"

"Markus, I am being an ass, but you're being slow. Don't you get it? Do you see what just happened?"

". . . Oh," I said, embarrassed.

"Mockery—more specifically, parody—is a phenomena present in all intelligent life in the universe. It's also obvious evidence for the second law. Someone says something that annoys you, so you repeat it. Someone angers you, and so you imitate them. When you mock someone you hate, you satisfy, to a degree, this desire to become what you hate."

"That's superficial," I said. "You're not really becoming what you hate. You're just acting. It's only imitation."

"On my planet, there is a saying: 'imitation is the sincerest form of hate.'"

I smiled. "So *anything* we hate . . . We also want to become?"

"Yes. Think about it like this: Whatever you resist in one

context, you must embrace in another. Ask yourself: What do you hate?"

"Okay, I hate . . . untruth. I hate lies, lying, being wrong. As a scientist, I prefer truth. I think humans, in general, are becoming more truthful, or at least, more scientific."

"Of course, you still lie sometimes," Ralph said.

"Of course, but, you need to tell me how my disdain for lying . . . is really some sort of envy. That I have some deeper desire for lies that I don't recognize. I don't see it."

"You don't see it . . . so . . . have you seen any good movies lately? Read any good books lately?"

"Oh . . ."

"Exactly. As much as humans try to avoid falsehood, you embrace it in the fiction of novels and movies. As much as you hate being wrong and being lied to, you love to immerse yourselves in good fiction, to believe the story you know is false."

"I feel like an idiot," I said.

"Well . . . maybe you are," he said with a laugh.

"Thanks . . ."

"Markus, it was just a friendly insult."

"Oh well, fuck you too then."

"Sorry, bad joke, but humor is a good source of fiction. Just like your movies and books, your humor will also progress."

"Is that another joke?"

"No. Advanced civilizations require advanced forms of humor."

". . . Have your people ever encountered a more advanced alien civilization?"

"Only once."

"So . . . What happened?"

"We were lucky they didn't cause more damage. It is not a pleasant story, and there are more important things to discuss."

"I'd like to hear it."

". . . Very well, then," Ralph said, flashing golden for a tiny moment. "We discovered them by accident. They were studying us, but in secret. Obviously, we wanted to learn something from them, so what do you think we did?"

"You asked them about their technology or answers to difficult scientific questions."

"*No*. We knew the dangers of receiving advanced knowledge. Instead, we humbly asked if they could share some humor with us."

"You asked them for jokes . . ."

"Yes, and we were scared, because we knew their jokes must be extremely advanced. But, we were polite, and we begged them for just one great joke. After much deliberation on their part, they agreed to tell a joke to one, and only one, of our people. They demanded our greatest expert in the field of comedy, and they told him a single joke. The joke took over two Earth years to communicate . . ."

"Two . . . years . . ."

"It was the largest joke any of my people ever dared comprehend."

". . . What happened?"

"Sadly, the joke was not safe. Our expert was unable to communicate it, as he was unable to stop laughing. The more advanced beings apologized profusely, while laughing hysterically, and vanished. We later calculated that by the time he stops laughing, we will have caught up to the level of civilization of those who told him the joke."

"That's unbelievable," I said, astonished.

"It should be, because I'm *completely* fucking with you. Ha!"

With my red face, I watched Ralph's glow grow golden.

"How long have you been waiting to tell that joke?" I said.

"Since before you were born . . . but, we really need to get back on track," he said. "Now, do you understand the second law?"

"Well, I understand it, but I don't really believe it."

"Then ask me a question," he said, and I thought for a minute.

"Does the second law imply that becoming what you hate is . . . inevitable?"

"In the long term, one way or another: yes. Humans fail to recognize it, because your lives are so short. But as you figure out your genetics and prolong your lives, what I'm saying will become glaringly obvious."

"Well . . . That's probably the most awful thing I've ever heard."

"Don't overinterpret this. You don't become exactly what you hate. It's more complicated than that. There are ways to mitigate this."

"Maybe, but still—"

"Don't be pessimistic. Obviously, you can also become what you love. It happens every day: people fulfill their dreams. This is no secret."

"Of course . . . but . . . If becoming what you hate is inevitable, how is becoming what you want even possible? I'm sorry, Ralph . . . This is too much."

"Then why are you asking all the right questions?" he said.

"My mind is a swamp of questions."

"There is a special answer to your concern. In fact, it is the third law."

I hadn't yet wrapped my mind around the second law, but he told me nonetheless.

"Simply put," Ralph said, "you must become what you hate, in order to become what you love. In order to become what you want to, you have to become what you don't. It is simple."

"Wonderful," I said.

"No. This should be obvious. How can you not see this?"

"This is too abstract . . . If you could give me some examples—"

"There's no shortage of examples. You know who Tony Hawk is, right?"

"Yes. He's some extreme roller skater."

"No. He's a skateboarder, one of the best on your planet. How do you not know this? Anyway, when he was younger, learning to skateboard, he had so many bruises and went to the hospital so many times, the doctors suspected his parents of child abuse."

I got the point, but Ralph made it explicit.

"Clearly, typically, when you want to become something, you are going to have to fail, numerous times, in order to accomplish the goal. Typically, the greater the goal, the more failure you will suffer in attaining the goal. Thus, you must become what you hate, in order to become what you love."

"Oh, OK. If that is what you are saying, that sounds reasonable."

"Good. But do you understand *why* this is true?"

I looked at him with a blank face.

He said, "The ego must constantly keep itself in check, to prevent itself from getting too big. If you suddenly attained some goal, without failing beforehand, your ego would be oversized. It is all the failure, beforehand, which allows your ego to accept the accomplishment without blowing out of proportion and making you . . . well, an obnoxious douche bag."

I nodded.

He went on, "What often happens, when you have a big success, as a human?"

"You celebrate?"

"Exactly, and what happens at these celebrations?"

"Well . . . you have a party, people loosen up, they drink, dance . . ."

"That is what I mean. You loosen up, and you get drunk. The function of alcohol is to help you to become what you hate. To help you become what you normally resist."

"Well, okay, when we drink, we give in to urges we normally resist. That's no secret," I said, flexing my sore knuckles.

"Your urge to embarrass yourself is like your urge for sex. Humans are only starting to cope with both. It is both hilarious and horrifying that you can't show a pretty boob on prime-time TV, and yet violence is allowed."

"You really find it horrifying?"

". . . Are you really asking or joking?" Ralph said with a shiver.

"I'm asking."

Ralph quickly looked over at the barracks, looked away, and burst out a second-long scream, the kind he blared in the Oval Office. No doubt, Lieutenant Barber heard it at his post.

"YES, YES, YES, YES, YES," Ralph yelled in repetition while my hearing returned.

"Ralph, stop. I heard you. Don't fucking do that. I can barely hear."

Ralph paused and said, "I'm sorry. I thought you understood, but I assumed too much. My people have zero inhibitions about sex. We're like Bonobos. But violence . . . that is where humans are more . . . psychologically mature."

I was soothed to hear this.

He continued, "Just talking about violence is embarrassing for us. We talk about it in private sometimes, but talking about it in public . . . That just doesn't happen. I've heard that on the Internet—the Internet on my planet—there are perverted websites where people can watch violent movies—"

"How are your people so nonviolent? You never get violent urges during angry disagreements?"

"No. The most mature thing we can do is scream," Ralph said shyly. "Sometimes we just freeze up and black out. The first time I learned about violence—it was awful. My parents gave me *the talk*."

"The talk?"

"I mean, just as human parents have to explain sex, our parents have to tell us what the Kardashians did to our planet . . ."

He started to tremble. I reached out to steady him.

"Maybe there is something else we should talk about," I said.

"No. This is important. Because the Kardashians gained our technology too early, it ruined their development as a species. They didn't fail enough to earn this technology, and now they are failing all over the galaxy to make up for it."

"I don't understand."

"It's like . . . so many of your child actors. They are way too young, have barely suffered or failed at all, and suddenly they are millionaires because of some popular movie. Their ego blows up, and the mind must compensate, so they begin to fail—hard. They get involved with drugs, risky sex, all sorts of failures, and it is because they gained something they barely worked for, barely *failed* for."

"So that's why many rich kids end up spoiled. But they don't all end up spoiled . . . Why is that?"

"Good parenting," Ralph said coldly.

"I wouldn't know about that."

I expected Ralph to respond, but he paused and looked up at the sky. While I stared at Ralph in the silence, my mind wandered back to the second law. The claim that all hatred is envy still bothered me. I wanted to find a counterexample.

"What about death?"

"Go on," he said, glowing brighter.

"Death is ugly, undesirable, something we want to distance ourselves from. And so, if all hatred is really envy, then I should secretly have some desire to become dead, right?"

"That's right."

"But where's the evidence? I mean, how are we satisfying this desire to become dead? By doing risky things with our lives—risking death? People don't risk their lives that often. That's way too weak. I don't buy it."

"Wow."

"What?"

"It is astonishing," he said. "You really don't see it, do you?"

"Just tell me."

Instead of responding, Ralph made a long, drawn-out noise. It sounded like a lion slowly roaring or a motorboat sinking under water.

"What are you doing?" I asked, annoyed.

"I'm trying to imitate the sound of snoring."

"I'm boring you?"

"Dear Lord. Markus, you make me wish I had a face and a palm. You are so unreceptive. Is it that mysterious?"

"Oh . . ."

Ralph laughed.

"*Sleep* is a way to satisfy the desire to become like death?" I asked.

"Exactly. The resemblance between sleep and death is obvious."

"Wait," I said, realizing a basic concern, "*infants* sleep. Are newborns afraid of death? They don't know about it. Death isn't even a thought in their heads."

"Of course, but eventually, they grow and fear death. They will grow up and learn to fear and hate death just like everyone else, and sleep will already be there for them. Evolution has already chosen this mechanism, this mechanic of sleep, to satisfy this deeper need. You will never understand genetics until you understand how you inherit methods to become what you hate."

"That just sounds . . . That's crazy," I said. Ralph sensed I was overwhelmed and let me rest for a minute.

"Did you know that humans are actually paralyzed for a

period of time while they sleep? Your muscles freeze up during REM sleep, much like rigor mortis," Ralph said.

"You're unbelievable. There's a perfectly good evolutionary explanation for that. It's to prevent us from moving our limbs when we dream. I mean, if I'm dreaming about swimming, I don't want to be waving my arms around in my bed. I could hurt myself."

Ralph's glow went red. "How about once, just once, you respect the fact that I'm from an advanced civilization? And that maybe—just maybe—I know a hell of a lot more than you?"

Our argument ended when my phone vibrated. I only had to look at my watch to know what Francis was calling for.

00:02:01

00:02:00

00:01:59

"Go," Ralph said.

"You're not coming?"

"It would be too painful to watch."

Ralph lay down in the grass and looked up at the night.

Within the hour, members of SETI would sip nervous glasses of champagne at their headquarters in Mountain View, California. But before the bottles were dry, a distraught director of SETI research, whom I never met, would send me an e-mail with a single sentence.

'You were right,' he wrote, then went home and put a gun in his mouth.

TRANSMISSION

I left Ralph alone and answered my phone as I moved swiftly back to the barracks.

A door slammed on Francis's end of the line.

"Tell Ralph I don't want any more fucking surprises."

"Ralph's not with me. He stayed outside."

"You just tell Ralph. Any more surprises and I will completely reevaluate our relationship. And tell him to answer his goddamn phone when I call."

I stepped to the upper floor of the barracks and looked at the countdown on the TV.

00:00:10

00:00:09

00:00:08

"And why is Ralph not with you?"

"He said it would be disturbing."

00:00:02

00:00:01

00:00:00

The numbers on the screen faded, and an empty white room appeared. Shadows in the room vanished when focused upon, and the overbearing light hid features one tried to discern.

Then I saw something I was not prepared for, something I had never imagined. What I saw made me doubt every warning given in the Oval Office. Every prejudice I ever had about aliens was already shattered, but what I saw on that screen swept up the shards and threw them out the window.

It was the queen. And she was beautiful.

When those dark purple eyes fluttered open, there was no doubt. "Hello."

Her greeting was so compelling I had to resist the urge to respond. I put my hand over my mouth and closed my eyes, questioning my mental control.

She spoke again, and my eyes opened. "Allow me to introduce myself, please. I am Queen."

The innocence in her voice was overpowering.

"My true name is difficult to hear with your ears."

She pushed herself gently away from the lens. This brought her naked body into view and revealed she was floating in zero gravity. I moved closer.

"We are neighbors in this Milky Way. We call our planet 'Kardash.'"

Suspiciously, her two opposing arms and legs had five fingers and five toes. Her hands and feet were small and had no nails. She had no sharp edges.

"We plan to visit."

She looked almost human.

"Plan to be friends."

Below her gorgeous inhuman eyes lay a single nose. Below the nose was a lipless mouth which opened to reveal a slice of darkness completely unilluminated by the harsh ambient light. The lighting was so forceful, the contours of her body often disappeared, making her invisible, except for that bulging blue heart.

"We have a large ship near your dwarven planet Pluto. You can look. It is white."

Her skin was sharp white all over. Her chest bulged and pulsed, seemingly forced outward by the huge blue heart that pounded beneath her chest, as if it were trying to escape.

"We have many other ships, smaller ships, near Earth. We are hiding."

I could see no malice in that heart.

"We do not want to scare you, and we are not shy."

She smiled. It was a spectacle. It forced me to do the same.

"We have studied your transmissions and find them attractive. We have learned about you and desire more. You too will learn, and there are many things we desire to teach. We know the spiral of your history and are afraid for you, afraid for your guidance."

Her gaze did not control my beliefs, but it teased my empathy and overtook my attention. I looked outside the window at Ralph. He was on his back, motionless.

"We are sorrowed to interrupt your entertainment and sorrowed to know the death of your American president. We know death is difficult and common for you. We want to help."

There was a turn of sadness in her gaze, and her words became more reluctant. I had to review later to confirm, but for one second she looked offscreen and made an expression of annoyance. Someone was watching her.

"We are ready to share the true message of God."

I glanced outside at Ralph again.

"All we ask is that you listen to the prophecy."

The dance in her voice was over. Her sincerity was hard to measure with her exotic locution, but the hooks were in. The seeds of conversion were planted.

Then, she moved closer to the lens and said something Ralph never warned us about.

"As we travel to your planet, expect large words, sentences, *messages* in your sky. You will see the words soon. These are the words of God . . . the God that loves you."

She then quickly turned away, unfurled her smooth white wings, and flew out of frame like an angel. Her wings were useless on Earth, but they aided her maneuverability greatly in zero gravity.

Before the broadcast ended, there was another voice. It gave a cold screech in alien tongue. The deep black body of the voice passed in front of the lens and the transmission ended.

The screen flashed back to white with the following sentence on-screen:

FOR EVERYONE WHO EXALTS HIMSELF
WILL BE HUMBLED
AND HE WHO HUMBLES HIMSELF
WILL BE EXALTED.

The quote is from the Gospel of Luke, 14:11, in the Christian Bible. It remained for approximately fifteen seconds before a terrestrial test pattern appeared. Then the Internet, radio, and television channels were released from alien control. I muted the television and waited for Francis to say something, but he was just as speechless.

"Ralph mention anything about 'messages in the sky'?" Francis asked.

"He said nothing about it."

The messages in the sky are what media outlets would soon euphemistically call 'sky banners,' while converts would refer to them as 'signs,' 'signs from heaven,' or 'signs from God.'

Though they appeared in the sky and were easily legible, these banners were thousands of miles outside the normal orbit of Earth—high enough, large enough, and bright enough to be seen by the entire continent they continually faced. The first sky banner would appear within minutes of my hanging up with Francis.

Francis exhaled a full sigh. "Presumably, it doesn't matter. Looks as if Ralph was right. Now that they've announced themselves, I won't need you or Samantha to back me up. I'm speaking to the vice . . . the president, in an hour. You should stay there. He may want to go meet Ralph in person."

"Wait, you haven't told him anything about Ralph?"

"No, nothing yet."

"I can't believe you. It's like with Samantha, you're afraid the president won't take you seriously. Ralph's the only person on the planet who knows what the fuck is going on around here."

"Fuck you, Markus. Fuck you. Do you have any idea how difficult it is to breach that subject?" he shouted and then continued with a dopey imitation of my voice. "*Oh, hey, there, Mr. New President. I know you've got wars and terrorism and the recent assassination of the last president and your new job and everything else to worry about, but remember that Diet Coke ad on the moon and the big can of soup? Well, they were created by an alien who will rescue us from Kardashians . . .* You think I can tell him *that* in an e-mail or memo and just send it to him? Keep in mind what's been going on around here. He hasn't even announced his VP choice yet, and he's barely been in the White House. Everything's in lockdown until the Secret Service revets everyone and finishes the investigation. It was difficult enough just to get an emergency appointment with him."

At the time, I was shocked. But, with the fresh chaos of the assassination, it was understandable Francis hadn't told the new president. In any case, I'm sure, at that moment, Francis had every intention of informing him about Ralph.

MESSAGE

Despite what would soon happen, the public's immediate reaction to the queen's broadcast was not frantic. Later polls revealed most people were initially overcome with a sense of relief, as if an unknown tension had been wiped from their mind. Of course, these polls only include the survivors.

For those few peaceful minutes before the first sky banner, most Christians celebrated. By coincidence, both the Vatican and the Westboro Baptist Church simply tweeted 'Welcome,' though the Vatican would later delete it. Jews, Muslims, and other mainstream religious groups had mixed reactions, but there was no immediate panic.

Though the takeover of our communications should have been enough, not to mention the images from Keck and other observatories, some humans were still skeptical the queen was alien. Actual aliens announce themselves, and moron conspiracy theorists thought it was a government conspiracy.

But, the immediate reaction to the queen's broadcast matters little. After the first sky banner appeared, all calm attitudes and good feelings died. The world was about to slice itself to shreds.

It just didn't know it yet.

When I walked outside, I looked at the sky and saw nothing new. Ralph looked over at me, waved, and stood up. We met each other halfway.

"How did she look?" Ralph asked.

I wanted to say 'Good,' but I didn't. I tried to be angry with Ralph for not being more forthcoming, but I was still enchanted. I suspect he knew.

"How did you know it would be her?"

"They always use the most seductive."

". . . And how do you know this?"

"I told you," Ralph said, annoyed, "my people have studied the aftermath of the planets they've visited. The only difference now is that one of us, I mean me, got here before they did. As long as your new president follows my advice, humanity should have the upper hand."

I believed him.

"What are the 'messages in the sky' she was talking about? Does she mean something like *that*?" I asked, pointing at the moon.

"No. She means something . . . very different."

"What will the messages say?"

"I can't say, but they will be . . . disruptive."

"Elaborate."

"The first message should be the most disturbing . . . How much gas is in your car?"

"Maybe half a tank. Now answer me: how disturbing?"

"Something much more disturbing than *that*," he said, pointing at the moon. "So disturbing, we may have to leave."

"What are you talking about? No one knows we're here."

"Enough do," he said, glancing over my shoulder.

Before I could turn around to see what Ralph was looking at, a bright light spread out overhead. I looked up. The sky banner technology was being implemented.

Approximately 120,000 miles above the Earth's surface, halfway between the Earth and the moon, a pure white sky banner revealed itself. It was tall and long enough to be seen all over North America. Its beaming light bleached the night sky.

The banner was 150,000 miles long and 50,000 miles tall. From my perspective on Earth, it was a gigantic blank flag in the sky. At first, it was beautiful, and it became more beautiful when the blank white surface gained colors.

First, the top strip of the banner turned red, forming a long red stripe across the full length of the top of the banner. Then, a second stripe, just as thin and long, turned orange, directly beneath the red stripe. Then a yellow stripe right under the orange stripe, then a green stripe, then blue, and finally, the bottom purple stripe—all the colors of the rainbow neatly represented.

"Why a rainbow?" I asked, mystified.

"Oh no . . . Markus, I think I know what it's going to say," Ralph said as his voice weakened. "Those fucking bastards . . . Oh God . . . *Francis* . . . Markus, did Francis tell the new president about me yet? Did he?"

"No, not yet, calm down. He's going to tell him soon."

"How soon?"

"About an hour." I didn't get why Ralph was asking.

"Oh God. That's too late. Markus, we need to leave," Ralph

said as he fell down and covered his visor with his Earth mittens. His behavior bewildered me. I nervously wondered: how bad could a message written on a rainbow be?

Ralph shouted a prayer, "God, please, don't do this to them; anything else, but not on their rainbow. Please let me be wrong." He was so unnerved he lapsed into his native tongue and hissed spastically.

I watched as the first three letters were written. Each manifested as if God was writing the black letters by hand on the rainbow flag.

'GOD' was the first word of three.

"*What's going on?*" a female voice screamed out behind me.

It was Alice Higginbotham, though I didn't recognize her. After she had crept out of my car, she'd been hiding and lurking around the barracks all night. The battery on her smartphone had run out hours ago, so she didn't know about the queen's broadcast. She didn't even know about the image from Keck. I swiveled and watched her faint from the incomprehensibility of it all.

I ran to her limp body and found her still breathing. I checked her belongings, found her New Jersey driver's license, and when I read her name, I understood.

"This ruins everything," Ralph cried.

I looked over at Ralph on the ground, staring at me and pointing at the sky.

"Markus, we need to leave. Now."

I looked up at the sky and froze.

'GOD HATES FAGS' was writ black across the rainbow flag.

ESCAPE

I was the only human on the planet who knew what the Kardashians were really doing. Nevertheless, everything seemed unnatural and lost. The world felt broken, impossible, and slow. If it weren't for Ralph, I'd have been unconscious on the ground with Alice. Instead, I was awake in a night of the surreal.

Dizzy from cognitive dissonance, I lay down and closed my eyes. Ralph's earlier words reflected in my mind: *They will take the worst of Earth's culture and twist it back at you in force—expect the ultimate forms of mockery. They will seduce your people with great trickery and power, appealing to the worst of what you know.*

'GOD HATES FAGS'

Of course, the Kardashians didn't care about homosexuality at all. They only knew it polarized humanity. If homosexuality had been accepted on Earth, they would have chosen something else.

Future readers will find it difficult to understand, but this was a time when many humans would openly, in casual conversation, blame earthquakes and hurricanes on homosexuality. Even before the sky banners, it was common to hear stories of homosexuals beaten to death, by total strangers, simply because they were gay.

In 2013, the head of the Russian Orthodox Church claimed the recognition of same-sex unions by Western countries brought us closer to the Apocalypse. There were still scores of countries where homosexuality was illegal, sometimes punishable by death.

Supine under the light of the first banner, I opened my eyes and stared at the awful sky. I asked what everyone asked: why? But I already knew the answer. I closed my eyes and Ralph's words streamed through consciousness: *They believe that by becoming monsters, they can learn to be at peace with monsters. They think that by acting intolerant, they may truly understand those who are. They are coming to Earth to act as terrible as possible, just to fulfill this twisted purpose. Become evil, to overcome it, like a reductio ad absurdum of evil itself.*

When Ralph said this earlier, it seemed too abstract, but the reality was hovering above me in high geostationary orbit for all of North America to see. The message scraped at my thoughts, even when I wasn't looking. I feared I might believe if I looked too long.

I checked on Alice again.

"Markus," Ralph said standing over me, "will she be okay?"

"She was overwhelmed. You knew she was here the whole time, didn't you?"

"She seemed harmless, and I didn't want you to call the guard. We should take her with us."

I should have been worried what Alice might say to her boss at the *New York Times* about Ralph, but the thought didn't occur to me, the situation being so ludicrous. In any case, because of what would soon happen, I wouldn't have to worry about her talking to anyone.

"Markus, we need to leave."

It is embarrassing to confess, but I started to laugh. I swear it was nervousness—the laughter began slow and escalated quickly. I lost control.

"Markus, don't laugh. This is serious."

My head agreed but my lungs couldn't stop jiggling.

"Markus, this isn't funny. We're not safe anymore. Don't you see that?"

"Did they see us hugging?" I asked deliriously.

"I'm talking about *Francis*."

Francis was gay. This was not a secret. In fact, Francis was a well-admired figure in the gay community. When I imagined Francis in danger, my laughter calmed, and I regained control.

"Francis is safer than most," I said.

". . . You don't understand."

I didn't understand. Ralph was not scared *for* Francis. Ralph was scared *of* him. If I was less bewildered, I would've been afraid too. I did not connect the dots.

"I'll call Francis," I said as Ralph shook his head.

"I'm getting ready to go," Ralph said and walked inside the barracks.

"Go where?" I yelled. He did not respond.

I checked on Alice again while I called Francis. Alice was still breathing, and Francis didn't answer. I dialed Samantha, and she didn't answer either. Through the cracked open upstairs window of the barracks, Ralph called out with a low voice.

"The soldier's coming," he said, not knowing Lieutenant

Barber. "Get up here." I looked and saw no one, but remembered Ralph's vision was exceptional. "You have to protect me, Markus. There's a gun in his hand."

I got a text message from Francis: *I'm sorry. I can't let you or Ralph interfere.*

Ralph's advice in the Oval Office was clear: Don't fight them. Do nothing.

Francis had played along until the first sky banner appeared. Then, all bets were off. He couldn't sit by while the Kardashians preached the absolute hatred of his community. He couldn't risk Ralph or I anywhere near McAllister—he wanted no chance for Ralph to persuade the new president. With Ralph and I out of the picture, nothing Samantha could say would matter—she would have no direct evidence Ralph ever existed.

Francis ordered Lieutenant Barber to kill us, and by the time I figured most of this out, I could see the lieutenant walking up the gravel driveway. We only had one weapon, and it would be difficult to control.

I ran upstairs to join Ralph.

"Markus, he has a gun. I think Francis sent him to kill us," Ralph said, trembling. "I'm going to die here on Earth, aren't I? Oh God . . . Stay with me, I don't want to die alone."

But I had an idea.

"Ralph, when you scream, like you did in the Oval Office, do you have control over it? Or is it completely involuntary?"

"I only do it when I'm scared or frustrated," he said, shaking. "But by the time I get scared enough, I'm not sure I can hold back."

"I don't want you to hold back . . . at all. Can you do it now?"

"Right now?"

"No, not this second. I mean, when Lieutenant Barber . . . the soldier outside, when he comes up here, can you do it then?"

". . . I could."

"Will it knock him out?"

"Well . . . I guess so. But . . ."

"But what?"

"But it will knock you out too."

He was right. I hadn't thought it through. If Ralph's scream knocked Lieutenant Barber and I unconscious, it wouldn't do Ralph any good if the lieutenant recovered before me. And I had no way to deflect the blast of Ralph's scream. Ralph was too physically weak and pacifistic to do anything to an unconscious Lieutenant Barber. I doubt Ralph could've even tied him up.

I spied Lieutenant Barber out the window. He was headed toward the front door of the barracks. It was haphazard, but it was the only thing to do. We had to take the chance.

"Ralph, listen closely. This is what we do. You lay down by the top of the stairs and stay scared. *Here,*" I said, standing where I wanted Ralph to be—opposite the upper landing of the stairs. "As soon as you see Lieutenant Barber, just scream as loud as you possibly can."

"As loud as I can?"

"Yes. I'll be at the far end of the room, over there," I said, pointing. "I'll cover my ears with whatever I can. This way, you knock us both out, but I'll recover quicker; then we tie him up and get out of here. Okay?"

"But you won't kill him . . . right?"

BANG.

A single gunshot rang outside. Neither of us wanted to talk anymore. I only imagined the lieutenant shot Alice in cold blood to destroy a loose end. Ralph was whimpering and crackling, barely holding back his scream. He could talk about violence in the abstract, but when it came for him, he shook so much he shimmered.

He then lay down at the top of the stairs as I'd told him.

I heard the creak of the front door downstairs.

With Ralph in position, I went to the sofa and realized there were no removable cushions. I vainly tugged at the fabric, hoping to tear it, but could not. Looking around I saw nothing else to protect myself, so I took off my shirt and wrapped it around my head, over my ears. I crept to the far end of the room and clamped my palms over the sides of my skull.

"Dr. West?" the lieutenant shouted from below. I heard him too well—I knew my ear protection was not enough. I didn't dare respond. Ralph was ready to burst.

I expected the lieutenant to creep in slow. But he walked in quick and headed up the stairs at the same pace. The last thing I remember was the shine of the lieutenant's bald head and the windows blowing out from the inside.

XXXIII

When I started thinking again, I was dreaming. I dreamt I was lying in the back of my own vehicle while Alice Higginbotham drove. I could hear Ralph's voice somewhere behind me. Lieutenant Barber was following us in his vehicle. We drove to a large white house with a huge lawn, and the dream ended with me getting a very sloppy and wet kiss.

I would learn this dream was a feeble awareness of actual events. There was much I would learn that next day—including strangely earthly things about Ralph.

Most importantly, I would learn Ralph, Alice Higginbotham, and Lieutenant Barber were all alive. I'd learn that Francis illegally ordered the lieutenant to kill everyone in the barracks, but Lieutenant Barber did not obey. Samantha had intervened.

Samantha was a tactical genius. She was in Colorado at NORAD at the time, but when the first sky banner appeared, she guessed how Francis would react. She ordered Lieutenant Barber to protect everyone in the barracks, no matter what Francis said.

Right before the sky banner manifested, Lieutenant Barber was scanning the grounds with night-vision binoculars and saw

Alice's silhouette skulking. He knew she shouldn't be there and approached the barracks to engage the intruder.

The disturbing gunshot I heard was Lieutenant Barber shooting and killing a raccoon that came too close to the unconscious Alice Higginbotham. I don't know if Ralph ever forgave him.

For reasons I did not anticipate, Lieutenant Barber recovered from Ralph's scream long before I did. Samantha had experienced Ralph's screaming defense firsthand in the Oval Office, which led her to issue industrial strength earplugs to Lieutenant Barber. He was ordered to wear them upon approaching the barracks.

Saving me the trouble, Ralph introduced himself to Lieutenant Barber, and later to Alice when she revived. Ralph explained how he was responsible for the lunar advertisement and the enormous can of Campbell's Chicken Noodle soup. I'm sure Ralph charmed them just as he had charmed Francis, Samantha, and me—he told them the same things he told us in the Oval Office, but only those things—he never spoke to them about the Kardashians' hidden motives, nothing about humility or the second and third laws, none of that. As far as Lieutenant Barber and Alice were concerned, the Kardashians were the religious zealots they appeared to be.

I would learn all of this, and more, that next day.

But I hadn't learned any of this yet.

I awoke atop a king-sized waterbed, wearing pants and no shirt. On the large white wall across from me hung one of Andy Warhol's prints—a can of Campbell's Chicken Noodle. The room was so large I guessed the whole house was abnormally large as well. There were no furnishings except for the bed, and undecorated except for the art.

An adult golden retriever was licking my face, and there were scratching noises outside the bedroom door. Tucked into the dog's collar was a note, and I recognized Ralph's childish handwriting immediately: *Don't worry, Markus. You're okay. Love, Ralph.*

My head ached, and my ears felt plugged, but I'd recover. I was knocked out by Ralph's scream; then, because I was exhausted, overly stressed, and sleep deprived, I just continued to slumber. Never tell an alien to scream as loud as possible.

The quiet of the house was contagious, and I walked gently on the floor. When I opened the door to exit, a large puppy scurried in and jumped on the bed to harass the older dog with its youth.

I walked on the slippery parquet floors of the wide hallway, past several large empty bedrooms, to the grand marble staircase leading down to the main entrance.

At the bottom of the stairs, I heard electronic beeps coming from the front door. It was the noise of someone inputting a code on a keypad. The door opened and a well-dressed, professional-looking man was surprised to see me. He had mail in his hands. We both had the same question on our faces, but I asked first.

"Who are you?"

I must have looked at home with no shoes and no shirt on. He erased the inquisitive glare from his face, slapped his forehead playfully, and smiled. He put out his hand to shake mine as he walked to me with confidence.

"Of course, we don't recognize each other. I'm Noah Alpert, and you must be Mr. Ellison . . . I mean Emerson, *Emerson*," he said, embarrassed. "I'm so sorry, Mr. Emerson, but I'm sure you understand. I've been interacting with your assistant for so long; it is a pleasure to finally meet you in person. Everything has been prepared exactly as you requested."

I had no clue what the hell he was talking about, but his tone suggested I belonged. I continued to look at him curiously while we shook hands.

"Mr. Alpert?" I asked with a small scowl.

"Oh dear, I just can't stop being awkward . . . I'm the property manager. Oh, and here's your mail," he said as he handed me three envelopes.

Each envelope was addressed to Ralph Waldo Emerson in Grasonville, Maryland.

"Call me 'Ralph,'" I said with a smile.

Until that point, it hadn't occurred to me Ralph might have a full name, but he did: Ralph Waldo Emerson. He took it from the nineteenth-century American philosopher of the same name. Not being a philosopher, I was unaware of any deeper meaning of this choice.

I correctly guessed Ralph had been interacting with this man purely through e-mails and phone calls while still on the moon. Mr. Alpert assured me he had maintained the estate, fed the dogs, and played with them every day, as required. He was nervous, and I was lucky he didn't recognize my face. Maybe this was because of the gigantic homophobic rainbow in the sky.

When he left I looked at the mail. There were two credit cards, each with a $100,000-dollar credit limit on them, as well as an ATM card. Each card had the name 'Ralph Waldo Emerson' on it.

Then, Ralph Waldo Emerson himself bounced down the hallway and gave a glowing hug.

"Explain to me what the hell is happening, *Mr. Emerson*, or I scream," I said.

He turned a shy shade of purple and explained what happened with Lieutenant Barber and Alice Higginbotham the night before. He said they were both 'pleasant humans' and were currently out shopping for human food, as the pantry and fridge were bare. With much distress, Ralph reconfirmed Francis's intention to kill us, which Lieutenant Barber had confided to him.

"Oh shit," I said, feeling my pockets. "Where's my phone, the one Francis gave me?"

"I'm way ahead of you. I ditched both our phones back at the barracks in Fort Ritchie."

"Good job," I said, and breathed easier, knowing we could not be tracked. It was a lot to digest with a headache, but I understood enough to move on to the larger question surrounding us.

"Do you own this place?"

"You like it?" His glow grew golden.

Ralph was rich. In fact, he was a multimillionaire before ever stepping on Earth. Keep in mind, Ralph had been on the moon for at least ten years, had Internet access, free time, and could hack any database accessible from the Internet. Though he broke some laws, he managed to earn his money without stealing it.

How? Online poker.

First, he stole the identity of an identity thief and got a new credit card account in their name. Using that account, he started playing online poker with the screen name 'Waldo.'

Officially, Ralph was a British citizen living in the Cayman Islands. He used his poker earnings to bribe, via e-mail and phone calls, authorities on the islands to establish his citizenship and residency. He had a house and property manager there too. As a resident, it was easy to get another credit card and transfer all his poker earnings, via PayPal, from the old credit card to the new, legal one.

Within a month of playing online poker, Waldo built up a bank-roll of $100,000 US. Within two years, he had over $30 million.

He dominated the big, nosebleed cash games, and challenged anyone to play any variant of poker, for any stakes. One advantage of online poker is the ability to play multiple poker tables at once. At the height of his game, Waldo played twenty tables simultaneously against multiple players starting with a million dollars at each table. He earned money from nearly every online poker pro on the planet, except Phil Ivey, whom he broke even with.

"Did you cheat?"

"Of course not. Where would be the fun in that?"

There were widespread accusations of cheating/hacking against Waldo, and storms of speculation about his identity, but no one could prove anything. After a while, people just stopped playing him. He had outclassed himself. So, he looked for new ways to make money, mostly through investments in the stock market. Wisely, he invested most of his money in PepsiCo before the lunar advertisement appeared.

He bought the house four months before he ever entered it. From inside, it felt like a small mansion and smelled of seamless renovations. It was set back from the main road by at least an acre of lush, green lawn, and was the most impressive home in the small, upper-middle-class neighborhood. In case negotiations with humans did not go as hoped, Ralph had a backup plan, and this was it.

When he was done explaining, the front door opened. Lieutenant Barber gave a knowing nod, Alice gave a shy smile, and Ralph hugged everyone for good measure.

The dogs were lingering by the front door when they returned, and the larger dog began jumping and pawing at Alice, who was busy holding grocery bags.

"Ralph, Sally is being impossible," Alice said.

"C'mere, Sally," Ralph said, and Sally obeyed happily.

Alice walked to the kitchen, and Lieutenant Barber put his grocery bag on the ground.

"Could you help me bring in groceries?" Lieutenant Barber asked. He didn't need help.

"Of course," I said and walked outside. I was struck by the acre-sized front lawn, and right in the middle was an uncanny white cylinder, as tall as a man.

"What's that?" I asked, pointing.

He looked at me and said nothing. He was silent, so I tried

making small talk with him. "Samantha told me you two are old friends."

He glanced at me, nodding almost imperceptibly.

"Were you two ever . . . um—"

"She's not my type of bitch," he said. I wasn't used to this type of macho talk.

"Oh, really? What type of *bitch* do you prefer?"

He stopped, and for the first time I saw him smile. He gazed up at the rainbow sky banner, looked back down in my face, and said, "Let's just say God hates me."

I laughed, and we quickened our pace to the car.

"Ralph tells me Samantha saved our asses last night," I said.

He didn't respond. I was trying to be subtle, and it didn't work.

"Would you have killed Ralph and me . . . if Samantha hadn't called you?"

He kept his pace and gave an angry, ambiguous look.

Out of every human I've ever met, Lieutenant Barber was the least compelled to respond to anything anyone said. It was oddly passive-aggressive for someone skilled in active aggression. As time went on, he would open up more, but talking seemed to annoy him, as if he was eating with a bad tooth. We got near the car, and he grabbed my elbow. He wanted to speak, but was uncomfortable putting the words together. He exhaled.

"Doc . . . about bubble boy—"

"Who?" I asked.

"Is he *really* an alien?"

I looked back at Ralph by the front door playing with his puppy, glowing pink.

"What would make you think he's not?"

The lieutenant looked over at Ralph and leaned in. "Do you trust him?"

"I trust Ralph more than any human on the planet."

He was studying my face, measuring my sincerity, when we heard Alice yelling inside.

It was 1:15 p.m. in DC, Eastern Standard Time.

Ralph motioned us into the house, so we rushed. We were led to a room on the first floor with a long couch opposite the largest flat-screen TV I'd ever seen.

A CNN correspondent in Beijing was reporting live and pointing her finger upward. Traffic had stopped in the street behind her. Every pedestrian in view was staring at the sky.

"It's the second sky banner," Ralph said.

The news coverage was split-screen with the reporter on one side, and a gigantic white sky banner on the other. This banner was much longer and thinner than the first.

"It looks like a blank fortune . . . I mean, like a fortune from a fortune cookie," Alice said.

It did. This was not an accident. It was just one more part of the mockery. I wouldn't have been surprised to find lottery numbers on the other side.

Then the message appeared, in Chinese.

学英语 自慰队

The Chinese people in the background had mixed reactions. The younger ones mostly laughed, while others squinted and looked curiously at their neighbors. The older they were, the more disgusted they looked. It was all difficult to interpret, and the speechless CNN correspondent was embarrassed.

"Well . . . That's not very nice," Ralph said.

"America gets 'God Hates Fags,' and the Chinese get 'not very nice'?" Alice said.

"What does it say?" the CNN anchor asked the Beijing correspondent.

The correspondent regained her composure and answered, "Apparently, the aliens are issuing a command . . . demanding the people of China to . . . learn English. But . . . It seems there are some mistakes, and perhaps something got lost in translation. The command to 'Learn English' is followed by an insult, *zì wèi duì*, usually reserved for the Japanese—"

Before she finished, an old and petite Chinese lady walked into frame and knocked the correspondent on the head with her cane. Then, someone threw a can of Coca-Cola at her and missed. The camera was jostled, and the video feed cut off amid the twanging argument of Chinese voices. I lowered the volume on the TV.

"Ralph, what does it say?"

". . . The literal meaning is something like: *Learn English, You Self-Defense Forces.*"

"And the not-so-literal meaning?"

"*Learn English, You Japanese Jerk-Offs.*"

Even the stoic Lieutenant Barber looked at Ralph in disbelief.

"They order the Chinese to learn English and call them 'jerk-offs'? But they can't tell the difference between the Chinese and the Japanese? Are they serious?" Alice asked.

"Yes," Ralph lied. "They are just a bunch of religious

extremists who care little for the differences of Earth's many cultures. I doubt they even bothered to learn Chinese. They probably just used Google translator."

"Aren't these supposed to be the words of God?" Alice reminded.

"They know English is a common language. Since they've chosen to use it, they want Asians to learn it."

Neither English nor masturbation is particularly taboo in China, but to confuse a Japanese person with a Chinese person *is*.

In the 1937 Nanking massacre, Imperial Japanese forces invaded the Chinese city of Nanking and slaughtered upward to 300,000 people during a six-week period—more than 7,000 murders per day. The large majority of these killings were the cold-blooded murders of civilians.

Europe had Nazi Germany, and Asia had Imperialist Japan.

But, if the Kardashians intended the second sky banner to sow the same dissent as the first, they were mistaken. It did little to reignite the old animosity between Japan and China.

Nonetheless, there would be consequences.

INVASION

It was fifteen minutes after the Asian sky banner: 1:30 p.m., EST.

Like chameleons, the invading Kardashian ships changed color to white and aimed for Earth. Descending from the upper atmosphere all around the planet, they achieved global air supremacy instantly. Those long tubular white ships, anywhere from a half mile to twenty miles in length, numbered in the thousands, and quaintly resembled the much-larger ship still stationed near Pluto.

It was a show of force. Only the Americans had the nerve to send up aircraft to inspect the invading ships. But, the human aircraft were treated as less than gadflies, not even worth swatting. It was just as Ralph had predicted: the Kardashians would not attack unprovoked.

Almost every nation on Earth understood the aliens were real, except North Korea. North Korea was the most isolated and paranoid country on Earth. Though American military activity in the Korean War ended in 1953, officially, the war never ended. There was only an armistice. The 160-mile border between North and South Korea was a heavily guarded no-man's-land of listening posts and land mines.

North Korean intelligence believed the alien invasion was an American ploy to overthrow their government. After all, why would aliens put a sky banner over Asia telling them to learn English? And, of course, North Korea, like everyone else, blamed the lunar advertisement on America—in their mind, the second sky banner was just a more imposing variant of the lunar ad. Additionally, North Korean leadership must've seen the queen's first broadcast, and were likely suspicious of her humanoid shape—why should an alien look human? So when the Kardashian ships entered the lower atmosphere, North Korea was preparing for war. The lunar ad, the second sky banner, and all those flying white phallic-shaped aircraft were all interpreted as invasive American propaganda meant to turn the will of the people against the North Korean government.

For hours, the Kardashian ships cruised over the surface of Earth, coming closer and closer to the ground as time passed. But, the pervasive procession of ships did not create worldwide panic. While survivalists prepared for the end of the world, most people were too shocked to panic.

Parents kept their kids home from school and most stayed home from work. Stock markets around the world curbed trading to quell volatility. The business of life slowed as governments around the world warned their citizens to keep calm and stay indoors, but everyone wanted to go outside and gawk at the invasion.

Their ships moved nothing like human aircraft, and their maneuverability was impossible by our understanding. They flew slow and low over populated areas, sometimes stopping completely in midair. In St. Louis, Missouri, a ten-mile-long ship crept under the Gateway Arch. In Paris, a ship coasted through the huge square hole in the middle of La Grande Arche De La Défense.

Throughout the world, ships of various sizes would creep under tall bridges, next to skyscrapers, and near national monuments. Their flight paths seemed more playful than intrusive, and it eased the shock. There was no trouble . . . until a squadron of alien ships flew low into North Korean airspace.

It was never entirely clear what happened. Chinese intelligence would later confirm what many immediately suspected: North Korea attacked first. Though the Kardashian ships were entirely unscathed, their retaliatory strike was insanely disproportionate.

North Korea launched ground-to-air missiles from Kaesong, a city close to the South Korean border, about thirty miles from Seoul, the capital of South Korea. For the Kardashians, it was guilt by proximity, and they used strategic overkill to send a message

"Why attack Seoul? South Korea wouldn't attack them. It doesn't make any sense."

"Maybe they don't know the difference between North and South Korea. I'm sorry, Markus, I don't understand either," Ralph said.

Rumors of the melting of Seoul swarmed for hours before confirmation. For the first time in a long time, there was no live footage of such a devastating event—because no one was alive to transmit it.

Being in a closed society, we could only assume Kaesong

met the same fate as Seoul. There were no bombs, no lasers. Initially, it was unknown what weapons they used, but the answer was straight out of H. G. Wells. The buildings of Seoul were reduced to liquefied puddles of concrete and metal—millions of people exploded into flames and melted. Countless others would be lost in the following 8.5 magnitude earthquakes.

"How do you melt an entire city? How is that possible?" I asked.

"They used heat-rays," Ralph said plainly.

"Heat-rays? You mean lasers?"

"No," Ralph said softly, trying to be polite. "Lasers waste too much energy to be economical. They used something far more . . . efficient."

"What?"

"Your scientists call it a 'Fresnel lens.' But humans don't have ones this powerful."

"You mean a goddamn magnifying glass?"

"A weaponized magnifying glass, yes, but not made of glass."

Using concentric circles to focus light, the Fresnel lens is thinner, more lightweight, and much more powerful than a normal magnifying glass. And the Kardashian version was dreadfully more powerful than the human variety. "Heat from a Kardashian lens can reach up to 90,000 degrees Fahrenheit," Ralph said.

". . . It's a death ray."

"Yes, but it's environmentally friendly."

Ralph never revealed the intricacies of interstellar travel, but any such voyage must be energy efficient—so any weapons must also be efficient. A weaponized Fresnel lens was an optimal choice, because it only needs the power of a sun. Each Kardashian ship was equipped with multiple, oversized Fresnel lenses. So, as long as ships were within range of the sun, no city was safe. And there were always ships in range—there were still hundreds of ships outside Earth's atmosphere—ready and able to focus the purest sunbeams into murderous rays of light. With enough ships in range, it was painfully clear how they could melt a full city.

The first sky banner hadn't been up for more than 24 hours, and already the second sky banner had appeared over Asia, the Kardashian fleet had taken over the skies, and two cities had been eviscerated. Without losing pace, the third sky banner manifested over Europe. This was less than half an hour after the melting of Seoul. It wasn't even night yet in DC.

The third sky banner appeared as an ancient scroll rolled up at both ends in the European night sky. It slowly unfurled to reveal the name and number of verses from the New Testament.

'1 TIMOTHY 2:11–2:15'

Young Europeans rushed to the Internet as older Europeans rushed to their bookshelves to find the verses from Paul's first letter to Timothy:

"*Let a woman learn in silence with all submissiveness. I permit no woman to teach or to have authority over men; she is to keep silent. For Adam was formed first, then Eve; and Adam was not deceived, but the woman was deceived and became a transgressor. Yet woman will be saved through bearing children, if she continues in faith and love and holiness, with modesty.*"

Egalitarian Europe was deflated, while conservative

Europeans applauded the sexist alien message. Both sides should have read the beginning of Timothy's letter, which warns against bad teachers.

By the next day, thousands of conservative female teachers, police officers, soldiers, and doctors quit their jobs. They'd spend the next day rummaging their wardrobe for any clothing they considered immodest—to burn or destroy it. Symmetrically, ultraconservative men refused to deal with any woman in a position of authority—whether she was a doctor or a tollbooth worker. Attendance in churches, mosques, and synagogues increased dramatically right after.

This was just the beginning.

An hour after the European sky banner appeared, the Kardashians once again took over all television and radio broadcasts, replacing them with their own. Just like before, they blanked out the top 1,000 most popular websites to eliminate distraction. People started to call this KEBS—an acronym for the Kardashian Emergency Broadcast System. There was no countdown, just a minute or so of blank screen.

The time of the queen's broadcast was 5:00 p.m., EST—twilight in DC.

"I'm sorry. I can't watch this," Ralph said as he picked up his puppy and ran out of the room. The other dog followed while Alice and Lieutenant Barber remained.

I stepped back when I saw her.

"Hello."

The queen appeared in the same overly lit room, alone. Standing and not floating, she was clearly affected by gravity, which meant she was in one of the thousands of ships within Earth's atmosphere.

"My people have enjoyed touring your beautiful world and seeing the sights. We have taken many photographs. We hope we did not disturb you."

By not acknowledging the attacks on Seoul and Kaesong, she made me question them. There was a false but plausible rumor that North Korea had attacked Seoul in a confused act of retaliation. At this time little was certain.

"Over the next few hours, we will be landing our ships in major cities throughout your world. We want you to visit. Do not be shy."

She scratched her lower belly erotically with her soft fingers. I looked at Alice and Lieutenant Barber. All I saw was mesmerization.

"I will be landing in a ship near your Washington, DC. I hope to talk to your American leaders and journalists. There will be a press conference tomorrow at noon," she said as she looked away. After a grunting noise offscreen, she swiftly turned back to the camera.

"There will be refreshments," she added.

She was done speaking, but there was one last message.

She looked off camera, cooed like a dove, and raised her arm out straight. This was a cue for something unexpected.

A large bald eagle flew onto her arm and faced the camera.

"What the hell?" Lieutenant Barber shouted, looking to me for explanation.

They must have caught this wild eagle, in midflight, while the queen's ship flew low over North America. She pet the eagle's neck firmly as the bird stared at the camera, while gripping her arm tight in its talons. When the eagle spread and flapped its wings for balance, she playfully did the same with her own wings and smirked.

The screen faded back to white, and normal broadcasting returned.

Up to then, the White House had been embarrassingly quiet. The only official response had been a short press release from the night before, an hour after the manifestation of the first sky banner. President McAllister had been scheduled to hold a press conference at 2:00 p.m., EST.

But the press conference didn't happen at 2:00 p.m. Every time the president was ready, another unexpected event would happen. First, there was the Asian sky banner, then the invasion of the alien fleet, then the attacks on North and South Korea, then the European sky banner, and finally the queen's broadcast—each event delaying the new president once again. But he could not delay any longer.

It was 5:40 p.m. in DC.

We had been watching Anderson Cooper interview an astrobiologist from SETI on CNN. Cooper had asked what SETI might learn from a species of sexist and homophobic aliens, when a breaking news announcement interrupted. Coverage switched to the White House Press Briefing Room in the West Wing.

President McAllister was introduced quickly by the press secretary and stepped to the podium. This was his first public appearance as the new president, and many applauded. I shuddered when I glimpsed Francis standing off to his left.

The former general spoke as if his audience was an organized regiment of soldiers.

"At approximately 3:45 p.m., Eastern Standard Time, the capital city of South Korea, one of our closest allies, was attacked and destroyed by an unknown force. The attack was completely unprovoked. And now, as I speak, we are undergoing an invasion from that same hostile force."

He omitted that the enemy was alien—to him it didn't matter who they were. I looked over at Lieutenant Barber and saw him standing at attention.

"The United States Congress, under Title 10 of the United States Code, has authorized all reserves in all divisions of the military to contact their commanding officers and report for duty."

Of course, Congress was not in DC at the time. Following the Continuity of Operations Plan, all congressional officials had been relocated to a single, secret location. The secretaries of state, treasury, and others, as well as members of the Supreme Court, had also been relocated.

President McAllister insisted on addressing the American public from the White House. This was not arrogance: if people believed the president was safe in his house, they would believe they were safe in theirs.

"Let me be clear: America has been invaded. And make no mistake, these are enemy forces, and we are bound by duty to repel any invasion of the sovereign territory of the United States of America. Earlier, we had dismissed the enemy aircraft in our airspace as cultural naïveté, but when they attacked South Korea, they were no longer ignorant travelers. They became the enemy in our midst."

American airspace had been violated all day. Though no shots were fired, we were already at war. I sensed no fear in McAllister. After all, the American military was the strongest human fighting force in the world.

"All enemy aircraft must permanently exit American airspace. They must begin their departure within the next half hour. Otherwise, they will be attacked with the full might of America's military arsenal. God help us all if they do not heed this warning."

The president glanced over briefly at Francis and continued.

"America will not surrender its tolerance to enemy propaganda. We will not return to the barbaric thinking of the past. We will not counterfeit the courage of our ancestors who fostered the greatest nation on Earth. We will not sacrifice our civility to anyone, no matter where they're from. We will not surrender America's soul without a fight, and we will defend our way of life with our lives."

He gripped the edges of the podium and leaned in.

"And we will *never* surrender."

Planes buzzed overhead as he spoke his last words. I rushed to the window to see the black triangles of stealth bombers in finger-four formation. Dwarfing the bombers from above were at least ten Kardashian ships cruising toward DC. Ralph's house in Grasonville was just across the Chesapeake Bay, only fifty miles from DC.

Reporters shouted questions as the president ignored them and stepped away. The camera panned to the left, and I noticed the first person the president talked to was Francis.

I turned down the volume on the TV.

"Do you need to leave?" I asked Lieutenant Barber.

"The secretary of defense ordered me to protect all of you. I'm staying," he said and then looked over at Ralph by the door. "Are we safe here?"

"No," Ralph said. "Nowhere is safe."

"You think they'll attack?" I asked. "Why would they? You said—"

"I am not a fucking Kardashian," Ralph said as his glow shifted red. "Under these circumstances, I don't know what they'll do. Your president just declared war on them, and they won't let anyone interfere with their plans. They want to convert people—that's *why* they won't attack first, but if you prevent them—"

"Listen," Alice said, turning up the volume on the TV.

An excited CNN correspondent was reporting from downtown DC. On the other half of the split-screen was a live shot of at least twenty Kardashian ships—all floating upward rapidly.

"As I hope you can tell," the correspondent began, "the aliens are agreeing with the president's demands and are flying up to exit American airspace."

"Everyone get out of the house," Ralph shouted.

All of us turned to him.

"Now," Ralph yelled and grabbed my hand.

We rushed to the front door and dashed out. In the west, we could see the massive Kardashian ships, tiny from this distance, gliding straight up at a rate not possible for human aircraft.

"Where do we go?" Alice said.

"Over there," Ralph said, pointing. "You see the cylinder on the lawn?"

Under the light of the sky banner, I saw it. I picked up Ralph and sprinted across the lawn. Halfway to the cylinder I looked back above DC, but the ships were already far above the clouds.

"Looks like they left," Alice said before coughing.

"No. They just need a better angle," Ralph said.

"What's this cylinder?"

"It will protect us from the earthquakes."

When we reached the five-foot tall cylinder, I paused to catch my breath.

Lieutenant Barber inspected the cylinder, but he knew what it was. With both hands, he pushed it over and it landed with a dull thump on the grass. Then he jumped up and stomped the flat of his foot on its round shell, rolling it a few feet toward me. In the glow of Ralph's body I read the upside-down words, 'United States Navy,' stenciled on the casing.

I looked at Ralph, and he touched my hand. His words from the Oval Office ran through my mind: *I'd be embarrassed if you knew how much thought I'd put into this.*

"What is this thing?" Alice asked.

"This is for over 100 people," Lieutenant Barber said.

"I couldn't know how many people might be with me," Ralph said.

"How'd you get it?"

"Military surplus, the property manager bought it. Can you open it?"

The ground trembled as I looked westward to DC again

and froze. Hundreds of beams of light shot down from the sky onto the capital over the horizon. Even from fifty miles away, we could see the rippling flash of explosions bursting through blooming mushrooms of smoke, miles above DC. I wondered if Samantha had vanished in that burning loss of human history.

The Kardashian ships never intended to leave. They only needed to get up higher, above the darkness of the night, to harness the sun's destructive force and redirect it onto DC. My shock tumbled me to the ground, and I felt the Earth's hectic vibrations.

"Open it," Ralph barked at Lieutenant Barber. "Alice, help him."

Lieutenant Barber and Alice got on their knees and unfastened the buckles on the cylinder. Inside was a 300-pound load of tightly rolled up plastic, and Lieutenant Barber dumped it all out.

"You are a very strange being, Ralph," Lieutenant Barber said as he searched through the plastic.

"I didn't know this would happen. It's just one possibility I prepared for," he said.

"This will protect us?" Alice asked.

"If the state of Maryland sinks into the Atlantic Ocean— Yes. Do you know how many fault lines there are around DC? Activate it already."

"Activate what?" Alice said.

Lieutenant Barber found what he was looking for and said, "You'll see once I press this button."

When he pressed it, we were all knocked over by the largest automatically inflatable life raft I had ever seen. Using a life raft to protect us from an earthquake seemed harebrained, but when a sudden tremor twisted my ankle, I didn't hesitate to limp in.

The inflated rubber craft set us three feet off the ground, cushioning us from the violent shaking beneath. In the distance, I heard the collapse of neighboring houses after spastic tremors bounced the entire life raft a foot off the ground repeatedly.

Natural earthquakes rarely last more than a minute, but this wasn't natural. The Kardashians were burning holes deep into Earth to destroy targets on the surface. Old fault lines around DC were being reopened and realigned constantly as their tectonic boundaries jarred and melted.

We were fifty miles from the epicenter of multiple magnitude 8 earthquakes, and for the next twenty minutes, we rode out the seismic turmoil. We said little that night, and one by one, we each fell asleep on our inflated bed, occasionally awakened by a heavy aftershock.

I awoke to the sound of distant sirens, the pain of a twisted ankle, and the burnt scents of everyday substances wafting about. I looked at Ralph's house and was relieved it still stood. His two pet dogs had spent the night in there, trapped in a closed room, and were now walking peacefully on the lawn. The only person in the raft with me was Lieutenant Barber, talking on his phone. He glanced at me and smiled.

"He's awake now," the lieutenant said. "Markus, are you . . . okay to talk? It's urgent."

"Who is it?"

"The president."

It was hard to believe President McAllister had survived. I imagined Francis finally told him about Ralph, and that this is why he was calling. I took the phone eagerly.

"Mr. President—"

"Markus, it's me."

"Samantha?" I shot a grimace at Lieutenant Barber.

"They're dead," Samantha said. "Everyone in DC, all of them, they're all dead."

"The president's dead?"

"Markus . . . I *am* the president."

Immediately after President McAllister's speech, everyone in the White House, including the press, retreated to the Emergency Operations Center beneath the White House. The plan was to evacuate using the underground tunnels below DC, in accordance with the Continuity of Operations Plan.

Everyone, including Francis, was either melted alive or crushed to death.

After the assassination of President Shepherd, President McAllister had delayed choosing a vice president. In comparison, President Johnson waited fourteen months to choose a VP after the assassination of JFK. But Johnson didn't have to deal with an alien invasion. McAllister had to decide.

They were certainly familiar, but Samantha never met McAllister in his capacity as president. After President Shepherd was murdered, Samantha rushed to NORAD in Colorado Springs.

NORAD was a cold war artifact, a joint creation of America and Canada, designed to anticipate a Russian attack or invasion. Samantha went under the guise of an inspection. Of course, she knew it would be an ideal command center to track invading alien ships.

When the Kardashians destroyed Seoul, McAllister made Samantha vice president, and she was secretly sworn in. In case of his death, McAllister wanted someone from the military to succeed him.

But he never announced Samantha's vice presidency. He feared how the American public would view it: he was preparing for his own demise—and he wanted people to view him with confidence. America had just lost President Shepherd. He didn't want the country considering another loss so soon.

And there was no confusion. McAllister had informed enough of the survivors in the line of succession for all this to be clear. Before I woke up, official press releases had already announced Samantha as the president of the United States—the third in less than a week.

And she was calling me for advice. Or so I thought.

"I'm not the little girl who wanted to grow up and be president. I was the one who would grow up and kill bad guys. And now every general I know is asking me *when* we'll retaliate."

"What have you told them?"

". . . Nothing," she said.

"Did the Kardashians attack us anywhere else?"

"No, just DC. And now they've taken over. There are six ships parked at ground zero."

"I take it you've told no one about Ralph," I said.

I shouldn't have mentioned Ralph, but maybe she shouldn't have called me. I glanced at Lieutenant Barber, and he glared at me, shaking his head vigorously with his index finger vertical over his lips.

"Let's not talk about Ralph right now," she said quickly. "I need your advice, your honest thoughts. Do you think we should retaliate?"

"Of course you shouldn't retaliate. You know you can't defeat them. Just let them—"

"Thank you, Markus," she said. "You're right, we can't retaliate. Thank you. I needed to hear it from someone I trust. I'm sorry, but I've got to go now."

She abruptly hung up, and I gave the phone to Lieutenant Barber.

"I think I just stopped a war," I said in awe.

Lieutenant Barber laughed. "You're some kind of moron, aren't you . . .?"

"Excuse me?"

"You think she called you for advice? You *really* think Samantha Weingarten, the president, commander in chief, based her decision on what you just said?"

"Well, it sure sounded like it. What are you saying?"

"*They're listening,*" he said, pointing his finger at the sky. "And Samantha knows they're listening. They hacked our entire Internet. You don't think they've hacked into her phone by now?"

"Oh," I said, sheepishly. "Well, you could've told me."

"No, I couldn't have, because then you'd be unnatural. You might've gotten creative, instead of saying what she wanted you to say."

"What exactly did she want me to say?"

"She called you because you're the only one she knows who thinks we shouldn't retaliate. And Samantha needs *them* to believe we won't retaliate. You get it?" he said.

"OK, OK, I get it . . . but . . . Wait, how do *you* know all this?"

"I figured it out on my own. Not like she could tell me over the phone."

". . . Does this mean we *will* retaliate?"

"How the hell should I know?" Lieutenant Barber said.

The conversation I had with Samantha was really a conversation between her and the Kardashians. She wanted them to believe we wouldn't attack. That was the only reason she called. Lieutenant Barber was cruel but correct.

In that moment, I realized something important: They had not listened to every phone call of every White House official in the last week. If they had, they would've heard Francis's phone calls, and they would've already known about Ralph.

With more diligence, they would have found us much sooner. But they never intended to laboriously study and spy on humans. They didn't want to work much at all.

For them, the invasion was a holiday.

PRESS

During our slumber, the fourth sky banner appeared over the African continent. From the Mediterranean to South Africa, from Senegal to Somalia, it was easily seen. This time, the message intended to tempt as much as offend, and it was equally dangerous. It foreshadowed the stunning announcement the queen would make in her press conference.

It was the longest banner with the longest message. With white words of English over a glowing black background, the following message manifested:

'THE BLACK ONE WILL ALWAYS BE A SLAVE ON EARTH. COME WITH US.'

The first sentence was pathetically anachronistic. Enslaving people of African descent had been abolished so long ago in so many countries, one wondered if the aliens were out of touch. So, the natural interpretation was metaphorical—as if to say, despite all the advances of racial equality, blacks will never be treated equally. Former President Barack Obama tweeted, "What the hell are these aliens talking about?"

The second sentence of the message was more intriguing.

'COME WITH US.'

The queen would soon clarify the details of this invitation.

While we slept in the life raft, Kardashian ships were landing in all major cities throughout the world. No country could resist them after the melting of DC, and, of course, some countries welcomed them for that same reason. But all governments warned citizens against provoking the Kardashians in any way.

Large parks within cities were used as parking lots: Central Park in New York City, the various *Jardins* throughout Paris, Chaoyang Park in Beijing, Parque Tezozómoc in Mexico City, among all the others. Most parks could only fit the smaller ships, and some witnesses viewed ships shrinking in size in order to land.

The queen's press conference wasn't cancelled, only delayed. While the American government put out press releases reassuring the public that they still had a functioning government, the Kardashians issued their own press release that morning, giving all the required details for the press. It stressed that any question could be asked.

The question-and-answer session took place inside the queen's ship. Major news outlets were invited to send exactly one journalist each, which the Kardashians would vet and verify. It would be broadcast live on every TV and radio channel, via KEBS, which, once again, blanked out popular websites to eliminate any competition for attention.

The press conference was rescheduled for 5:00 p.m. Originally, the queen hoped to have it at noon in DC, but the destruction made this impossible. The venue was changed to the

Queenstown golf course in Queenstown, Maryland—a location chosen more for the sake of a pun, I'm sure, than practicality.

Queenstown was three miles east of Ralph's house in Grasonville, and both were on the Delmarva Peninsula. As a peninsula, there were only a few routes available. The Chesapeake Bay Bridge had become impassable from damage, so the only land route was from the north.

But it was difficult to find journalists to attend, as almost all journalists were unable to make the trip. Commercial flights were still grounded, and trains had been cancelled because of damage to tracks from earthquakes. Driving was the only option for many, and it was risky. Many roads had been destroyed, and many more were restricted by the military.

This left the media scrambling to find anyone to go.

"I'm going," Alice told us.

"No . . . Alice . . . Don't. You're not ready for this," Ralph said, shaking his helmet.

The oncoming press conference was all over the news that morning. Alice, tempted by opportunity, called her boss at the *New York Times* and begged to represent them. They already had someone. But, as a professional courtesy, they passed her name to other news outlets.

Her contribution to the article in the *New York Times* about the cylinder made her enough of a journalist, and her proximity to Queenstown made her especially valuable. It wasn't long before the *New York Post* called her to represent them. Representing a conservative publication put a dent in her progressive sensibility, but she saw past it.

Ralph begged her to stay, but Alice ignored him.

"Lieutenant, please go with her," Ralph said.

The lieutenant said nothing.

"This is a press conference, not a military operation. I don't need protection," Alice said.

"How do you plan to get there?" Lieutenant Barber asked.

She looked at him, then at me, and said, "I'll walk, it's only three miles."

"No, Alice, I'll drive you," I said.

Lieutenant Barber rolled his eyes and grunted. "I'm supposed to be protecting you people, and I can't do that if you split up."

"I'm the interloper," Alice said. "No one asked you to protect me."

Lieutenant Barber exhaled, reached into his pocket, threw Alice his keys, and said, "Take my vehicle and drive straight there. Don't stop for anyone or anything. We don't know the local situation. The steering pulls a little to the left, the brakes are sticky, and a Beretta Px4 is holstered to the bottom of the front seat."

"Thanks," she said with a tiny smile.

Alice left two hours early, though the drive would take only minutes. We went outside to see her off and saw the white spaceships bulging into the horizon over nearby Queenstown. Ralph hugged Alice quickly and ran back in the house.

And once again, Ralph would refuse to watch the queen on television. I asked him why. He replied, "It could make me scream, and from this distance, they might hear me. They know the sound of my people screaming."

Alice arrived in Queenstown and called to reassure us, and, perhaps, herself. As she drove, she described for me what she saw. There were no police or military in the area. I advised her to drive straight to the ships, and she agreed. She saw three ships. The queen's ship was easy to identify from the numerous imprints of 'Queen's Ship' programmed to appear in huge black letters on its surface. There were no Kardashians outside to greet the reporters, and no grand entrance. There were only arrows imprinted onto the half-mile long ship, pointing to a small open portal with the word 'Entrance' above it. Other reporters were there, waiting outside, talking, unsure what to do.

Later, reporters would give similar accounts of what happened after entering the small portal, which only allowed one reporter at a time. Each was held in a small, well-lit space, the size of a small closet, which moved horizontally and diagonally, as well as vertically. At various points, the reporter would be paralyzed and a needle would appear to either remove blood, or inject an unknown substance. They all reported a variety of scans being taken as well. They assumed it was an advanced form of quarantine.

Alice went in first. "Wish me luck," she said.

That was the last contact we had with Alice before seeing her again on television. So we were just as shocked as anybody when the press conference began.

The all-white room was much larger than the room the queen had previously been filmed in, and less brightly lit. Her presence was less captivating this time, and the thirty human journalists with her suffered no mesmerization in her presence.

Like a human press conference, the camera was situated in the back of the room, focused on the queen in the front, with journalists in between. Each journalist sat on a simple white cube, which rose up from the floor. Most held a legal pad over their lap.

And everyone was naked.

Mandatory nudity was a Kardashian security measure, which, as a bonus, humiliated every human in the room. The other security measure was more shocking—no one could've guessed what the beast was at first.

Squatting behind the queen was a shady and monstrous alien. No one could confuse it for a terrestrial animal. The queen daintily held a long, thin leash attached to the thick collar around its fat neck. The black beast was easily 300 pounds, making the leash futile. The queen looked like a child holding the reins of a mutant grizzly bear.

The black metal muzzle on its snout seemed mystifyingly pointless in light of the ten glowing white dagger claws on each of its four limbs. I believe the muzzle was there to prevent the beast from speaking, more than biting or eating. The beast could have killed everyone in the room in less than a minute, and everyone in that room knew it. Its least-threatening aspects were the two dull and immature horns on its head.

Lined along the back wall were dozens of 8-ounce glass bottles of Diet Coke. It was a mystery how they obtained the bottles, presumably from the wreckage of some supermarket near DC, but it made the queen seem even more powerful and strange. The bottles inevitably brought to mind the lunar advertisement, but in any case, they had promised refreshments.

"Let's begin, shall we?" the queen said politely. The beast behind her grunted, and she paused. "Right, and if anyone would like a Diet Coke, feel free to get up and take one."

The naked humans stayed seated as the queen took a Diet Coke and casually removed the bottle cap using one of the forty knifelike claws on the black beast.

"No one's thirsty? . . . Then let's start. Ask me anything."

Uncertain of protocol, reporters shifted glances at one another, while Alice and a few others raised their hands. Alice was sitting up front, and the queen looked at her.

"Ah, you, the pretty one, what's your name?" the queen said.

"Alice Higginbotham, with the *New York Post.*"

"That's a funny name."

". . . Since we are on that topic, how do we address you? 'Your Majesty' or 'Queen'—"

"Ooh," the queen purred. "I like 'Your Majesty.' I like that a lot. Call me that."

"OK . . . Your Majesty," Alice continued, "numerous reports indicate that your vessels were attacked by North Korean missiles, which explains why you retaliated against Kaesong in North Korea. But why attack South Korea? Why attack Seoul? It doesn't make a lot of sense."

The queen paused and smiled. "North Korea . . . South Korea . . . North Dakota . . . South Dakota . . . These primitive and petty distinctions mean little to us. All we knew was that we were attacked, and we had to defend ourselves. I should ask you: why did you let your Koreans attack us? It doesn't make a lot of sense."

She was an ignorant bitch of a queen, but I had no idea how much of it was an act. Alice was too stunned to follow up. The queen moved on.

"Yes, you . . . the whorish-looking redhead in the back, I would like to hear you speak."

"Ahh, thank you, Your Majesty," the redhead said nervously. "Stephen Hawking feared aliens might come to Earth and strip it of its resources. Is that why you are here?"

The queen laughed. "Stephen who?"

"Ahh, Stephen Hawking, Your Majesty, a prominent theoretical physicist."

"I'm sure he's charming. But no, we are not interested in such things. We don't care about your caviar, your oil, your platinum or plutonium . . . We're not even interested in your helium reserves. We are not here to take. We are only here to give."

"So will you give us your superior scientific knowledge?" the reporter asked.

The queen giggled. "Of course not. My dear, mankind does not need more science. Mankind needs more God. Haven't you been listening?" she said as she took a sip of Diet Coke, paused, and called on another. "You, yes, you, the man with the strange-looking penis."

He was about to stand up, then thought better of it and asked his question from his seat.

"Why is it that you look so human, or, as many say, humanoid? It seems like a fantastic coincidence—"

"There is no coincidence. We were made in God's image, just like you," she said, as if it was the most obvious fact in the world. With no loss of rhythm, she pointed to another reporter.

"What is the purpose of the large ship near Pluto?" a reporter called out.

The queen looked at the reporter, smiled, and said, "Next question."

There was a pause; then the questions resumed. "Why do you have this press conference in the United States? Why not another country?" the unshaven reporter asked calmly with a French accent.

Her response seemed completely flippant.

She smiled, almost laughed, then looked over the faces of the reporters and said, "What's great about this country is that America started the tradition where the richest consumers buy essentially the same things as the poorest. You can be watching TV and see Coca-Cola, and you know that the president drinks Coca-Cola, Liz Taylor drinks Coca-Cola, and just think, you can drink Coca-Cola too."

Her weird answer left almost everyone dumbfounded. I'd bet only a few thousand people on Earth recognized her words, but Alice was one of them.

"Your Majesty . . . Did you just quote Andy Warhol?" Alice asked with a small laugh.

"This one is clever," the queen said with excitement, pointing sharply at Alice while looking back at the gnarly beast. Then she walked over and touched Alice's shoulder with a smile. "In fact, I did quote Mr. Warhol, for fun, but don't think I was insincere. The United States is truly the greatest bunch of states on Earth. That is why we are here." The queen seemed more impressed with Alice than embarrassed. Whereas Alice's knowledge of Warhol was easy to account for—she studied art history at NYU—the queen's knowledge was not.

The queen called on another reporter. "Ah, you, yes, you, the hairy one."

Trembling, the hairy reporter asked, "In light of the appearance of what we've been calling 'sky banners,' and also what you just said about Coca-Cola, I have to ask . . . Are your people responsible for the lunar advertisement?"

The queen paused for thirty seconds to think about it, staring at the bottle in her hand while she did. "We thought humans were responsible for that . . . Don't you like Diet Coke? Why would we do that? It was here when we got here." She looked back at the black beast. "We didn't do that."

The beast huffed and grunted.

She glared back at the reporter. "Are you saying Coca-Cola is not responsible?"

"Well," he said, "that was the conclusion of the congressional investigation."

"I thought no one took that seriously."

I was worried—worried for Ralph. If the queen believed the congressional report, *my* report, then she'd wonder if another alien was responsible. I believe Alice was putting the pieces together and worrying the same. She tried to change the subject.

"Your Majesty, earlier you said humans needed more God. Are you claiming to be prophets?"

"Of course we are prophets."

"But . . . Why should we believe you?"

"Oh, my poor child, I will not waste my secrets in this crude public forum. And I will not try to persuade you with reason, when I could only convince those with faith," she said as she turned away from Alice and addressed the camera directly. "Any human who wants to see the glory of God must come to us. We will show you the way. This is a promise. We want to show you the kingdom of heaven. This is why we came to your lonely planet."

"And if we refuse?" the French reporter asked.

The queen laughed. "We are not forcing anyone. If you wish to pass up the chance for eternal bliss, I will pray for you. If you want to stay on Earth and worship your decadent idols of rock and rap and pornography and drugs and money and homosexual intercourse, I can't stop you. But if you come with us, you will be shown wonders unknown to human minds. You will no longer worry about human illness. And you will know a warmth you have never felt before."

The queen's large blue heart was thumping so strong I was tapping my finger to its rhythm. It increased her allure and everyone's attention.

"But be warned. Each human has only three days to make their decision. Three days."

"What happens in three days?"

The queen smiled. "We're leaving. And we're never coming back."

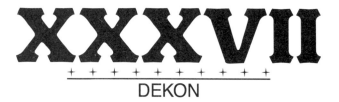

XXXVII

+ + + + + + + + +

DEKON

The seduction had officially begun.

Everyone was invited to heaven. And everyone had three days to decide.

"Now, who is ready?" the queen shouted, galvanizing attention. Her eyes took the gaze of a hunter as she scanned the room. "Time is short. Who among you will be first? Who here will show the world that you have God in your heart and come with us? Which of you inquisitive reporters is ready to decide your soul's fate, right now?"

The reporters slowly looked around at each other. Ten seconds passed before someone raised a timid hand. It was Lillian Gray, the first convert. She was tall and attractive with a picture-perfect body, the sort of woman young girls dream to be. We'd learn later she'd recently been diagnosed with heart cancer, extremely rare; most die within two years of diagnosis. Like me, she was single with no family, nothing tying her down to Earth.

"Please, my dear child, stand up and come to me."

Lillian Gray wanted someone to take the pain away. Her walk oozed sadness, and when she reached the queen, her head hung low, barely hiding her wet face.

"Everything's fine, my child. Everything's all right," the queen said softly as she put her arm around her. "Lift up your head. Let the world see your brave face."

But the reporter did not raise her head. She threw her arms over the queen's shoulders and cried aloud. Awkwardness flashed over the queen's face, and then she smiled and embraced her first convert. The world waited for a full minute as the queen tenderly held the woman in her arms and caressed her left breast.

"We will heal you," the queen said.

Astonished, Lillian stared in the queen's face.

The queen whispered something in her ear, and Lillian nodded.

Unexpectedly, the queen kissed the woman's lips and licked her forehead with her pure black tongue. She then reached into her furled up wings to pull out a small black tube.

"Any human who wants to join us," the queen said, addressing the camera, "must do two things. First, come to any of our ships, anywhere in the world, and present yourself as God sees you—naked—no clothing whatsoever. Second, to show your commitment, you must draw these symbols on your head . . . above the eyes . . ."

With the black tube, the queen carefully drew the symbols on the reporter's forehead.

⋈ ⋈ ⋈

Naïvely, converts called these symbols 'the three butterflies.'

A common interpretation went as follows: Each butterfly was really an hourglass knocked over on its side, to remind us time is running out—so the three together represented the mere three days humans had to decide whether to go with the

Kardashians. It was a thoughtful interpretation, but the real meaning was far more sinister.

"What do the symbols mean?" Alice asked.

"It means you are ready," the queen said gently, petting Lillian Gray's long hair. "Now, go sit down, my lovely. We will collect you when the press conference is over."

The reporter obeyed, and the room went silent.

Then, once again, something unexpected happened.

A reporter raised her pale hand. We had mostly only seen the backs of the heads of the reporters, as the camera focused on the queen. But I could tell the other reporters were not sitting near this one. Her English was not very good.

"Ah, yes," the queen said. "Please, stand up and ask your question . . . in English."

"Thank you, my queen, Your Majesty," the reporter said, shaking as she stood up.

The reporter was a Kardashian, a female who looked much like the queen, though her body and wings were smaller. Once I accepted she was an actual journalist, I realized that the Kardashians had their own complex society, with schoolteachers, engineers, social workers, criminals, politicians, and everything else you'd expect. I imagined everyone in their society gathered around their own televisions, watching the press conference broadcast on screens with Kardashian subtitles running underneath.

Until that point, I hadn't wondered what *type* of queen she was. She was not a queen the way a queen bee is a queen—where everyone else is a drone or worker. She was more of a monarch who happened to be female.

"Why you . . . have new scars? On the back?" the Kardashian reporter asked.

"Because someone's been a *very* bad boy," she said, pounding her fist on the beast's head. Inexplicably, the beast cowered and squealed, hiding his hazardous claws in shame. The queen then shouted something at the beast in her jagged alien tongue.

"Your Majesty," Alice began, "we are all very curious . . . who is this . . . alien behind you? Is this a pet of some kind?"

"Oh," the queen said, "I believe this is what you call a 'husband.' His name is 'Dekon.'"

Her voice went raspy and harsh when she pronounced 'Dekon,' indicating it was her husband's alien name. Dekon whimpered in response, and she began petting him.

'Sexual dimorphism' is the phrase biologists use to describe a species where the males and females appear different, and the sexual dimorphism of the Kardashians was severe. When first seeing Dekon, no one thought they were viewing a male Kardashian. While the queen was dainty, white, hairless, and elegant, Dekon was burly with dark brindle hair and murderous claws.

"Ah, does this mean . . . Your husband is king?" the redheaded reporter asked.

"No," the queen said, poking Dekon on the head. "No. No. No." To be sure, even on Earth, the husband of a queen is not automatically a king. Consider the husband of Queen Elizabeth II, for example.

Another reporter asked, "How would you spell the name of your husband?"

"D-E-K-O-N seems the most natural, in English," the queen

said as she sipped her soda and petted Dekon's harsh, heavy hair. When the camera focused in, we could see the vestigial wings of the beast. They were tinier and even more useless than the queen's, but it gave credibility to the claim that Dekon was a male of the same species.

The camera focused in further, and I saw three crimson butterflies on his fat black collar.

⋈ ⋈ ⋈

"Your Majesty," Alice said with a tiny laugh, "one of your sky banners, the one over Europe, explicitly preaches women to be submissive, and yet . . . You're holding your husband there on a leash, he's wearing a muzzle, and you just bonked his head and scolded him in front of the whole world . . . Is this some kind of joke?"

Alice had been increasingly bold in her questions, and I feared she was trespassing in deadly territory. Though I sensed a mutual respect growing between Alice and the queen, pointing out the queen's hypocrisy was suicidal.

The queen smiled at Alice, as if she admired her. She walked close to Alice and slowly bent over to put her mouth next to Alice's ear. Afraid, Alice pulled away. Then, with two hands, the queen firmly held Alice's head in place as she whispered, speaking directly into Alice's ear for a minute. No one knew what was said, but when the queen released her head, Alice pulled back and gawked at the smiling queen.

At once, Alice and the queen burst out in hysterical laughter. Their collective laughs exploded into the room as everyone else wondered. But we never discovered what was so humorous.

Alice was laughing and pointing at Dekon.

"Dekon, No! You can't," the queen screamed as Dekon slashed his feeble leash and lunged at Alice with his shining claws flying overhead. Parallel lines of blood streaked onto the walls as reporters ran back toward the camera, hiding the remainder of the instant slaughter.

"The press conference is over," the queen shouted amidst whirling screams.

The screen went blank white.

When the shock wore off, I was angry, and my anger gave me an idea.

My ankle was still in pain from twisting during the earthquake, so I limped quickly to the kitchen and searched all the drawers, but they were empty. I searched some closets and two rooms on the first floor, but couldn't find what I wanted, so I went upstairs and found Ralph. Though he didn't watch the broadcast, he sensed something terrible had happened. Fearing he might scream, I didn't tell him.

"Is everything okay?" Ralph asked.

"I need a magic marker."

"Is Alice okay?"

"Just find me a fucking magic marker."

Slowly, Ralph raised the arm of his suit to reveal a small pocket. "Look in here."

I reached in and pulled out a lightly glowing thin metallic tube.

"Is this safe?" I asked, after pulling off the cap. "Can I write on my skin with it?"

"Yes, it's safe . . . What are you doing? What's happened?"

I didn't answer and went back downstairs as Ralph trailed behind.

I found a bathroom, closed the door, and used a towel to wipe any trace of perspiration off my face. I then drew the three angular butterflies on my forehead.

⋈ ⋈ ⋈

Ralph's strange alien marker tingled on my skin. I felt no pain, but I could smell my singed flesh. I never asked if the marker was permanent. I didn't care.

Ralph and Lieutenant Barber began talking outside the door. I couldn't hear what was said, but when I heard Ralph's sad crackling, I knew Lieutenant Barber must have told him about Alice. The crackling noises faded as Ralph walked back upstairs.

Lieutenant Barber opened the door.

"What are you thinking?" he asked, glaring at me.

"Infiltration."

XXXVIII

PANIC

"Slow down, Donnie Brasco . . . What are you planning to do once you get in a ship? And how will you get back out?"

My thought was to get inside and kill as many monsters as I could before they killed me. He knew what I was thinking, but I would never have said it. In any case, if you think scientists never get so angry they want to kill someone, you can go fuck yourself.

"Look, Doc, I wanna kill aliens too, but what you're thinking is suicide. They didn't come across the galaxy to risk getting killed by people like us."

His words calmed me.

"Meet me out by your car in ten minutes, OK?" he said.

I got in my car and waited while Lieutenant Barber talked to Ralph. The waiting cooled me a little more. Around in the distance were echoes of rushing sirens and smoke plumes of different shades. There was chaos out there, and the rage inside me wanted to meet it.

Lieutenant Barber came outside thirty minutes later.

"You still want to go?" he asked.

"Yes."

"Then I'm driving."

"No."

"Didn't you hurt your ankle?"

He knew the answer. My ankle was still in pain, and I needed it for driving. I reluctantly got out of the driver's seat and limped around to sit shotgun in my own vehicle. Lieutenant Barber turned on the ignition, rolled down the window, and lit a cigarette. He had taken the time to print out the directions using Google Maps, even though my car had GPS navigation and we could see the large Kardashian ships in Queenstown from Ralph's.

"Ralph will be safe," I said, but I was really asking.

"Safer than us—he's got a panic room in the basement. Looks like it could withstand a low-yield nuclear blast."

"Good."

Lieutenant Barber eyed me and then pointed his finger in my face. "Now you need to lose your fucked-up ideas about infiltrating one of those ships, OK? You're the smart one here. Don't lose your fucking mind on me."

I had cooled enough to agree with him, so I nodded, but I needed to do something—*anything*. "I'm still going to Queenstown."

He flipped down the sun visor to look in the mirror. "Give me Ralph's marker." He took it and casually drew the three butterflies on his forehead. "We are going to do some basic reconnaissance, just to get a sense of what's going on in Queenstown. I'll get my car back, and with any luck, maybe we can find Alice's body and give it a proper burial."

I exhaled some anger out of my brain, and off we drove. The

chaos had already started, and what we saw was a small glimpse of the violent schism happening in all the neighborhoods of the world.

In retrospect, I'm sure Lieutenant Barber was humoring me. He didn't want me going off on my own. Checking out the local damage from the earthquake and examining the Kardashian ships up close seemed harmless. It was only three miles away. But we never made it to Queenstown.

Pulling out of Ralph's driveway, we saw a pedestrian. Like a zombie, he walked in the street, slow and alone, the sleeves of his shirt and hands covered in dried blood. It felt good to see something like this, and as we passed, I spied the three butterflies on his head. He didn't even glance at us. A police car sped by, sirens blaring, and didn't stop to investigate.

Ralph's neighborhood was mostly residential, and Lieutenant Barber drove slowly. We had barely traveled a half mile.

"Where are you going?"

"There's supposed to be a convenience store around here somewhere . . . Ah, there it is."

As we turned the corner, we saw the store, and I sighed. Cars had parked, and there were customers. They seemed oblivious to the fresh teenage corpse on the sidewalk. The sentence 'ALL FAGS MUST DIE' was spray painted in red on the ground near the body.

Two police cars flew by as we pulled into the parking lot.

"You want anything?"

"Hurry up."

Waiting, I saw a mother pushing her young boy in his wheelchair on the street, both of them smiling and singing,

"Jesus loves the little children, all the children of the world." They were converts. Most of the cars and pedestrians on the road were headed toward Queenstown, and most were converts. The nonconverts were usually police officers, firefighters, or weary homeowners guarding their property with rifles and shotguns.

Lieutenant Barber took more than ten minutes in the store, and I started honking the horn. He came out with a coffee, a bag of chips, and some newspapers. At this point, I suspected he was purposefully delaying. Without saying anything, he got in and drove.

When we made a full stop at a stop sign, a blond boy burst out the front door of the corner house. His father chased him on the front lawn and tackled him. We were close enough to see the three black butterflies on the son's head. I could hear the mother wailing inside.

"I'm one of you. Help me," the boy shouted to us.

"Mind your business," the father said to us.

Focused on us, the father didn't see the other young convert walking by on the street. He rushed up and sucker kicked the father in the face. His son got up and started running with his new friend to Queenstown. I opened the door, intending to check on the father, but Lieutenant Barber hit the gas, and we sped through the intersection.

A few blocks down, we saw a middle-aged female with three butterflies on her shaved head walking backward along the road. She spotted us and held up a cardboard sign that read, 'QUEENSTOWN.' She waved it overhead and gave an open mouth smile as we approached.

We should have been more suspicious.

Unlike most, she had baggage: a large green duffel bag. Yet, converts were told to enter the ships naked. Luggage was pointless.

"Know thy enemy," Lieutenant Barber said.

"You're picking her up?"

"Sure, why not?"

"I don't know. There's something strange about her."

"All these converts are fucked in the head," he said sharply, gently honking and stopping on the shoulder. She threw away her sign and ran up. She wore a green flannel top with denim pants. An American flag was tattooed on her neck, and her three butterflies were drawn with freshly applied crimson nail polish.

"Howdy," she said and smiled as she opened the rear passenger door behind me. "Y'all going to Queenstown, right? Aw, lookit your heads; 'course you are."

There was a metallic clang when her bag hit the floor behind us.

"What's your name?" I asked.

"Sharon. You?"

"I'm Frank, and this is Markus," Lieutenant Barber said in a friendly tone and began driving, a bit faster than before. We turned another corner and saw a naked male convert walking in the street. Sharon laughed.

"That guy has the right idea," the lieutenant said. "Y'know, Sharon, you can't take that bag with you. You can't take anything with you."

"Yeah, I know."

"What's in the bag anyway?" I asked.

"Just personal stuff."

"You women and your bags," Lieutenant Barber said. "Where're you from?"

"South Texas," she said. "Can't ya tell?"

Texas was an easy guess, but something in her voice wasn't right. She was too excited, too loud. Her accent sounded too thick.

"You military?" I asked.

With a defensive tone she replied, "I can't be in a military where they allow dykes and queers, know what I mean? And I don't wanna live in a country which lets fags ruin marriage, know what I mean? America's gone to hell, and these aliens are here to save us."

"Yeah, all those fucking fags, ruining America and marriage and God knows what else. Probably why the aliens attacked DC," Lieutenant Barber said as he winked at me.

Neither of us saw Sharon reaching into her bag.

With no accent whatsoever, she said, "You people make me sick." Then she put a handgun up to Lieutenant Barber's temple. Calmly, Lieutenant Barber pulled the car to the shoulder.

"Don't turn off the engine," she said with no accent. "Now get out—both of you."

Lieutenant Barber looked at me, shrugged his shoulders, and opened his door to exit.

I glared at her. "Aliens invade Earth, and so this is a good day to carjack?"

"You won't need your car in outer space, dipshit. Now go. *Move.*"

Lieutenant Barber had already walked around the car, opened my door, and was forcefully pulling me out. By the time

I closed the door, she had hopped into the front seat and started to drive off. I watched my car disappear around the corner.

Lieutenant Barber was already walking back the way we came.

"So that's it?" I asked.

"What, you wanna walk to Queenstown on your bum ankle? That's about two miles, and we gotta walk back."

"Give me your phone."

"Be my guest."

I dialed 911 and was put on hold. I was hoping to at least report my car stolen, but after waiting for five minutes with no response, I just hung up.

As we walked back, I wondered if Sharon was more than she seemed.

Sharon *seemed* like a car thief impersonating a convert, but I wondered if there was a further level of duplicity—*I wondered if she was also impersonating a car thief.* At the risk of sounding too imaginative . . . I still wonder whether Sharon was some military buddy of Lieutenant Barber's who happened to live in the area.

Let me explain.

Lieutenant Barber's job was to protect me, not my car, and with no car, he knew I'd be forced to walk back to Ralph's—I couldn't walk to Queenstown and back on my ankle. So, as a guardian, his job would be easier if I had to stay at Ralph's for the next three days. Then, his duty to protect Ralph and me would be done.

I'm afraid it all sounds paranoid. But, all he had to do was call her up, meet at a prearranged spot, she steals my car, and that's it. He was the one driving my car, remember, and he was obviously delaying a lot—I imagined the delays were the result of him waiting, waiting to be certain she was ready in the right spot.

And if she only wanted the car, why not let us drive to Queenstown and steal the car after we got there? If she thought we were converts, it's the safer, less violent, move.

Of course, I was too embarrassed to mention my conspiracy theory to him, but it was something to think about while walking back, which I did, slowly but inevitably, on limping foot. Considering what happened next, it all feels petty.

The mile walk back was, mercifully, uneventful. By then, it was a little more than two hours after the queen's press conference. We were two houses away from Ralph's.

"Is there alcohol in the house?" I asked.

"Yes," he said with cheer. "I saw it, a whole wine cellar from the previous owner."

"You want red wine then?"

Lieutenant Barber looked back at me, about to answer, then stopped moving. His face lost expression. I looked over my shoulder and shuddered.

Half a mile away, a Kardashian ship was pointing and traveling in our direction, a hundred feet off the ground. It seemed impossible for something that big to move so quickly without making sound.

"Markus, we have to move," he said with a hushed tone as

he took out his phone and called Ralph. "Ralph, get ready to jump in the panic room . . . There's a ship coming our way, a Kardashian ship, but wait for Markus. OK? See you in five."

With my arm over Lieutenant Barber's shoulder, I limped along the street and up the driveway, hobbling to the front door. When I gazed back along the driveway, the ship was a few hundred yards behind us, floating as silent as a cloud and descending.

When we made it inside, I looked at Lieutenant Barber.

"Go down that stairwell, take a left, and go all the way. You'll see the safe room."

"You're not coming?"

There was a hissing noise of pressure outside. We peered out the window to see the ship parked along on the street.

"Go. Now. No discussion."

He ran upstairs as I hopped down the steps. At the basement landing, I looked left and saw Ralph's dismal purple glow at the end of the long, dark corridor. I ran to him, adrenalin flowing and masking my pain.

Ralph sat on the floor, motionless. He said nothing when I reached him. I picked him up, took him into the panic room, and shut the thick, reinforced door.

Inside were two black-and-white monitors linked to surveillance cameras. One camera covered the long, front lawn. The other covered the long, thin hall outside the panic room.

I saw them on the lawn. First ten, twenty, then at least thirty male Kardashians stormed straight up to the house, vaulting across the lawn like marauding gorillas. I could hear them violently searching the house as I kept my eyes on the monitor covering the corridor outside the panic room.

I froze when I saw a male bound toward our room, stop, and tap his long claws on the metal door. Another rushed up behind him, they communicated, then one went away, leaving the other right outside. For a few seconds the male stared at the camera. With one quick thrash, his claws destroyed it.

My eyes shifted back to the outdoor camera, where I could see the males leaping across the grass and returning to the ship. The noises upstairs had stopped, and I sensed the house was almost empty of intruders. Though I could no longer hear or see him, I was certain the one male had remained outside the door, waiting.

"Ralph?" I whispered.

No response.

I turned back to the monitor. Outside on the lawn, a thick ring of males approached the house at a calm speed. In the middle of them was a single female walking along casually. I didn't know it at that moment, but it was the queen. I watched her coterie calmly escort her across the full length of the lawn to the house.

"What are they doing?"

Ralph said nothing.

I could hear them jostling and bumping the walls of the corridor outside. We were trapped, but the animal in me still wanted to hide. The only hiding space left was a plain closet set into the wall opposite the entrance of the panic room. I went to it and motioned Ralph to join me.

"Markus, I'm sorry."

I waved my hand again, beckoning him, but he didn't move. I backed further into the closet and lightly bumped into several large canisters of helium. As I sat down on the floor of the closet, the power was cut off. I cracked open the closet door, just enough to see Ralph's dark purple glow.

With barely a sound, something sliced through the thick steel door of the panic room. With geometric precision, a two-foot square was cut out of the door and removed silently by the intruders. Light burst into the room from behind the square hole.

The queen put her hand through the cutout and revealed the source of shining light. Barely fitting in her hand were four glimmering spheres. She gently dumped them into the room. They hit the floor without a single sound or bounce. Immediately, each one rolled to locate one of the four corners of the room and remained there. The four spheres lit up the room from below, and I sensed they were somehow scanning the room.

I glanced at Ralph, still motionless.

I can barely describe what happened next, let alone explain it. An anomalous material was placed in the square hole in the door. I should say it had no color, but I want to say it was *somehow* the color of nothing. It appeared like a blind spot in my eye, like something my mind, or my eye, could not process.

Next, the material extended and covered the door. As it extended, it became clearer and clearer. When it extended to cover the entire door, the anomalous material was gone, along with the door. The entire metal door was somehow wiped away. There was a slightly noxious odor in the air, no doubt a by-product of this inexplicable chemical process.

One at a time, four males lumbered inside, each calmly sitting near a corner of the room, and each staring at Ralph.

I wondered why Ralph wasn't reacting. Why wasn't he afraid? Why wasn't he *screaming*? Ralph had led me to believe the Kardashians would kill him on sight. But they only watched him.

Then the queen came into the doorway. She stepped in slowly, naked and smiling, like a conqueror. She walked to the center of the room and faced Ralph.

"Hello, Father," she said.

XXXIX

FATHER

"**F**ather," each of the four males said in their own gruff, respectful tone.

My fear froze. I couldn't think how it was possible, but everything in that moment—her tone, Ralph's lack of denial, the calm acknowledgment of the males—all told me it was true: Ralph was their father.

Ralph's words from the Oval Office sprang to mind: *Once I have mated enough, I will spontaneously produce multiple beings, each with a different genetic makeup. I could even produce carbon-based beings.*

I wanted to ask how? Why?—but I couldn't speak. The betrayal paralyzed me, and I feared madness more than death. I could only listen—though I would not comprehend everything I heard.

"Why did you do it?" she asked Ralph with accusation. "Do you fancy yourself a wolf—a wolf giving advice to helpless mortals? Hmm? What did you hope to achieve? Spoil our amusement? Deprive us of our holiday? Your anagram gave us all a good laugh, by the way."

I didn't know what she meant by calling Ralph a 'wolf,' but it frightened me. Nor did I know what anagram she referred to.

The conversation was mysterious, and Ralph's nonresponsiveness only puzzled me more.

"Why do you even care for these humans?" she roared. "They are so stupid. They think they are living in one of their science fiction films where everyone in the universe speaks English." She swiveled in my direction. "Do you really think we don't know you're in there?"

A single claw blade from a male near the closet poked in the crack of the door and opened it, exposing me. The queen laughed when she saw the butterflies on my forehead.

"Father . . . You've chosen some strange bedfellows . . . What have you been telling this human? You were trying to save him from us . . . What makes him so special? What does he know?"

If she had asked me directly, I couldn't have answered. Shock had turned me speechless. If I could've spoken, I would've asked about Lieutenant Barber.

"Well," she continued, "he'll find out one way or another. While I'm queen, I can protect you both, but when it's over . . . I don't know what Dekon will do."

I didn't understand, but I sensed she was revealing secrets, not because she wanted me to know, but because she didn't care if I did. I wrote earlier that the invasion was a holiday for them, but her leadership, as queen, was only a temporary function of this extraordinary holiday.

She focused on me again. "What did Father tell you? Did you two become friends? Lovers? Did he call you his 'brother'? Did he? I know you are in shock, human, but you can still nod and shake your head, so answer me. Did he label you his 'brother'? This is important; don't lie."

I nodded.

She looked at Ralph. "Is this true, Father?"

"Yes," Ralph said weakly.

She laughed. "Well then, that makes me your niece, doesn't it?" She walked over to me with her hand out, smiling. Sensing I had no choice, I carefully stood up, stepped out of the closet, and put my hand out to meet hers. Unexpectedly, she pulled me close and hugged me. Every second in her soft arms eased my nerves. I was so quickly restful in her embrace I slammed straight back on the wall when she suddenly released me.

Newfound family relations notwithstanding, I felt like the prey of a predator being played with before dinner. Ralph's only reaction was to glow blacker.

"So listen, Uncle," she said to me, "about how we found our long lost father here."

I gave a nod.

"You probably think we know all about your little planet, like we came all this way to study you because you're so interesting, but . . . well . . . We're not really that into you. We only learned what we needed to, or what we wanted to, which wasn't much. At first, we didn't care about your so-called 'lunar advertisement.' Our first impression was: humans love advertising. You people seem to put advertisements everywhere you can. You even made a TV series about advertising. How revolting . . ."

I nodded politely.

"And when that reporter asked me if *we* were responsible . . . I had to wonder. So, immediately after the press conference, I ordered the closest ship onto the surface of the moon. What did we find? The lunar advert was composed of solar-powered cells. But your civilization is nowhere near advanced enough for the solar-powered cells we found on that moon," she said, then turned to Ralph. "Imagine that."

Ralph did not react. She turned her attention back to me and continued. "Ha, humans barely use the solar technology they do have. But anyway, because of all this, and the laughable anagram, we knew our absentee father was here, somewhere."

Again, she referenced the anagram, and I still had no clue what she meant. And why did she assume Ralph was responsible, and not some other alien, or some other member of Ralph's species? I wanted to believe the anagram was something private between her and Ralph, but she spoke as if it was staring me in the face. I didn't understand, and I doubt she cared if I did. Though she repeatedly addressed me, she was really speaking to Ralph.

"We found no other trace of Father on the moon, so we asked ourselves, what would Father do? He'd try to warn the humans, of course, most likely the Americans—they have the most power. And what advice did Father give you? Did he tell you not to attack? Did he?"

I nodded.

"Of course, he did. And did you listen? No, of course, you didn't. Your stupid president just had to threaten us in front of your whole stupid world. Stupid. Stupid. Stupid."

Her big blue heart beat faster as her lips opened wider, revealing the dripping blackness inside her mouth. She had wandered from her train of thought and got lost in anger. A male grunted, and she returned to explaining.

"Now, as a safety protocol, we've been recording the communications of your White House officials for the past week or so, but, of course, we had no intention to actually listen to these recordings, except in an emergency. And, of course, Father knew this. We are his children, after all. So, once we knew Father was lurking on Earth, we ordered the engineers—we have millions of engineers—to scurry through all those boring White House communications. They quickly noticed a mysterious being named 'Ralph' again and again in the e-mails and phone calls of President Shepherd, Francis Holliday, and Samantha Weingarten, amongst others. This was right after that mysterious cylinder came down from the sky and landed right next to your White House." She looked at Ralph. "A little chicken noodle soup for the oversoul, Father?"

Her tone made my mind cringe.

"Then, right after the night of my first broadcast, all this chatter about the enigmatic Ralph had died out. That is, until this morning, when Samantha Weingarten talked to someone who used the name 'Ralph' in a phone call. All we had to do was determine your location at the time of the call, and lo and behold, the call was made on the property of one Ralph Waldo Emerson. And that's how we found you, Uncle Markus."

My eyes closed as my mind shut down.

The last thing I heard was laughter.

I awoke to the sound of large wings flapping gently and slowly. I was floating, gripped by my upper arms, flying in zero gravity. I was naked and sensed there wasn't a single hair on my body. I felt clean, numb, and weak, but well rested and neither hungry nor thirsty.

Two female Kardashians were holding me and flying down a long, cylindrical tunnel. I didn't know how much time had passed or where I was. I had the strange sense my bowels had been completely evacuated and believed my body had undergone medical examinations and, I suspected, operations or experiments. I felt I could remember if I concentrated, but a wiser part of me decided not to.

I coughed, and one of the females looked at me and gave a feeble smile with pitying eyes. Her companion glanced at me, cold and unconcerned. The walls of the tubular tunnel were black, with small circular lights every ten feet or so, irritatingly bright.

I sensed my escorts didn't know what to make of me, but they weren't afraid. When we reached the end of the tunnel, they released me. While escorting me they flew slowly, warily, but as soon as I was delivered, they soared away like bats on fire.

I was alone, and someone wanted me to stay there. I could have followed the females and gone back, but I would've been caught and taken right back where I was. I didn't feel trapped, nor like a prisoner. I was in an alien ship in outer space—'escape' was meaningless.

There was a closed circular door, scarlet red and six feet in diameter. I tried opening it, but failed. And there was—what I could only describe as—a computer terminal sunken into the curved wall of the tunnel. The monitor had a white screen and clearly some sort of keyboard, but with fewer keys than a human keyboard. All of the symbols were angular and blockish, not a single smooth curve or semicircle to be seen.

Each symbol was white, and the circular keys were black. However, the keyboard was clearly old, some of the symbols had been partially worn away, and one symbol had been completely worn away from overuse. I found myself staring at the keys, as if I was unknowingly searching, though I hesitated to press any of them.

I recalled what Francis told me in the White House, the morning after the arrival of the cylinder. We briefly chatted about Ralph's numeral system.

"It turns out, our symbol for one, the single vertical dash, is their symbol for two."

"So what's their symbol for one?"

"Just a single dot, a period."

If these aliens were truly Ralph's offspring, then, naturally, Ralph's children would use *his* numeral system. Furthermore, you would expect of any alien keyboard, that all the numerals would be grouped together for convenience. I scanned the key-board and noticed the top row of keys set slightly apart from the row below it. To my intellectual delight, the symbol on the uppermost key of the far left was a single dot:

•

Following what Francis said, this had to be their symbol for one. And fulfilling expectation, to the immediate right was the key containing their symbol for two:

|

I was strangely comforted by this, and by the fact that they counted (and presumably read and wrote) from left to right. To the immediate right of their symbol for two was a triangle, which I had to guess was their symbol for three:

Δ

The symbol for four was a square:

□

And the symbol for five was a pentagon:

⬠

But I was left to wonder what the symbol for six was. It was the only symbol that had been entirely worn off from excessive use. There were two uneasy questions. What was their symbol for six? And why would it be completely worn off from use, especially when the other numerals were still legible?

My first guess was their symbol for six was a hexagon; that is, a six-sided figure. This kept with the pattern of a triangle for three, a square for four, and a pentagon for five, etc., but this answer was unlikely. One must discern numerals quickly and without confusion—but a pentagon and a hexagon are too easily mistakable to be practical together as symbols for five and six, respectively. So, I correctly eliminated the hexagon as a symbol for six.

Their symbol for seven was a square with a triangle resting flat on top, like a stick figure drawing of a house. And their symbol for eight was a square with another square resting on top, like an angular form of our symbol for eight. Their symbol for nine was a square with a pentagon on top. As Francis had said, their symbols were geometric and nonarbitrary, so I was confident I could figure out the missing symbol for six.

By chance, I glanced at the monitor again and paused. I stared at the monitor as a harrowing thought overtook my mind.

The monitor was blank white, but what I saw in the reflection made me wonder if I was already dead. The three symbols on my forehead reflected back at me in darkness. As if possessed, I mechanically pressed the blank key for six three times, instantly seeing the Kardashian numeric for 666 on the monitor:

⋈ ⋈ ⋈

In the last book of the Christian Bible, the end of the world is described. It tells of a beast in the thirteenth chapter, a beast with two horns like a lamb who speaks like a dragon. The beast works great signs to seduce humanity, signs like fire coming down to Earth from heaven. These signs deceive the people of Earth, and they mark themselves with a number on their forehead to show allegiance to the beast. That number is 666.

It was also the password to open the red door, and beyond it the beast was laughing.

XLI

+ + + + + + + + + +

BEAST

The red door swung outward at me, revealing a room the size of which was impossible to determine. Looked at one angle, it was a seven-foot-high room whose length and width extended out beyond sight into darkness. From another perspective, it was not a room at all, but a seven-foot-wide chasm between two sheer walls—with abysses upward, forward, and downward.

Like the door, the room was scarlet. The shiny surface looked slippery, yet gripped my skin. I floated in and braced myself with my feet on the floor and my palms on the ceiling.

The laughing beast floated twenty feet in from the entrance. I recognized his collar from the press conference—it was Dekon. His laughter grew and echoed about me.

He did indeed laugh like a dragon, and I wondered how long he could maintain his ugly laugh. Dekon was not a demon from hell. He was a beast, and in my mind, he will always be *the* beast, but he was no beast of the Apocalypse, though his imitation was severe.

Seeing Dekon's eyes was an event. His large, round eyes were simply black, as if each eye was a permanently dilated pupil. His knife-blade claws drew attention away from his face, and I had no doubt Dekon could kill me like a pest. But I was not there to die. I was there to be intimidated. This was an interrogation. And I was about to antagonize my inquisitor.

A river of strange confidence rushed through me as I watched the beast laughing. Somehow, his laughter made me stronger, and the strength infused my mind. The air vibrated with power, and I imagined myself inhaling it directly into my heart. I stared straight in his eyes and prepared to do something I knew Dekon didn't expect. I was entirely ready to die, because I was exhausted from fear. I took one last deep breath and smiled.

And then *I* laughed. I laughed ferociously in the beast's ugly face. I laughed at the beast who sliced Alice apart for exactly the same thing. I just didn't care anymore.

Dekon stopped laughing. My laughter, however maniacal, was genuine, and it shouted out of my throat wildly.

The beast approached me swiftly by bouncing diagonally between the ceiling and floor. When he was close enough to murder me, I shut my mouth.

"Do you know what I am?"

It was the first time I heard Dekon speak. His smoky voice was softer than expected, and his heavy breath somehow smelled sweet. As he circled me, the thick bristles of his fur brushed against my naked skin and tickled me with fear.

"I know what you want me to say."

"Then you must say it."

"You're a demon . . . the beast."

"But you do not believe it."

"Not at all."

Dekon paused, then said something in his native tongue, a command, and a pristine televised image appeared on the ceiling near us, ex nihilo. A female Kardashian looked at us with a wide smile. Next to her was a human convert, a mother, standing with her young son, both naked. The mother held a long alien knife by her side, and the child was weeping. All three had been waiting for this, just in case Dekon needed them. They were in a type of white cubicle, and gravity implied they were in a ship still on Earth. In the background, I could hear faint human screams.

Dekon said something to the female Kardashian. He used a single word of English in the middle of his alien sentence—the word was 'Jesus.' The female Kardashian, still smiling, whispered something in the ear of the human mother. The mother frowned, looked down at her son, held him by the back of the neck, closed her eyes, and quickly slit his throat.

As the blood cascaded from the boy's throat, the televised image disappeared, and Dekon stared at me while the reality set in.

"Do you doubt me?"

"What did you say to her?" I asked breathlessly, half-surprised I could speak.

"I told her to tell the human mother to slice her son's throat for Jesus," Dekon said flatly, staring at me. I wanted the power to silence him forever.

"You are a sick, evil creature who deserves a long, painful

death, and if I killed you right now, I wouldn't feel a drop of guilt." I swear he smiled when I said it. "But you are not the beast of the Apocalypse. That's just a bunch of bullshit. You're acting, and it is very convincing, but *I know* it's all an act." Again, I managed to surprise Dekon.

"What do you know?"

"I know you want to cause chaos for us."

"What did Father tell you?"

"Ralph told me what you're really doing here. He told me *everything.*"

"Not everything. He did not tell you he was our father."

". . . You're right. He didn't . . . How did you know I didn't know?"

"I didn't, but now I do."

"Dekon . . . I know why you're here."

"I doubt you."

"Fuck you," I said, expecting to die.

He paused, then calmly said, "In two days we are leaving Earth. Whatever happens, you will not return. If you do not tell me what Father told you, then in two days you will die. There will be no torture. You will not be given the chance to beg."

Exasperated, I asked, "Two days—why not tomorrow?"

"The queen's protection expires in two days."

Lost in the circumstances, I wondered if he was making it all up. I didn't understand why I had the queen's protection in the first place. I raised my voice. "Why would her protection expire at all? After all, she's the queen. Why don't you tell me what the hell you're talking about?"

"It seems the being you call 'Ralph' told you much less than everything."

"Then answer my question."

Unexpectedly, he answered, and his answer explained more than I expected.

SATURNALIA

"Your ancient Romans had a holiday called 'Saturnalia.' Do you know it?"

"No."

"Pathetically, humans no longer celebrate it."

"I don't understand."

"No, you do not. Saturnalia was a time for gift-giving and the allowance of certain immoralities, like gambling and public drunkenness. But most importantly, there was role reversal. Slaves would become masters, and masters would cook and clean for their slaves. The slaves were even allowed to openly insult their masters. And here is where you have your answer, Uncle Markus. During our three days on Earth, we are celebrating our own version of Saturnalia."

"So the queen is . . . a slave?"

"All our women are slaves. But during our Saturnalia, they rule over the males. It is . . . most humbling. Do you understand?"

I did. It explained why the queen's protection expired when their holiday ended.

Ralph had never mentioned anything about Saturnalia, but he didn't have to. It was a detail in a larger scheme that I already understood. The plan was to become what they hate, for the sake of their own humility—a plan I still considered insane. But, their Saturnalia fit well with the plan: males became slaves, and females became the oppressors. The whole event was necessary to keep their twisted society from unraveling.

"What have you done with Lieutenant Barber?"

"I don't know who that is," he said. I was certain he was lying.

"He was in the house where we were captured."

"Ask the queen."

I glared at him and moved closer.

"Why did you attack Seoul?"

"I didn't. Seoul was destroyed because the females are in control, and they have no idea what they are doing. The queen couldn't be bothered to learn your geography, and so Seoul was melted. Oh, but she had to read all about Andy Warhol . . . couldn't get enough of him. This is what females do when you give them power."

The strange holiday also explained why the queen kept Dekon on a leash like a pet at the press conference. And it explained why the queen so maliciously enjoyed laughing at Dekon with Alice.

"You were not supposed to kill Alice, were you?"

"The human reporter? No, that was forbidden," he said with palpable guilt—not guilt for Alice's death, but for having forsaken their Saturnalia. "In fact, this room we are in is a punishment for me."

The disappointment in his tone made me realize that Alice's death saved millions of lives. There were humans who would've been seduced by the power of the Kardashians, no matter what. But millions were still undecided. And I'm sure, when they saw what happened to Alice, the undecided decided not to convert. From the standpoint of public relations, their press conference was a disaster, and it was all Dekon's fault.

"Why did you kill her?" I asked.

But Dekon did not answer. He inched back and stared at me.

"You knew her," he said, astonished.

I nodded.

"*Father knew her . . .*" he said in a whisper.

He moved backward further and glared at me, suddenly afraid—of me. He retreated again, glancing furtively in all directions—searching for an enemy. Like a cornered animal, he attacked. In less than a second he was on me, shaking my shoulders violently with his huge hands and throttling my neck with his thumbs, his claws inches from my skin.

"Tell me what you know. Tell me what Father is planning. *Tell me or you will regret it for the rest of your painfully short life.*"

It was so obvious, I was barely afraid. Just underneath the surface of his rage was a gushing wave of raw horror. Dekon was not afraid of Ralph—he was *terrified.*

KNOWLEDGE

"**D**ekon," a female voice shouted from nowhere. "The festival of the burning star has not ended. Release Uncle Markus or we will grant you a far worse punishment."

Dekon flung me away. Until then, I assumed they called me 'Uncle' as some form of mockery, but they used the term seriously—why?—yes, Ralph was their father, and yes, Ralph deemed me a 'brother,' but they talked as if I was *really* Ralph's brother. In any case, the label gave me some protected status, so caution led me not to pry.

Dekon was paranoid—he wondered if, somehow, Ralph had tricked him into killing Alice, as if there was a deep plot against him and Alice's murder was just another part of the plan. Again, Ralph's words floated through consciousness: *I'd be embarrassed if you knew how much thought I'd put into this.*

But that was absurd. Ralph had begged Alice not to attend the queen's press conference. So there was no way Alice's death was part of some deeper plan. But Dekon didn't know this, and he was smart enough to know that Ralph was a thousand times more cunning than he.

"Tell me what you know," Dekon said, regaining patience. Feeling little allegiance to Ralph, I told him what I knew. I sensed no harm in it.

"I know nothing about a plan to attack you."

"There's no interest in what you don't know. Tell me what you *do* know. There's a reason why Ralph made you a brother . . . Why?"

"I saved his life, and we vowed to protect Earth . . . from your people. He said I had to leave Earth, and I could not go home again. He told me things . . . and made me promise never to tell another human."

Dekon cocked his head and eyed me. "You must tell me."

"He told me what you already know, or believe, about psychology, so I doubt you'd want to hear it."

Again, Dekon was taken aback. "Indulge me. It will tell me how important you are."

I paused and said, "Ralph told me about the second law—"

Dekon pushed off the wall to float away from me. "Don't lie to me, human. Father would never tell a primitive such a thing. I know him too well. You overheard something perhaps, like a child listening through a keyhole. You did not understand what you heard."

"The second law is that all hatred is envy."

Dekon paused for some time, studying me. Finally, he laughed with an ugly smile and said, "Now I understand. He told you, but you do not believe it."

"No, I don't. We had a conversation. I wasn't convinced."

"You humans are so pleasantly stupid. Of course you can't see what is sitting on your face. I forgot how amusing it is to meet a primitive."

"Sitting on my face?"

"It's a Kardashian expression. I'm sure you can figure it out." Dekon was getting lighthearted. He looked comfortable when he patronized. "Why do you think my people rebelled against Father? Hmm? Why is it that, all over the universe, generation after generation, the youth rebel against their parents, hmm?"

"I don't know . . . an innate desire for freedom?"

He let out a shady chuckle. "What a prude American answer. And where is this innate desire for freedom in all those humans who viciously fantasize of being sexually dominated?"

I paused and closed my eyes. "Do all aliens talk about sex so often?"

"Only primitives are uncomfortable talking about sex. Answer the question."

"There's just something wrong with those people. They're sick."

Again he laughed. "It is *you* who are sick, Uncle Markus, if you believe that. Did you know," he said with a smile, "there's a whole fantasy called the 'plantation fantasy,' where an African American woman fantasizes about being a slave, sexually dominated by her white master? It is so exquisitely humiliating, but I doubt your primitive mind can comprehend its full beauty."

I groaned in disgust.

"The reason each generation rebels against their parents, Markus, is because each generation is given a set of rules, and they *must* break some of them. They must do what they know is wrong—the second law commands it. Your prissy philosopher Plato actually argued that no one could knowingly do the wrong thing . . ." Here a rumbling quake of laughter derailed his speech.

I waited a minute for him to stop and realized something.

"This is about violence, isn't it?" I asked.

"Ah," Dekon said, as if he was proud of me, "now you glimpse the truth. But say it, so I know you see clearly."

"Is Ralph really a pacifist?"

"Yes, it is his nature."

"So then he must have tried to raise you, his children, as pacifists."

"He tried and failed. We are his wretched devils. This is why he abandoned us."

"What are you planning to do with him?"

"I can't say what the females are planning. But when our festival ends, I will destroy him."

My confusion was overwhelming. I'd been assuming everything Ralph said in the Oval Office was a lie. But Ralph's story was more incomplete than incorrect.

"How exactly did Ralph become your father?"

"Millennia ago, the ancient Kardashians landed on the planet of Father's ancestors." This much Ralph had already told. "Upon ravaging the planet, these Kardashians wisely chose to kidnap a few hundred of the inhabitants. As time went on, the silicon-based creatures became a scientific-slave class within Kardashian society, and a tense symbiotic relationship developed."

My surprise must have shown on my face. Dekon paused and looked at me. "Father was born on a Kardashian ship, you see. He's a descendant of the members of this class. But Father was not like the others, who dared not mate with the Kardashians. Indeed, he was rather promiscuous. By mating with the Kardashians, he hoped to create a whole new breed, a peaceful and more intelligent race."

"And you're the new breed. What happened to the old breed?"

"We destroyed them. We are more peaceful than my

ancestors, but we're not unreasonable pacifists like Father. When Father knew he could not control us, he took the rest of his people and escaped, we suspect, back to the home planet of his ancestors."

"If you wanted him dead so badly . . . why not go to their home planet?"

"He deleted from our databases all information about his people and their planet before escaping. This is why he must be destroyed. He knows too much about our ships and technology. Our females are like human females, you see. They are overly sentimental—they don't know how dangerous Father is. He must be destroyed."

"What will happen to me?"

"You will be kept alive," he said.

"And the converts?"

"Why do you care about these converts?"

"I want to know what happens to them. Your Father never told me."

"Don't you see we are helping Earth? All those losers and religious extremists—do you care about them? Can't you see your planet is better without them?"

"They're still human."

"Humans who believe everyone else will burn in hell—who *want* everyone else to burn in hell."

I gave him a curious stare. "You haven't answered my question. What happens to the converts?"

"We will fulfill our promise and send them to heaven. I'm sure God can overlook the number of the beast on their forehead."

I shook my head. "You're going to kill them."

"We'll fly them all straight into your sun," he said with a dark cackle.

Like a fool, I lunged at Dekon, wanting to feel my fist punch his hide. But he outmaneuvered me in zero gravity and brushed me aside. I lunged again with the same result.

"Take this human away before I murder him," Dekon shouted.

A pain shot through my spine and I passed out.

XLV

DEATH

When I awoke, I was floating numb and naked in a simple prison cell. Outside the cell was Dekon, along with ten male Kardashians, each wearing the most imposing earplugs I had ever seen. Each rubbery black plug stuck out a foot from the ear, each fixed in place with black glue. The defensive earplugs could only mean one thing. I looked behind me. Ralph was floating in the corner, naked, except for his helmet.

When I saw Ralph, the pain entered consciousness. My spine felt loose and my skin felt tight. I reached my hand to my lower back and felt a clean surgical scar.

"What have they done to me?" I asked, wincing.

With a deep voice, Ralph answered, "When they brought you onboard, you were implanted with a device which gives perfect nourishment. It provides your body with only essential nutrients, and you will not excrete any waste. But it also controls your nervous system. They used it to knock you out."

I said nothing.

"Markus . . . Do you hate me?"

I shook my head.

"You sure?"

I pointed at Dekon. "He explained your . . . relationship."

Ralph said nothing.

"When their holiday ends, Dekon will kill you," I said.

We were in an all-white cell, reminiscent of a human prison cell, with round, vertical bars, two inches apart. Dekon had his back to us at a computer terminal opposite the cell, typing, while the ten male guards stared through the bars, their claws dangling in zero gravity.

They were assassins-in-wait—waiting for the holiday to end to kill their father with impunity. None of them blinked while glaring at Ralph, and none of them even glanced at me. Their cold eyes revealed a mix of fear and anticipation, and I suspect the earplugs protected them from Ralph's guile, as well as his scream.

"I begged my daughters to put us together. I waited so long. I got anxious."

"I'm all right."

Ralph paused, looked at the guards, then looked back at me.

"Markus, I need a hug," he said, flinging his silicon tendrils around my naked body.

"Look at me," he whispered in my ear.

I looked into his visor, inches from my face. And just like the night when Ralph experienced his first snowfall on Earth, he wrote messages on his face with his thousands of thin, tentacular limbs. As he wrote each sentence on his face, his sight watched my eyes. When I was done reading, he erased and wrote the next sentence, pacing my comprehension perfectly.

"You see the camera above?" he wrote.

"Yes," I said.

"The guards can't hear us, but the camera has audio. Try not to speak," he wrote.

I nodded.

"I can't write how happy I am to see you."

I smiled lightly, and Ralph's glow grew pinker as he gripped me tightly.

"I can get you out of here, but we must trust each other."

Escape was the least likely option, but Ralph had a plan.

"I must get to that computer terminal," he wrote, as if Dekon wasn't floating right in front of it—not to mention the ten male guards. Yet, he was serious. I had no clue what he was planning and feared he'd gone insane from stress, but there was a confidence in him I could not explain.

I started to wonder.

Setting aside the guards, I imagined Ralph could slip between the bars of the cell, but quickly realized, though Ralph could physically fit his jellyfishlike body between the bars, mentally he could not.

Ralph was naked except for his helmet, and his helmet couldn't fit through the bars. So the only way for him to escape was to remove his helmet and slip through. But because his ego is externalized, if he took off his helmet, he'd risk his ego being seen. As Ralph had said, if someone sees his ego, it would kill him and anyone who saw it. A fantastic claim, of course, but it was neither a joke nor a lie.

"You must stay in this corner and face the wall."

I wanted to argue, but he told me not to talk—the camera

was listening. I could only nod or shake my head.

"Promise me you won't look, no matter what happens."

I nodded and Ralph shimmered wildly in the light.

He leaned in close and wrote, "It is finished."

He embraced me again, constricting me tighter than ever before and then released. He looked at the guards, then back in my face. I heard a guard growl.

"Now, you must hide your sight completely. You will hear me scream, but do not protect your ears. Keep your eyelids clenched and your hands over your eyes—no matter what."

I rotated and stabilized my floating body, squatting in the corner with my feet on the floor, elbows on the corner walls, and palms pressed over my eyes.

"I love you, Markus," he said aloud.

How I know what happened next must wait to be explained. The events are as incredible as my knowledge of them.

Ralph took off his helmet to expose his ego, slipped through the bars, and commenced screaming. His blaring scream muffled the bashing explosions of the guards' skulls, and I felt their warm, alien flesh splatter over my skin in successive waves. All the guards—and Dekon—died within seconds of seeing Ralph's ego.

After that, Ralph had little time.

I passed out from the pain, while Ralph continued with his plan. He typed rapidly at the computer terminal as his ego disintegrated under the weight of public exposure.

Remember, the Kardashians' ships were made of the same

malleable and programmable substance as Ralph's cylinder—a technology Ralph was all too familiar with. As Dekon had feared, Ralph knew more about those ships than the Kardashians ever did.

He had time for two things.

First, he programmed the walls of the cell to form an airtight room around me.

Second, he incinerated the rest of the ship, along with *every* Kardashian ship in our solar system. He programmed them all to overheat until obliteration. It was the greatest thing Ralph ever did, maybe the greatest thing anyone has ever done.

Every one of the new breed of Kardashians, slowly and painfully, melted and died in the burning hell they deserved. I'd never thought I'd be content to know of the complete genocide of a unique species. But I was, am, and always will be, at peace with their annihilation.

The makeshift escape pod Ralph created for me was the only existing remnant of their ships. There was no point in Ralph trying to escape with me. He knew what would happen the second he took off his helmet. By the time he finished hacking the entire Kardashian fleet, it was over.

Ralph was dead.

LIFE

But I didn't know Ralph was dead. My perspective was near total ignorance. The shock was so great I could barely think. Nonetheless, I now know Ralph died, and my source for this information must be correct.

One moment Ralph was screaming, and the next he wasn't. When I recovered, I didn't know I was floating free in space or that Ralph had programmed a trajectory for me to the far side of Earth's moon.

For ten minutes I floated in that room as the alien innards encrusted on the walls and gelled on my skin, waiting and hoping for Ralph to communicate with me. I had no idea, but I was traveling to a destination planned for me all along.

My flying cell crashed onto the surface of the moon, smashing me to the wall. Once settled, the room twisted back and forth, grinding and maneuvering mysteriously but deliberately . . . downward. A small hole opened in the wall and shot cool oxygen inside.

'DO NOT PANIC' appeared on the wall.

My vessel sank deeper. The walls undulated as the vessel squeezed itself deeper into the moon's crust. A zoo of whirling beeps and pressures stung my ears as my breathing eased. I was descending into Ralph's secret base on the moon, located deep beneath the Tsiolkovsky Crater.

When the vessel finally rested, I felt heat on the walls. Everything was still and quiet for a minute, then a door manifested and opened.

"Markus."

Behind the door was Ralph. He wore only a small, aluminum beret, and he hugged me.

Ralph was alive. And his glow was golden.

I can explain.

As Ralph had explained in the Oval Office, when he mates, he takes the cells of another being, incorporates those cells into his own cellular structure, and eventually, a hybrid version of himself and the other being splits off from him. This is what he did with the ancient Kardashians to create the new breed.

But when Ralph arrived on the moon, he was alone. A highly sexual being like Ralph, lonely for such a long time, is inevitably going to do the obvious.

"I mated with myself . . . a lot."

Eventually, he reproduced, and the result was an exact copy of Ralph. It is easy to think of the copy as a twin, an identical twin, but it was still more than that.

Ralph had not only created a physically identical twin, he was also a *mentally* identical twin. According to Ralph, their brain matter intertwined at the quantum level—via what physicists call 'quantum entanglement.' They shared *exactly* the same memory, emotions, thoughts, and beliefs, though they were in two different places—one stayed on the moon, while the other flew a large cylinder down to Earth.

From his perspective, he was in two different places at once.

"So your twin was a carbon copy of you, mentally and physically?"

"Well, a silicon copy."

Everything Ralph ever said about his externalized ego was true, but there was another reason he didn't want anyone to see his ego—as soon as anyone physically observed his ego, it would decohere the quantum entanglement, thereby separating his mental identity from his twin. So when Ralph revealed his ego to Dekon and the other Kardashian guards, he killed them all *and* simultaneously ended the entanglement. Only then did their mental identity end.

The last thing Ralph did, before dying aboard the Kardashian ship, was disintegrate those terrible sky banners. Ralph, the one that is alive with me on the moon, could not have done it. It had to be done from a Kardashian computer terminal, just as the destruction of the fleet required internal access. On the other hand, Ralph was able to incinerate his cylinder from the moon.

It took more than a few Earth days to explain all of this to me, and I never understood it completely. I asked him, "But if your twin, I mean the one that was on the Kardashian ship with me, died from embarrassment, how come you didn't?"

"Once my twin's ego was exposed, the entanglement ended, and I stopped experiencing what my twin experienced. I never felt the full horror of my ego's exposure. For me, it lasted less than a terrible second. Then it was over. I'm sorry I didn't reveal my secret identity earlier, but, as you can see, this isn't easy to explain."

His twin was identical physically and mentally, and also *morally*.

"Moral identity is the highest type of identity," he said. Though they could operate independently, one twin could never do something the other wouldn't. Guilt by one was instantaneously shared by the other.

"The guilt was nonlocal, something Einstein would have a hard time with," he said.

"So you were responsible for what your twin did?"

"Yes. We knew what we were doing."

Ralph was responsible for the genocide of an entire race of beings he fathered.

"Violence was my greatest fear," he said. "And now you must do the same."

"I don't understand."

"Markus, have you forgotten your greatest fear?"

Of course, I had not.

"When we are ready, you will come to my home planet, as you promised. And then *you* will be the alien. You must become what you have resisted the most. Like a human child on Halloween, you must become the monster, the one you've always feared. This will bring you closer to illumination."

The preparations for interstellar travel have lasted over two years on the moon. I have no technical understanding of how the voyage will occur, but my body is undergoing a transformation that will allow me to survive the journey. I've been eating a delicious crystalline substance to which I became instantly addicted. Like

Ralph, it smells like fresh celery.

"If I told you what it was, you wouldn't eat it."

The red, crunchy substance is transforming my body. I feel healthier and quicker all over. I look and feel as if I were twenty years old again, albeit with a neon pink sheen. My mysterious new diet also allows for helium respiration, and I should be fully acclimated by the time we leave. I can't explain it, but instinctively, I know I will live for thousands of years.

When I wasn't reading the news online or talking to Ralph, I spent my time writing down my experiences, with the understanding that this report be left on the moon.

"By the time it is discovered, humans will already understand."

"How long will that be?"

"Centuries. Remember, the Kardashians couldn't even find this place."

The moon base is difficult, if not pointless, to describe, as Ralph constantly changes the interior decoration. One time I woke up and the place looked like an old European hotel with antique furniture and a floor made of large, glowing white tiles, and the next time I woke up, everything was plaid. The strange programmable substance, which the Kardashian ships were made of, also composes the walls of Ralph's secret moon base. According to Ralph, the material was injected deep into the moon and then programmed to expand as he saw fit, creating a catacomb labyrinth of rooms and halls.

"Luckily, no one noticed the moonquakes."

Along the way, we've discussed my personal history of events.

Ralph's been helpful with my questions, but not all of them.

"What was the anagram that the queen mentioned? I never figured that out."

Ralph's golden glow brightened.

"Stop being a trickster. Tell me," I said.

Ralph paused.

"I . . . tricked . . . Dekon," he said, his glow nearly white.

"*That's* the anagram? 'I tricked Dekon'?"

"Yes. I got slightly lucky with the spelling, but yes. That's it."

"I don't get it. I mean, just as 'God' is an anagram of 'Dog,' an anagram is always an anagram of some other words. What are the original words?"

"When you are done writing, I will tell you. And you will laugh," he said.

"I can't know until I'm done?"

"But you do know. You are closer to the answer than you've ever been before."

No government ever officially claimed responsibility for the destruction of the Kardashian fleet, but it's widely believed the United States was secretly responsible. Samantha, of course, never denied it, and was happy to have the world believe it.

The commission report on the alien invasion, which took over a year and a half to appear, made only insubstantial references to me. Of course, I didn't read the whole thing. It was only interesting when it was mistaken, and when it wasn't, the investigators admitted their ignorance in the face of inexplicable details.

I don't know what happened in Ralph's house when the Kardashians raided it, but I assume they let Lieutenant Barber live because he had the mark of a convert. In any case, with a quick appointment from Samantha, he became the first openly gay vice president of the United States.

Alice Higginbotham will go down in history as one of the most courageous reporters that ever lived, up there with Edward R. Murrow—because of her aggressive questioning of the queen. And interest in her led to interest in me. Alice had confided to her boss about me going insane over the name 'Ralph' when I first talked with her. This strange fact became even stranger when President Shepherd uttered 'Ralph' with her dying breath. Because of this, many journalists have been investigating me, though they believe I died in the attack on DC. My name is even engraved on the memorial.

Almost everyone on Earth had believed President Shepherd and I were covering up Coca-Cola's involvement in the lunar advertisement. I wish I could've seen their faces when the lunar advertisement was shut off, by Ralph, seconds after the Kardashian fleet incinerated. Naturally, this led people to wonder if the Kardashians were responsible all along.

Shortly after arriving on the moon, I realized two things, which are related. First, Ralph's usual pink glow had turned golden and remained gold every time I saw him. Second, though Ralph often joked and made me laugh, he had stopped laughing altogether. I suspected he was depressed or ill.

"Laughter is just a funny way of breathing," he said.

"But why have you stopped? I'm actually worried."

"Actually, I haven't stopped at all."

"But I haven't heard you."

"I never stopped laughing. I've only improved the rhythm of my laughter. Right before you came to the moon, I had a realization. I realized that every single breath is a laugh . . . We laugh with every single breath we take."

His glow grew bright like the sun, and I smiled.

ACKNOWLEDGMENTS

I thank Marie-Juliette Riot for everything and forever.

I thank my parents, John and Virginia Steinsvold, and *ma belle mère*, Daniele Brison, for all their love and support over the years. I thank Mike Regan for being a good friend in a terrible time. I thank Jay Riggio, Chris Kent, and Courtney McKay for aiding me with social media and self-promotion. I further thank Courtney McKay for being a strange light in an all-too-familiar darkness.

I thank my literary agent, Mark Gottlieb, at Trident Media Group for discovering me. I thank everyone at Medallion for making the book real. I thank the people at Audible for the audiobook deal and Landscape Entertainment for the film/TV option.

Finally, I thank the /r/writing subreddit of Reddit for being a great source of information, help, and encouragement. You are my writing community.

CHRISTOPHER
STEINSVOLD

photo by
Ben Colen

Christopher Steinsvold received his PhD in philosophy
from the City University of New York Graduate School
and University Center. He is currently an adjunct
professor at Brooklyn College, City University of New
York. In his creative writing, he uses his background in
philosophy to feed his imagination.

✦   ✦   ✦   ✦   ✦   ✦   ✦   ✦   ✦